Leah's
Faith

JOANNE
LEHMAN

Leah's Faith
by Joanne Lehman

Copyright © 2025
All rights reserved.
Published by Masthof Press

This is a work of fiction. Names, characters, businesses, places, events, and incidents are either products of the author's imagination or used in a fictitious manner. Any resemblance to actual persons, living or dead, or actual events is purely coincidental.

Library of Congress Control Number: 2024944395
International Standard Book Number: 978-1-60126-956-0

Masthof Press
219 Mill Road | Morgantown, PA 19543-9516
www.Masthof.com

Dedicated to
Edie

ACKNOWLEDGMENTS

At first, writing felt like a lonely occupation. Eventually, I found community among various writers' groups—journalists, poets, essayists, fiction authors, and more. I can mention here only a few of the many who helped me become a fruit-bearing writer.

The idea for *Leah's Faith* began with a vineyard tour. Inspiration followed as I thought about Jesus' words, which are far more radical than many realize. We Christians are tangled together, growing and twisting in many directions. Yet each branch is part of a productive whole, growing, rooted, and grounded in love. We are *Gemeinschaft*, a community, branches of the True Vine.

I am most grateful to the Amish friends who have shared their lives with me. Our mutual Anabaptist and rural heritage was ever-present as we conversed about gardens quilts, and livestock. I also experienced first-hand how my Amish friends deal with complexity—physical disabilities, mental illness, and tragedy.

Thanks to the Women's Fiction Writers Association for matching me with my critique partners, Nanette Littlestone and Pam Raleigh. Without their help, this book would still be sketchy pages in a three-ring binder. Their thoughtful reading and insightful responses to all my first drafts continue to help me develop as a fiction writer.

Wooster neighbors who enjoy Amish-themed fiction volunteered to read a completed version of *Leah's Faith*. Thanks to Colette Mosier and Delores Ivan who read my manuscript and gave useful feedback. Thanks also to Barb Reinford, director at New Leaf Center, a medical clinic for special children, in Mt. Eaton. Barb read *Leah's Faith* and helped with cultural sensitivity. I'm most grateful for the comments of writer and editor Sue Weaver who set me straight on which Amish groups ride bicycles and which wear aprons, along with many other details about contemporary Amish life.

Thanks to our daughter, Laura Lehman, for joining me on a winter weekend to design and launch my author's website. I continue to rely on her marketing skills and social media advice. My niece, Cami Okey, made taking photos a joyful adventure as we trekked through parks looking for the perfect backgrounds.

I am blessed with family and friends who patiently wait to read my finished stories yet listen willingly when I talk about my half-finished projects. My sisters Karen Cobb and Melva Huebert might find a family memory or two on these pages. Lois Bontrager and Marilyn Rossiter are the kind of lunch and coffee friends every writer needs. Friends at Summit Mennonite Church routinely pray for me and ask for updates on my writing. And thanks to my Pilates guru, Maggie Klintworth, a positive force in my life who helped me straighten my spine and stretch toward my dream.

My husband, Ralph Lehman, is the most avid reader I know. Although I don't write his preferred genres, he is willing to read when I hand him a manuscript and is quick to offer an idea when I'm stuck. Thanks for being there through all the ups and downs of my writing life.

Finally, I am thankful for Masthof Press and Liz Petersheim who accepted my book for their traditional publishing program. She's an efficient administrator and her cover design hits all the right notes. I look forward to working with Liz and Masthof in the coming months as we complete the Benville Community Series.

I'm grateful for each one, named and unnamed, who has blessed me with your presence on this journey of mine.

LEAH'S FAITH

I am the vine;
you are the branches.
Those who abide in me
and I in them
bear much fruit,
because apart from me
you can do nothing.

JOHN 15:5 (NRSV)

CHAPTER 1

Leah Troyer

Leah stretched to water five new hanging baskets of petunias that graced the Troyer home. They brought eye-catching color to the porch that spanned the width of the otherwise plain-looking white house in the little Amish crossroad community of Benville, Ohio. It was late May. In the garden, pea vines were in blossom. More rows of young plants—onions, green beans, carrots, and red beets—hinted at a summer of abundance. Tomato and pepper plants had been set out along with cucumber, squash, and potatoes.

After dinner, the noonday meal, seventeen-year-old Leah and her slightly younger sister, Susan, sat on the porch swing, shaded by an old trumpet vine. The sisters had quickly washed up the dishes while *Maemm,* their mother, put away leftovers. Then everyone rested after a long morning in which they'd each done the seasonal chores. Susan had thinned the small carrot plants and weeded long rows of peas and beans. *Maemm* had trimmed the raspberry canes and put fresh straw beneath the strawberry plants. Leah had scrubbed the front porch.

"Looks like we'll have a nice crop of berries this summer," said *Maemm.* "I saw little berries out there—even in the new row we put in last year. Let's hope the almanac is wrong and we won't have all the rain they predict."

"Why don't you want rain?" Susan asked. "I thought gardens needed rain."

"Well, yes. But not too much or the berries will get soft and mushy. The lettuce is sure nice right now," she added. "We'll have plenty of lettuce for salads in the next few weeks."

Susan had harvested a bowl of bibb leaf lettuce and green onions for dinner. While Leah rinsed lettuce and made the salad, *Maemm* mixed dressing using mayonnaise, sugar, vinegar, and milk. She had no written recipe, but it was always perfect. They'd eaten the salad with canned beef with noodles and home-canned applesauce. For a half hour or so, they'd sat together at the big kitchen table, the seven of them—*Maemm, Daett*, Leah, Susan, and the three younger Troyer siblings. After they'd eaten slices of rhubarb pie, *Daett* said a second prayer over the meal. He rested and read the newspaper before returning to his job at the K&T Woodshop where the Keim and Troyer families made beautiful, handcrafted hardwood tables. Meanwhile, the women took a break on the porch.

For the women, the hard work of the morning was behind them. While *Maemm* and Susan worked in the garden, Leah had finished the last of the spring cleaning. *Maemm's* instructions that morning had been clear: "Susan, you come out to the garden with me and pull weeds. Leah, after you take care of the break-fast dishes you can wash down the front porch good and then do the porch windows inside and out. You don't need a ladder for that. And I don't want you hurting yourself lifting anything heavy. Don't use much soap or the floor might get slippery. We don't want you to fall."

Leah couldn't remember a time when she hadn't been instruct-ed with these cautions and reminders. *Maemm* gave her the easier inside chores and always plentiful warnings.

"*Maemm*, I'm not a cripple," Leah said. But her pleading got her nowhere.

"You know what the chiropractor said. No heavy lifting. Stand tall. Straighten your spine."

From a young age, Leah's parents were concerned about Leah's scoliosis. Leah's curvature of the spine—a birth defect—was known to affect their extended family. This condition would be with her for life, and it was a matter of faith to accept it as *Gott's* will. Her parents constantly warned and protected her, wanting only the best for their eldest daughter. Still, everyone, even Leah, feared the worst. Scoliosis in a young person could lead to disability in later life.

Dawdi Troyer, Leah's grandfather, talked about *Gott's* will almost any time something big went wrong, whether it was a bad growing season, a horse and buggy accident, or the death of someone precious, like *Mommi* Ruth, their grandmother. There was a reason for every sorrow, and *Gott* never gave you more than you could bear. But from Leah's perspective, at times it did feel like too much. It was so hard to understand.

Maemm's constant reminders annoyed Leah, who tried in vain to accept her imperfections. And when she went somewhere, there were different reminders. Just last week, at the Benville Grocery, she'd caught Aaron Keim, the most handsome young man in the neighborhood, observing her while she looked for cake flour in the bulk food section.

Leah had felt his eyes on her and met his glance. She'd said a polite "Hello!" and he'd answered kindly and then turned quickly to examine a display of flashlight batteries. Leah thought she'd read pity in the depths of his remarkable blue eyes. Their schoolteacher had once described them as "cobalt." It was a new vocabulary word that Leah still remembered.

Now, as they rested on the porch during the heat of the day, Leah, Susan, and *Maemm* watched a robin build a nest in the maple tree. From the porch, Leah could survey much of the small Benville settlement whose name didn't appear on any map. Simple white barns with low-pitched eaves sheltered buggy horses and pony pets.

"It looks like rain," said *Maemm*. "Maybe if it rains it will cool off." She fanned her face with her apron.

Leah shifted in her chair to ease the cramping in her shoulder. A whiff of lingering honeysuckle and spruce drifted onto the porch, despite the stifling heat.

"We won't work as hard this afternoon. Let's hem our new dresses and then take a break until suppertime," said *Maemm*.

"I already pressed my hem up," Susan said.

Susan was talented at sewing. Each pleat in her skirt was perfectly even. Leah envied her sister. From Susan's small waist, the skirt fanned out over her body, falling gracefully to the hem—a perfectly straight hem. Leah's sewing wasn't quite as perfect, and her dresses never looked as good on her crooked body.

Susan was the beautiful one. But Leah had never heard anyone say it. She was sure people noticed when she and Susan stood side by side at church. And Leah's dress often sagged lopsidedly from her right shoulder and hip despite the extra effort they took when sewing the hem.

"Let's go inside," said *Maemm*. "Leah, you put on your new dress, and I'll get the yardstick."

Leah emerged from the enclosed sewing porch with its eight windows, the new dress draped over her arm. She went to her room and changed, then came back downstairs wearing the periwinkle blue dress she'd sewn from a thin polyester knit bought on sale last fall. All three of the Troyer women had made dresses from the bolt of material. These dresses would be kept for good, worn when you needed something better than an everyday dress.

"Come over here in the light. Stand up nice and straight," said *Maemm*.

Leah shifted her weight slightly and tried to stand tall. *Maemm* placed the end of the yardstick on the floor and crouched down. She decided on the length and put in a straight pin marking the fold of the hem. Carefully, she moved around Leah in a circle, measuring and keeping the skirt the same length as she made her way.

"Okay, then," said *Maemm* at last. "You can go change now. Heat the iron and press it. You'll need to trim it on the right side where your hip is higher. Just make a two-inch hem all the way around."

Leah sighed and did as she was told. By the time she joined Susan on the shady front porch, her younger sister was almost finished hemming her dress.

"We can wear these to the Children's Relief Auction next week," said Susan.

"If I go," said Leah.

"Of course, we're going," said Susan. "You're not getting out of that one, and you know it. You need to get out more."

Leah dreaded the upcoming auction, which was a benefit to raise funds for Amish families with large medical expenses. The Amish who attended looked forward to seeing old friends and relatives, eating, visiting, buying each other's hand-made crafts and furniture and making donations of all kinds. It was the biggest event of the summer. Even people who weren't Amish liked to come just for the food and beautiful crafts.

"I don't want to go to that auction this year," Leah said. "It's always so hot, and no fun. All we do is help Aunt Fannie sell needlework in the big tent." Leah cringed at the thought of the massive crowd. The stealthy glances and curious stares of strangers made her nervous, even now.

"You have to get out and have a little fun once in a while," Susan said. "Meet some new people."

Susan was so pushy sometimes. *Couldn't she understand?* But Leah knew she wouldn't get out of this one. The whole family went every year.

After her dress was hemmed and supper was over, Leah sat on the porch swing with her parents and Susan. Her young brothers Jake, Andy, and Adam had helped *Daett* all afternoon at K&T. Now they were in the yard trying to teach their dog Toby to fetch. He was a smart dog, a yellow lab. The air was hot and sultry. Dark clouds hovered in the west. A storm was brewing.

"I'm going up now," Leah said.

Susan looked peeved. "Really? It's only eight o'clock."

But her parents nodded their agreement. They understood.

Leah made her way up the stairs and put on her nightgown. She took off her *kapp* and brushed her hair. There was no escaping the oppressive heat and humidity of this day. *Why can't I just be like Susan? Everything is different for me. I'm different.* Thank goodness she could live in other worlds in the pages of a book.

Leah read until Susan came into the room. Soon, they were both sound asleep.

CHAPTER 2

Susan Troyer

H ours later, a loud boom of thunder and a flash of lightning awakened them. It was raining hard. Susan got up and ran to close the window.

"Come here! Look! K&T is on fire!" yelled Susan.

Leah jumped out of bed and ran to look out the window. Across the field, flames rose from the roof of the woodshop where her father and the Keim family built hardwood furniture for a living.

"There's a fire at the shop!" yelled *Daett.* He was already dressed and halfway down the stairs.

Susan switched on the LED lantern and the two sisters dressed quickly in their everyday dresses. They dashed down the stairs, Susan going two at a time. The girls were still far behind their younger brothers.

K&T Woodshop was small, but it provided a livelihood for Mose Keim, Albert Troyer, and their five sons. The Keim sons, Aaron and Ben, were in their late teens. The Troyer boys were much younger but also had daily chores at the shop. The Keim and Troyer properties joined at the back where their pastures met. Now the Troyer family took the shortest route across the field. *Daett,* wearing a headlamp, led the way. Susan slowed her pace to stay with Leah.

From every direction, neighbors hurried through the downpour toward the fire. Sirens and blaring horns signaled the arrival of the fire department. Everyone stood in the rain and billowing smoke, watching as firefighters dragged their hoses to the dry hydrant near the old pond. They attached the bulky hose to the hydrant. Susan saw the hose bulge as it began to fill with water.

"Look! There's Aaron! What's he doing?" Leah nudged her sister who stood watching the billowing smoke and flames.

"Where?"

"Over there." Leah pointed to the front door of the shop. Aaron was running toward two firefighters who were dragging the large hoses. They were about to enter the burning building. Aaron gestured to them, as if giving instructions. They disappeared up the steps and into the smoke.

"I can't imagine how he's feeling," Leah said. "He works there every day. He must be devastated."

"*Daett,* too. And Mose. I can't believe this is happening." Susan wiped rain and tears from her face. The rain had finally slowed to a drizzle.

The firefighters came through the shop door lugging Mose's large, old oak roll-top desk. Aaron and his brother Ben helped them carry it down the steps and into the yard.

Flames engulfed the shop roof as the firefighters hacked through a window and carried some of the shop's unfinished tables out to the loading dock where others grabbed them and stacked them under the maple tree. Fire hoses poured water onto the roof while sparks showered around the building. Susan felt sick, knowing how this tragedy would affect their family and the entire neighborhood.

Just then, Ruthie, Susan's school friend, approached them. "I can't believe it. Can you?" said Ruthie. "I think we should help, but what can we do?"

She steered the two sisters to the porch of the Keim's farmhouse and away from the firefighters who were now hosing down the horse barn to keep it safe. Thankfully, the horses were all out to pasture this time of year.

"Fannie's standing over by the fence," Susan said. "She mentioned something about getting food for this crew. Stay here. I'll check if she needs us."

Fannie Troyer, their unmarried aunt, owned the nearby Cozy Corner Quilt Shop and lived in a small house near the Troyer home. Her shop was one of only two small stores that served their little community, the other being Benville Grocery and Dry Goods.

In no time, Susan was back. Fannie, their tall, willowy aunt, was with her.

"Now, you three, I can use your help. It looks like the fire is under control," Fannie said. "I'm going home to get some food for the family. You girls can help carry stuff. Everyone will be hungry after this."

They headed back to the pasture gate, the closest route to Fannie's house. "How did the fire start?" Ruthie asked.

"I don't know. Maybe this heat, sawdust, maybe lightning." Susan thought of the flash of lightning that had awakened them. How long ago had that been? An hour? Longer? It was hard to know.

Susan, Leah, and Ruthie tried to keep up with Fannie as she strode off across the pasture field in the dark. She led them to her little house beside the quilt shop. Everyone was out of breath by the time they arrived.

The screen door slammed. Once inside, Fannie grabbed a large dishpan and began filling it with things from her icebox—a wheel of cheese, loaves of sliced bread, a frosted cake in its flat pan with only a couple of pieces missing.

"There's lemonade mix in the pantry," she gestured. Ruthie opened the door. "Get a jar of peaches from the cellar, Susan. My goodness, what else do we need?" She pulled a bulk-sized box of granola bars from a low pantry shelf.

Fannie stopped rummaging in the icebox and fanned her face with her apron. As always, she was wearing purple. Her favorite color. "Let's see . . ."

The four of them carried the food, along with paper plates and cups, to Fannie's porch.

"Put them here," she told the girls, gesturing toward the garden cart parked near the door. "It's good I emptied this last evening."

Susan grabbed the handle as soon as it was loaded. She didn't want Leah to struggle with the cart. She had to be exhausted from running across the pasture—twice.

This time, Fannie and the girls took the road back to the Keim farm. It was longer but easier. Fannie had found her headlamp and fastened it to her forehead over her head scarf.

"We'll get there quicker with some light. Follow me."

The noise from the crowd increased as they got closer. The acrid smell of burning wood and plastics, along with the flammable furniture stains and solvents, filled the air. The chemicals had fed the fire. The damage was unmistakable in the brilliant floodlights the ladder truck beamed over the shop, but the shop hadn't burned to the ground. Weary firefighters stood about, removing their bulky protective gear. The danger was over.

Fannie bustled into the Keims' kitchen, and the girls followed her. Mose and Anna Keim, along with *Daett*, were catching their breath. "Now you just sit down, and I'll take care of things," Fannie announced. "Anna, do you have a big pitcher? Is there still a little ice in the cooler yet? I brought cheese for sandwiches, cake, and fruit." Susan mixed lemonade and gave a paper cup to *Daett*. He looked defeated.

Mose Keim splashed water on his overheated face and put his hat on, then stepped out onto the porch. He knew better than to stay in the kitchen if Fannie Troyer was taking over—and it appeared she was.

Susan opened the peaches and dumped them into a bowl. Leah put forks in the jars of pickles and red beets. Ruthie grabbed a platter and began slicing cheese. Soon the table was piled with the food from Fannie's house. More food arrived, carried in by the good-hearted neighbors who knew what to do when tragedy struck.

Food—it eases all worldly woes. Susan said a prayer in her heart for everyone whose life would be touched by this terrible fire—for Mose and Anna, their sons Aaron and Ben, the little Keim children, and her own family who had suddenly lost their source of income, even if only temporarily.

It wouldn't be easy to clean up the mess of the burned shop or build another one. Everyone already knew the neighbors would help *Daett* and Mose rebuild. That's what the Amish community did. Even now, as they stood around the table, fixing a bite to eat, their presence consoled the Keim and Troyer families.

The fire department loaded the last of their equipment and left. Some of the workers took the time to eat a sandwich or grab a cookie. The rain stopped and cool breezes wafted through the screen, overtop the smoke and dampened embers.

"Can I get you two boys plates?" Susan asked Aaron and Ben. "You must be bushed!" The boys came toward the table, barefoot. They had dark smudges on their foreheads. Aaron had what looked like a black eye, but it was only a spot of soot.

"Where's Leah?" Aaron asked as he filled a plate.

Susan looked around for her sister. "I don't know. I hope she's okay. We were running so fast to get back here with the food."

Aaron nodded. "Well, when you see her, tell her I said thanks for this. It means a lot."

"I will. We were glad to help," Susan said.

CHAPTER 3

Fannie Troyer

Standing at the counter of Cozy Corner Quilt Shop in Benville, Fannie Troyer counted the money from last week's sales. It was pitiful, but she would never admit to anyone that her retail store was not turning a profit. In the fall, a few tourists stopped in, and locals occasionally came by for sewing notions or Amish remedies, but the quilt shop had never even come close to breaking even.

I need different things to sell here.

Fannie opened the store at ten o'clock. After counting the cash, she stood looking around the room. The largest quilts hung from a hinged display rack made by her brothers for her birthday the year she opened. Besides these quilts, there were smaller decorative ones tacked to the walls. On a table, she displayed handmade aprons, stuffed calico toys, faceless Amish dolls, and woven potholders. But the room needed something else. *I don't have much to spend, but I could borrow from my nest egg. What would be nice is small wooden toys—marble games, wooden blocks, and holders for folded quilts. And why haven't I thought about quilt racks? That makes perfect sense.*

As Fannie stood there pondering this, her niece Susan Troyer dropped by. "Fannie, do you have any dark blue thread?" she asked without preliminaries.

"Well, yes. Surely, I do. Let's look," said Fannie. She pulled a polyester curtain aside and Susan followed her into the back room where one small window let in a little light. She found a sturdy cardboard gift box holding spools of thread arranged from darkest to lightest. At least half of them were shades of blue. Susan held out the scrap of cloth she'd brought with her. Aunt and niece peered intently and moved closer to the window.

"Why are you sewing in the summer, Susie Q?" For some reason, Fannie had taken to calling her niece Susie Q. Who knew why? That was the thing about Fannie. She was her own person.

"I like to sew, Fannie. I know I should wait until winter to make another dress, but really, *Maemm* is glad if I sew now because I'm finished when she starts sewing the boys' school clothes."

"Well, if you've got that much time on your hands, why don't you come over here and help me a few days a week?" Fannie asked. "You could sew here in my back room and come out when customers drop by. I've been thinking of trying to find some small wooden items to sell here. You know . . . the things they have at the Children's Relief Auction? The older men make such nice stools, wooden toys, and the like." Susan nodded and Fannie kept talking.

"If you help me out here, I could keep the store open and get a driver to take me around to pick up some things. It's too far to take the horse and buggy in the summer," Fannie added.

Together, Fannie and Susan hatched their plan. Fannie would pay her niece something—not much to be sure. It would only be for a couple of days each week.

"*Maemm* needs me in the garden. She doesn't let Leah work outside much," Susan reminded Fannie. "But I'm sewing anyway. I might as well do it here," Susan said.

"*Yah*! She babies Leah a little, doesn't she? I don't know as it would hurt her to work in the garden. But it's none of my business, I guess." Fannie usually spoke her mind.

"Leah's not very strong. *Maemm* worries about her. Especially about what will happen when she's older," Susan said.

"I know. It's a worry. Yes, it is," Fannie agreed. "I can't pay much but I'll let you pick out one of these quilts for your hope chest at the end of the summer. How does that sound?"

"I'm sure *Maemm* won't mind. She said she'd like both me and Leah to work somewhere this summer, but just part-time," Susan said. "I won't have far to go to work, will I? I can probably start tomorrow. We're caught up in the garden for this week."

"That would be just fine." Fannie nodded her head enthusiastically. "We'll have you come on Tuesday and Wednesday. Now you stay here. I'm going to call a driver for tomorrow." Susan took a seat on Fannie's stool and Fannie pulled a cell phone from underneath the counter along with a sliver of paper with a handwritten phone number on it. She planned to try the new driver, Hank Kratzer. People said his minivan was very clean and had tinted windows—always a plus.

She turned toward the window and spied two women—the deacon's and bishop's wives—driving in together in an open buggy. Her phone call would have to wait. "Oh, nevermind," she said to Susan. "Looks like I have customers."

Susan stepped out into the bright sun.

"Don't forget your thread!" Fannie yelled.

"I almost did! Thanks!" Susan stepped back inside, and Fannie dropped the spool into her niece's hand.

Fannie quickly put the driver's phone number away. She hid the cashbox under the counter and glanced at her *kapp* in the hand mirror she kept there. Everything was in order by the time the women had tied the horse. Fannie greeted them as they came through the door.

"Good afternoon! How are you today?"

"Not too bad," said Anna Yoder, answering for both of them. They began nosing around, pretending to look at the quilts, even though they had quilted three or four of them. They lifted embroidered pillows from the shelf and talked in quiet tones about the printed aprons. Fannie knew it was a bit odd to sew *Englischer-style* aprons, but she'd discovered tourists liked the lower-priced hand-sewn things. For a while, everyone wanted the pin cushions filled with sand that had a scrap bag attached. They were handy at the sewing machine. Then someone showed her how to make a hand towel to hang from the oven door handle, and she'd made a couple dozen of them from bright printed towels. Crocheted cotton dish-cloths were also popular.

These neighbor women didn't buy any of these things. If they wanted such a thing, they would make it themselves. They had come to snoop—plain and simple. They'd been sent by their husbands to find out if she was making enough to support herself or if she would need some aid from the church. Fannie never let on that she understood. "You just go ahead and look around," Fannie said. *Not that they need telling.* She tried not to notice or overhear their conversation, but it was a tiny store. She wished she could play music like they did in *Englischer* stores. It would be more comfortable for everyone. But, of course, the Amish didn't have radios or a way to access a streaming service.

The women took their time, so much so that Fannie began to fuss with the bags under the counter just to look busy. She took out a cloth and began polishing the counter. She rearranged the pens and pencils and noticed it was almost time to turn the calendar page.

"Well, Fannie, you have a lot in here. Have you been busy this spring?"

They know very well exactly how many customers I had. They probably counted the cars sitting in my parking lot and kept a running list, as if cars at my store were like the birds at their bird feeders.

"Oh, I can't complain," Fannie said, trying to make her voice sound both humble and a bit happy.

"We wonder sometimes how you do it. You're here so much. Is it hard to get your work done at home?" Lizzie Maust, the bishop's wife, asked.

"I don't need much. I get up early and do what needs doing. Besides, I'm going to have help after next week. My niece, Susan Troyer, is going to come two days a week to help me out here."

"Really? Susan? Is she the hunchbacked one?" Anna asked.

"No. That's Leah. Susan's the younger one."

"Oh, she's a nice girl," Lizzie said. "Well, we wondered how it was doing here. The men said we should stop by once and see your place. We drive by so often, but we're always in a hurry."

Deacon Yoder's wife, Anna, picked up one of the sunbonnets that were in fashion with the *Englischers* two summers ago. Unfortunately, the hats had already fallen out of favor.

Fannie thought she would donate them to the Children's Relief Auction. She had too many. People would notice that they still hadn't sold. *It's embarrassing. That's exactly why it would be good to have some wooden toys and such in here.*

"Well, now we can tell the men we were here," Anna said.

"*Yah,*" said Lizzie. "Fannie looks like she's getting on just fine and even taking on a girl to work for her. That's good." They spoke as if Fannie wasn't standing right in front of them.

The women slowly made their way to the door, pretending to look at things they weren't going to buy, picking up dishtowels and then putting them back down. Plucking a stray thread from a dark pillow or brushing an invisible piece of lint from a potholder. With-out saying much more, the two women looked briefly in Fannie's direction and pushed open the screen door. The bell jingled as Anna and Lizzie clutched their black plastic purses and adjusted their head coverings. They had done what they came to do—make sure Fannie didn't need any help from the church. Fannie had assured them she was doing fine. She sighed with relief, knowing the annual visit was over and she was on her own for another year. It wouldn't do to have to take charity from the church.

Fannie watched as they climbed into the buggy and Anna shook the reins. She could only imagine what they were saying as the horse trotted quickly out onto Clear Creek Road.

Whatever they were saying, it wasn't about the new wood-en toys and games Fannie would have in her store next week. Even though Fannie knew those two could spread the word faster than anyone, she hadn't told them about her plan to bring in some new merchandise.

She looked up the hill at the charred siding on K&T and felt a pang of sympathy for the Keim family and her brother, Albert. Her memory of the night of the fire was mostly a blur, except for the sooty smudge that made Aaron Keim look like he had a black eye. Her nieces could do worse than end up with a Keim husband. Peo-ple like the Keims, who had money, didn't hold off rebuilding; and everyone from the district pitched in. "Every day we can't work is money out of our pockets," Albert had said. Fannie knew her brother was right. Handmade quilts weren't selling these days, but handmade furniture—that was a different story.

It was already past closing time. Fannie locked the door and pulled out Hank Kratzer's phone number. It was finally time to make that call.

CHAPTER 4

Leah Troyer

L eah stepped outdoors, carrying a dishpan full of peapods, radish tops, and outer leaves from the head of lettuce. All left from making dinner. Just then, *Dawdi,* her grandfather, appeared from the backyard garden shed with his pruning shears. His small house was connected to the Troyer home by a front porch, so he was usually nearby.

"*Maemm* says you should come over for dinner," Leah said. The Troyers gathered at noon for the big meal of the day that they called dinner. It was always when they heard the whistle blow from the fire station in the next town.

"That depends. What are you having?" *Dawdi* asked with a twinkle in his eye. Leah knew he would come almost anytime they asked him, but on busy kitchen days, when they were putting up beans or canning peaches, he sometimes got his own dinner.

"Look," said Leah. "This will about tell you."

Dawdi looked in the dishpan. "I think I'll just eat at home today if you're having pea pods, radish tops, and slug-infested lettuce."

Leah laughed. *Dawdi* liked to tease her. They both knew *Maemm* and Leah were making a good spread—meatloaf, fresh green beans, and lettuce with poppy seed dressing—homemade. And canned peaches from last summer.

"What are you doing with the loppers?" Leah asked. "It's not time to prune the grapes, is it?" Leah always liked to watch *Dawdi* prune the grapes and apple trees. He seemed to know just what to do to make the grapevines and fruit trees produce the best. Last March, as soon as the ground began to thaw, she'd helped him at the arbor.

"Just a little final early summer pruning. The vines are growing too fast this season. With all this beautiful weather, if we don't watch, the grapes will suffer."

Leah pitched the contents of the dishpan over the fence and set it on a cement block beside the windmill. Curious, she followed *Dawdi* to the arbor. He began at the far corner and examined each vine carefully.

"See, last fall we did the main pruning. Now we just look for the vine shoots that have grown more than yea big." He stretched his arms about three feet apart. "We keep the branches close enough to the vine to produce good fruit."

Leah thought of the words of Scripture—repeated so often she had them memorized. *I am the vine; you are the branches; abide in me and you will bring forth much fruit. Dawdi* had quoted these verses in the spring at pruning time. Maybe that was why he liked pruning— it made him think of God.

Leah was puzzled. "How do you know which ones to cut? What if you cut too much? Does it hurt them?"

Dawdi looked at her, his caterpillar eyebrows curled over the cuff of his blue knit stocking hat. Leah thought for an instant that pruning them a bit would be in order, but she didn't say so. "Everything in its time," said *Dawdi*. "We are *Gott's* caretakers, doing what must be done. I don't know as pruning can hurt the vine. We do it to help, don't you know? I don't think vines have feelings. Do you?" Leah shook her head as if she agreed, but she still wasn't sure the vine was happy when *Dawdi* came at it with those huge loppers.

"Look." *Dawdi* pointed at a vine that had shot out away from the arbor. "Yes, I need to trim this *loppisch* vine." He clamped the sharp pruner beak over the unruly shoot. "See here?" he said, pointing to another vine filled with several small buds. "We keep this one. It will bear fruit. But these empty shoots just sap strength from the others." The empty vine fell to the ground and Leah picked it up. She followed *Dawdi* as he made his way around the arbor looking for suckers and worthless growth that his practiced eye could see, even when Leah's could not. She watched, wordless, lost in her world of questions.

I'm a useless vine. I'll never bear fruit—have a husband or children. I'll be laynich—*alone. No one will want me.* She consciously tried to straighten her back. Yet she knew it was useless to try to stand tall. She would always be a hunchback, as crooked and twisted as a grapevine. *When you are a girl with a crooked back, there is no gardener with a pruner handy.*

The little bit of effort seemed to make *Dawdi* tired. He was getting up in years. Last month they celebrated his eightieth birthday. He carried the pruner to the glider under the arbor and sat down. Maybe he'd sensed Leah's thoughts—deduced from her moodiness and shifting posture. Leah sat on the bench across from him and pushed the glider slightly with her foot. *Dawdi* sighed and Leah noticed a faraway look in his eyes. He was thinking about *Mommi* and heaven, she thought.

Dawdi looked up through the grape leaves that shaded them and began quoting: "My well-beloved hath a vineyard in a very fruitful hill: And he fenced it, and gathered out the stones and planted it with the choicest vine, and built a tower in the midst of it, and also made a winepress . . . and he looked that it should bring forth grapes, and it brought forth wild grapes . . ."

"What is that verse? I don't know that one. The last time you said the one about 'I am the vine; you are the branches,'" Leah said.

"*Ach, yah*, Scripture is full of verses about vines. *Gott* puts many lessons in the vine when we listen. The one I just said is from Isaiah. The people strayed from God's ways. A useless vine is such a disappointment."

Is that me? A useless vine that won't bear fruit? Leah quickly suppressed her bad thoughts. "I think we both like the other one better. 'Abide in me and you will bring forth fruit in season.'"

It seemed as if *Dawdi* sensed her dark thoughts. He focused his rheumy eyes on the knotted base of the vine growing up from the ground near the arbor posts. "The roots of this vine grow deep. If the branches stay close to the vine they will bear. Always remember that. Keep the branches close to the vine. It's the vine that gives life."

Sitting with *Dawdi* under the arbor on a fine summer morning was a memory Leah always wanted to keep with her. Someday he would be in heaven, but she must remember *Dawdi's* kindness to her and his gentle lessons. They were so much better than her gloomy thoughts. She wanted to be more like he was as she sat in his presence. She would accept the life *Gott* gave her.

She would never marry and would live alone like Aunt Fannie. *Gott's* ways were always right. She would try to make the best of it. She knew without him saying so that *Dawdi* would want her to accept her imperfections and eventual disability.

"Look!" *Dawdi* pointed. His voice was almost a whisper. A tiny hummingbird was hovering over *Maemm's* hanging baskets, drinking nectar from the petunia goblets. "I think they have a nest somewheres nearby."

Just then the whistle blew, and it was dinnertime.

CHAPTER 5

Hank Kratzer

H e was slowly gathering a following of Amish needing a ride somewhere. He'd settled into a condo last winter, bought insurance, and was getting to know the highways and byways of his new home. Here, in the beautiful rolling hills of Holmes County, it was easier to let go of his old life, ordered by the semester calendar. The simplicity of driving Amish folk created a rhythm for his own life as he became part of theirs.

A routine had developed effortlessly, as his schedule filled with driving young mothers and their children to the doctor, taking energetic Amish entrepreneurs to meetings, and most interesting of all, having at least one weekly run with Fannie Troyer, owner of Cozy Corner Quilt Shop. She was different from the others, though. For one thing, she insisted on calling him Henry. After a couple of tries, he gave up correcting her.

Fannie had subtly drawn him into her project of finding new merchandise for her little shop. He looked forward to their weekly adventures into the farthest corners of Amish Country. Often their trips included a restaurant meal, an ice cream stop, or at the least, a home-baked treat from Fannie's kitchen. He was on his way to her place now. He smiled at the thought of the circuitous path he was certain lay ahead. They would spend the day looking for just the right pieces to add to her inventory at Cozy Corner Quilt Shop.

It was not a mistake to say "they." It had very quickly turned into a joint project between the two of them. Today would be another daylong effort to satisfy what seemed to be the extremely discriminating tastes of this eccentric woman—eccentric yet appealing in some indefinable way. He shook his head in dismay as he realized he was looking forward to being with her. He felt at home with her, perhaps even a bit attracted to her, if that was possible. *But she's Amish! What are you saying? Get a grip, Hank.*

Fannie's nieces were both at the shop today. He had met Susan early on. The young girl reminded him of some of his former students at Ohio University—a bit too self-assured, overly eager to please, and having the flawless skin and fine features of blossoming youth. Her waist was tiny, offset by the clunky athletic shoes that most OU girls reserved for running. Hank wasn't sure why Susan reminded him of them unless it was just that youthful exuberance that seemed so far from his own life at this stage.

"Did you ever meet Leah?" Fannie greeted him with a question as she gestured toward another young girl. "This is Susan's older sister, Leah."

"Pleased to meet you," Hank said, tipping his straw hat. She nodded her hello and stepped towards the door. Leah was shorter than her sister, and when she turned to leave, he noticed the unsightly twist in her spine.

Fannie gave Susan quick instructions and soon they were in the van. Fannie adjusted the seat to fit her tall frame. Hank adjusted the air conditioning. It was going to get warm today.

"So, you have two nieces?" Hank asked by way of conversation.

"More than two, of course. Susan and Leah are my brother's girls." Today Fannie was wearing a lavender dress that reflected her glowing complexion.

"Looks like Leah has a condition with her back," Hank said.

"*Yah*, she has a curvature of the spine. Other Troyer relatives have that, too. It's not *goot!*" Fannie said.

"I don't know much about it," said Hank. "But seems like there should be a medical treatment for her. What do they do for it?"

"The doctors talked about a brace once, but I don't think Albert and Elma went for it," said Fannie.

"That's too bad. Seems like something could be done to help her," said Hank.

"I guess Leah's parents just don't know what to do, other than make sure she doesn't work too hard," Fannie said.

They drove south from Cozy Corner, as Fannie laid out their plans for the rest of the day. "I'm wanting to go to Woodcraft Village over in Charm, and then to Sugarcreek. There's a place there somewhere, although I don't know exactly where, but I have the *Budget* with me. I'll look it up; they usually have an ad for it," said Fannie. She settled into the passenger's seat, the Amish newspaper in her hand.

Hank was surprised at the distance she'd asked him to drive. *Does she have any idea how far apart these two places were?* It was as if she was asking him to drive from the north pole to the south pole of Amish Country. Should he say something? This was going to be an expensive trip for her. But surely she knew what she was asking. It wasn't up to him to talk her out of it.

Not that he could if he'd wanted to. It hadn't taken him long to realize Fannie was a woman who knew what she wanted. He turned on the radio to the local NPR station.

"Do you get WKPN?" Fannie asked.

"Oh, yes, I suppose. You feel like country western music?"

"Well, it doesn't matter, I guess," she said.

But Hank knew it did. "Sure, we can listen to country. Why not?" So he tuned in and settled back in the leather seat, easing his achy breaky heart. They surged along, energized by Kenny Chesney's "She Thinks My Tractor's Sexy." *Does she think my van is sexy?* Hank smiled inwardly at this strange twist. *Was she listening to the words?* It was distracting to be riding with an Amish lady in this lyrical air. Hank turned down the air conditioning and focused on the double yellow line.

They rode companionably in silence for a bit. Sometimes when he was with Fannie he forgot she was Amish. Their conversations ebbed and flowed so effortlessly, and there was something between them—a depth of understanding that felt both strange and familiar. The music request was in the strange department. But Fannie seemed adept at asking him questions that moved from the surface to a deeper place.

Fannie broke the silence. "Where did you work before you moved here?"

"I was a university prof at OU—Ohio University." *How could she possibly have any idea what that meant?* Hank turned the radio down.

"What did you teach?"

"Humanities."

"What's that?"

"Well, it's really history, I guess you could say."

"Like Abe Lincoln and George Washington."

"Well, yes, in a way," Hank responded. "The idea is that we talked about the *human* part of history. Not so much the wars and changes in maps, but the way human civilization—arts and culture—moved from one era to the next."

"Oh, progress."

"I guess you don't think much of progress," Hank said, feeling suddenly nervous about the direction the conversation was headed. The Amish had bypassed progress, to his way of thinking.

"We Amish have our own kind of progress. Of course, no one ever calls it that, exactly. Things change for the Amish, too. Just the way they do for the *Englischers*."

Hank negotiated the van around a slow buggy going up a long hill.

"What kind of changes have you seen in your life?" Fannie asked.

"Well, for instance, constant upgrades to technology in the classroom. I finally decided to leave OU because I was expected to move from a chalkboard to an overhead projector to a smart board."

"You lost me there," Fannie said. "Right after the chalkboard."

"Don't worry; it's not worth learning about it. For me, life wasn't *progressing,* especially after Elaine died. I couldn't seem to find a good way to live life without her. That was the end of progress for me for a long time. Finally, I decided to move."

"Maybe that was the beginning of progress. Could it have been the beginning of a better life here in Holmes County?" Fannie asked.

How insightful. Why would she have thought of this?

"I wanted a simpler life," Hank said. "And I think I found it here. I must admit that at times it seems far more complex than I imagined when I first came, but I know it's changed me. And I'm no longer compelled to entertain students while I teach, or attend long meetings where people try to impress other people with their esoteric viewpoints and start arguments just for the sake of arguing." *This must sound strange to her.*

Hank leaned forward to turn the country music down again.

Another notch lower. It felt wrong to have it blaring into this comfortable conversation.

Fannie's hand reached out just as Hank grasped the radio knob. She caught his hand in her own and looked over at him in surprise. He quickly pulled away and put his hand back on the steering wheel. "Do you want it that loud?" he asked.

"No, that's okay. Go ahead, turn it down," Fannie said. "Henry?"

"Yes?"

"I'm sorry about your wife."

"Me, too. I think I'm getting better now. I needed a change of scenery." Hank gestured towards a hayfield where a team of workhorses plodded up a hill. Boys labored alongside men, using pitchforks to pile hay onto the wagon. A young girl was driving the team.

"Would you look at that?" he exclaimed. "Just this—sun, basic labor, green trees, grazing cattle. Horses and hillsides. And everywhere—I have never seen such flowers. It's a place to heal. It's the real world."

Fannie became quiet for a mile or two. They sat in a companionable calm, listening to country on the radio. In the songs, Hank suspected they both heard the truth. That pain, suffering, and regret were part of life. And yet the result was music.

CHAPTER 6

Aaron Keim

Something had changed for Aaron, Mose Keim's eldest son. It was as if he had grown up overnight. Perhaps it happened when he'd saved the old desk and the business records on the night of the fire. Even so, he felt the loss of their shop deeply, knowing it was the source of both the Keims' and the Troyers' incomes. It was a hardship for their families. And the fire had turned his *Daett* into someone Aaron didn't recognize.

Mose and his two eldest sons worked side by side. "What is all this trash still doing in here?" Mose Keim slapped his hand down hard on a door frame causing it to break loose, dragging the door with it. "How will we ever fill our orders on time?" he grumbled. "If we can even find the orders in all this mess."

Aaron tried to ease everyone's nerves. Being the eldest son, he knew one day this shop would belong to him. "*Daett*, I know it seems bad now, but just wait. We'll be done and have this place back together in no time." *Daett* barely acknowledged Aaron's words.

Aaron was encouraged when, at once after the fire, men from the church came and made a first pass at clean up. The job wasn't finished, but their presence had reminded Aaron that the Amish way was to reach out and help church members in times of need. And they had. They carted away the melted vinyl siding and broken windows and sorted the damage into manageable piles.

31

Leah and Susan's father, Albert Troyer, was both a neighbor and business partner. This morning, Albert had taken a couple of tables to a neighboring woodshop, where they could be finished. What was left was scrap.

"*Ach!* Look at this!" *Daett* raised pieces of once-beautiful cherry lumber now swollen with sooty watery film. Beautiful lathe-turned cherry table legs and grain-matched tabletops sanded to perfection were ruined.

Aaron grimaced and stopped what he was doing to watch his younger brother. Ben grabbed a broom and began scraping sodden sawdust and shavings out onto the loading dock. He pushed them over the edge onto the concrete below where they landed with a satisfying plop.

"The framing crew is bringing the new trusses on Friday," said *Daett*. "We need to get this cleared out today." He made a sweeping gesture in a half-circle.

Again, as he surveyed the rubble, the enormity of the situation settled into Aaron's gut. He tried to stay positive.

"I'm sure glad we hauled that cherry trestle table to the finish shop the day before the fire," Aaron said. "At least we saved that one." It was a new design he'd mastered. A work of art. Secretly, he'd called that table MOMA—Museum of Modern Art. But he kept that to himself. *Daett* always said: "Pride goeth before a fall." But those words didn't explain *this* misfortune, in Aaron's view. Pride or humility, it hadn't made a difference. K&T Woodshop was destroyed. At least for the time being. And *Daett* would also say: "Rain falls on the just and the unjust."

Were the K&T owners unjust or just? Aaron wasn't sure life could be so easily summed up in a couple of well-worn proverbs.

"We're going to have a pile of backorders now. The whole neighborhood will be affected by our fire. You know that don't you?"

Daett grunted. He shouldered the weight of the fire for the entire community.

Aaron knew *Daett* was looking to his eldest son for extra support. Maybe it was a new start. A time for Aaron to begin taking over what would one day be his business. This woodshop was part of a larger whole. K&T built tables, and a shop down the road made chairs and benches. Another neighborhood shop made cabinetry. Everything was hauled to a neighboring shop where stain and finish was applied. Working together, each doing their part, the little neighborhood of Benville could make a dining room furniture set.

"I predict the new shop is going to be way better than our old one ever was," Aaron said. "You said yourself we're outgrowing this one." He tried to put the disaster in the best light, hoping to improve *Daett's* mood.

"Look what I just found." Ben held up a length of new tubing still coiled in its packaging. "I can use this to replace some of the melted parts." Aaron was the draftsperson and artist. Ben was the mechanic who kept their nonelectric tools in working order. Compressed air, produced by a generator, powered table saws, lathes, drills, joiners, and belt sanders.

"*Yah*, that's good," said *Daett*. "Almost every tool we had in here is damaged."

Ben carried the coiled tubing over to the makeshift table on sawhorses where the damaged equipment was already lined up waiting for repairs.

"I can replace a couple of these damaged air hoses this afternoon," said Ben.

"Tomorrow Albert can take the equipment Ben can't fix to Air Products," *Daett* said. He kicked a melted plastic bucket towards the trash pile.

"Shall I clean up your desk?" Aaron asked.

"Might as well have a go at it. If you think you can manage that."

Aaron made his way to the old roll-top that he'd helped rescue the night of the fire. Sitting under a shade tree, its surface was stacked high with soggy papers and soaked invoice books.

"Save anything that looks important, like orders or bills," *Daett* said.

Aaron's pulse quickened when he realized he was being invited to oversee the shop's paperwork, even if it was part of the cleanup. Usually, *Daett* and Albert took care of that business. Aaron had thought *Daett* even seemed a bit secretive about the financial side of K&T.

"I'll put some of it on the picnic table in the yard. Maybe the sun will dry it out," Aaron said. He set to work, stacking things that were dry and throwing catalogs and old papers into the trash barrel. He glanced briefly at the stack of flyers advertising the Children's Relief Auction. Now that was something he looked forward to. A chance to see people, eat good food, and get away from the soot and smoke for a change.

At noon, when the firehouse whistle blew, the crew broke for dinner. Mose and his boys went up to the house where Anna had a good dinner waiting. Aaron carried a box of papers from the desk and detoured to the picnic table. He spread them out to dry and began looking more closely at what he'd found. It would be interesting to read the account book. He was curious about the woodshop's finances. For just a moment, he considered taking the record book and looking it over, but dinner was ready, so he placed it on a bench and went to wash up.

While they ate, their younger sister, Sovilla, distracted them from the morning's difficult work by telling them about the Troyers' yellow lab, Toby. The neighbors had adopted him from the Humane Society, and this was the second time he'd run off.

"I told you it was foolish of them to get a dog from the pound," *Daett* said. "Those dogs are spoilt indoor dogs that don't want to live outdoors. You don't know what you're getting at the pound. They should have taken my advice and picked up one of the puppies they were giving away free out in front of the Mt. Hope auction last week."

"He was gone for a week last time, but then he came back," Sovilla said. "Leah likes him so much. I think that's why they haven't given up on Toby."

"They could take him back if it isn't working out," Ben said.

"They have to find him first," Sovilla said.

Aaron felt bad for both the Troyer family and for Sovilla. Even though Toby wasn't her dog, she was already attached to him.

"He does tricks. He can catch a ball and he can beg for treats," Sovilla said.

"They think he understands *Deutsch,*" Ben added. Everyone laughed.

Aaron knew that for children there was nothing as fun as chasing a dog in circles on a cool summer evening, running off the *kinnah's* remaining energy before bedtime. And dogs did understand *Deutsch* just as easily as they understood English.

"After dinner, I'll go down the road with you, Sovilla," Aaron offered.

"Don't be gone long. We start back to work at 1:30."

"Sure thing, *Daett.*"

Aaron knew it was unlikely Toby was still in the neighborhood, but Sovilla would feel better knowing they'd tried to find the dog. They kept to the edge of the pavement on Clear Creek Road. A blue van, driven by Hank Kratzer, slid by them. He was taking Fannie somewhere again today. Aaron and Sovilla looked to the right and left as they walked down the road. As they came by, their neighbor, Leah, was at the mailbox.

"Did you find the dog yet?" Aaron asked. "Sovilla wanted me to help her look for him."

Leah kept her head down as if the mail in her hand was more important than Aaron's question. "He's not back yet. Last time he was gone for a week." She looked off across the field and Aaron sensed her discomfort. *Why didn't she want to talk?* She used to be friendly when they were younger.

"Thanks . . . for looking . . . Toby's still gone . . ." Leah's voice trailed off and she looked like she might cry. "He came back before. But he was so thin. I hope he's okay."

A soft spot opened in Aaron's heart as he thought about his school friend, Leah. She was always so kind to everyone. But just now she seemed shy, or sad, or both. He wished he could whistle, and Toby would come running. He wished he could make Leah smile. Aaron let out a sharp whistle. "Here, Toby, boy! Here, Toby!" They watched the field and looked down the road. But Toby didn't appear.

Leah gave Aaron a weak smile and without another word she turned and made her way up the lane. Aaron watched her for a moment and then followed Sovilla up the road. There was something about Leah that tugged at his heart. Why wouldn't she talk to him?

After another quarter mile, Aaron and Sovilla climbed the neighbor's metal gate and headed through the pasture back to the shop.

"That dog will come home when he's ready, Sovilla. Don't you worry, he'll be back before long," Aaron assured his younger sister.

"I hope so," Sovilla said. "He's such a nice dog."

"He is," Aaron said. Then he headed for the shop and Sovilla went back to the house.

Aaron wished he'd thought of saying something hopeful to Leah. Maybe she would have talked to him more. Maybe she would have at least looked at him.

CHAPTER 7

Leah Troyer

A thundercloud was gathering in the west, and *Maemm* sent Susan to the clothesline to gather in the dry clothes. Leah stood on the porch looking up. The sky was quickly changing from bright to deep blue. Everything in the yard became still. Trees suddenly showed the undersides of their leaves, and the horses made their way to the fence in the corner of the pasture. When it rained, the house became cool again. Leah went upstairs to lower the open windows and found the book she'd been reading. Just as she picked it up, *Maemm* called to her from the bottom of the staircase. "Leah, will you go check on *Dawdi?* I told him we'd look in on him later. He was feeling poorly this morning. Quick, before it storms!"

With the book still in her hand, Leah made her way to the kitchen and opened the front door to the passageway that led to the *Dawdi haus.* She spoke to him through the screen. He was near a window, leaning down to look out at the sky.

"Leah, come in, come in! Looks like we're getting a thunderstorm."

"*Maemm* said you weren't feeling well. Are you okay?" *Dawdi* didn't look as if he was sick.

"*Ach*! It's just my arthritis acting up again today. Now I know why. Weather coming."

"I felt sore this morning, too," said Leah. "I thought it was from scrubbing the front porch."

Just then a giant rumble of thunder crashed, followed by a flash of lightning. Leah jumped and then settled herself onto the couch, laying her book aside. *Dawdi* rocked gently in his old rocker and looked toward the window. "Just stay here a little and keep me company. I don't see enough of my little girly," *Dawdi* said.

Leah always felt so calm in the presence of *Dawdi*. The clock ticked the minutes away and his rocker squeaked, but no noisy children were running about, no dishes clattering.

Leah was happy to stay.

"My, my, another summer here already. Where does time go? Seems not long ago you were just a little thing. Look at you now, almost grown." *Dawdi* glanced lovingly at Leah and stroked his beard.

"Susan is going to work at Fannie's store," Leah blurted out.

"Well, now, is that so? You don't say?" *Dawdi* paused, but Leah didn't say more. The clock ticked away another minute while the two of them listened to the rain on the tin roof of the *Dawdi haus*.

"I'm going to help Aunt Lydia and stay for two weeks after the Children's Relief Auction," Leah finally said.

Dawdi nodded. "That's good! Summer is a season of growth and change. You will learn from your time away from home," he said. He picked up his large Bible and put on his glasses.

"That puts me in mind of what I read here this morning. Ecclesiastes: To everything, there is a season . . . ahh, you know all of that!" He waved his hand. "And then this: He has made everything beautiful in its time; also, he has put eternity into man's mind, yet so that he cannot find out what God has done from the beginning to the end."

Everything is beautiful in its time. Leah savored the words as they hung in the air around *Dawdi*. The clock struck the hour. Leah felt her heart open. If only she could say the things she was thinking. If she could say them to anyone, anywhere, it would be to her *Dawdi*. Here.

As if he knew she wanted to talk and didn't know how to start, *Dawdi* placed the worn Bible over his knees and looked across the room at her. "And you, Leah. You are beautiful."

It was such a surprising thing for him to say.

"I don't feel beautiful. I don't feel beautiful at all!" Leah exclaimed. "I stand crooked, and walk crooked, and people stare at me when I go places. I dread going to the auction. Even to Aunt Lydia's. People stare. Susan can't wait to go to the Children's Relief Auction, but I dread it!"

Dawdi looked surprised at Leah's outburst, as violent as the thunderstorm. And Leah was as surprised as he was. She had never said such a thing to anyone. But then no one had ever told her she was beautiful.

"*Ach*, Leah. I'm sorry you must carry this burden. In all the important things you are beautiful, and you are beautiful in *Gott's* eyes. You are *Gott's* beloved daughter." *Dawdi* paused as if to let his words sink into Leah's wounded soul. "It's not for us to know *Gott's* times and seasons, only to follow where *Gott* leads. You must never think of yourself as being less than *Gott's* handiwork." *Dawdi* folded his hands together as if he were ready to pray. He said nothing more for a time.

The rain pounded on the tin roof, and the harder it fell, the more talkative Leah became. The floodgates opened somewhere deep within her and now her words were raining down, watering the space between them with her deeply felt pain.

"I don't know why *Gott* made me this way and Susan and all the others are straight and tall. Why is it me?" She didn't say anything about Susan's blonde hair, her fair skin, or the pleasing chatter and laughter that always surrounded her younger sister.

Dawdi sat quietly, just looking at her with deep love in his watery blue eyes. Leah could feel it the way she could feel the sun on her skin or the cool breeze at twilight. She sat silent, too, waiting for what would come next. She noticed how calm she'd become—just because he listened and didn't chide her for these feelings that seemed so wrong. She was unaccepting of the cross *Gott* asked her to bear. She knew that. But *Dawdi* never said it was wrong of her to wish she could stand straight.

"*Ach,* Leah. I don't know why either. Can you remember this?" He looked straight into her eyes, which were spilling over with tears she didn't expect. "Scripture says there is a season for everything, and *Gott* has made everything beautiful in its time. Look how green everything makes since this rain."

Leah noticed now that the rain had all but stopped and the house was quiet again—with just the ticking of the clock. *Dawdi* placed his Bible on the table with the pages still open. Leah rose, picked up the unread book, and smoothed her skirt. The moment had passed with the thunderstorm, leaving her feeling cleansed and renewed. But neither of them mentioned it.

"I guess I need to go back now. *Maemm* will need my help folding the clothes."

Dawdi only nodded as she made her way to the screen door. She felt his eyes boring into her back, tracing the crooked spine. She knew he was tenderly holding her in his vision, the angular shoulder, and the sagging hemline of her gray skirt. As she walked, she stood a little taller.

Beautiful, she thought. *Beautiful. Everything in its time.*

CHAPTER 8

Dave Woodruff

The Lakewood Farmers' Market linked the city to the country, where Cleveland met Amish Country. Dave and Monica Woodruff discovered the market after their couples' counselor suggested they find things to do together as a family. Monica once said it had saved their marriage. Dave wouldn't have put it quite that way, but he knew his wife nearly left him soon after their daughter Kylie was born. Who knew? Without this weekly ritual, by now their family might have joined many ambitious medical professionals who lost their marriages to medical careers.

Instead, Doctor Dave Woodruff, Monica, and their two girls, Kylie and Skye, had discovered simple abundance in the outdoors as they mingled with good people and gathered good food. Wednesday mornings, spring through late fall, were sacred. Although Dave and Monica still didn't agree on a lot of things, this time together was a healing retreat from their busy lives.

Every Wednesday in early summer, from their Shaker Heights home on Briarwood, the Woodruffs coiled through midmorning traffic toward the lakefront in their black SUV. Monica had a list in her canvas tote, and Dave had a wad of small bills in his pocket—collected from the hospital ATM just before he'd crossed the bridge to the parking garage the night before. The girls wore sundresses and Skye sported a hat that looked like a sunbonnet. It was a souvenir from an earlier trip to their current destination. They turned at the intersection of Arthur Extension and Detroit Road, and Dave started looking for an empty parking spot in the area near Edgewater Park.

"I want to see Ellie," said Kylie, who would be four in December. She took another sip from a box of organic apple juice. Dave reached over the console and took Monica's hand in his. "We'll see her soon, sweetie. We're almost there. Daddy's looking for a parking spot." Monica smiled and squeezed his hand.

"Ellie! Ellie!" echoed Skye. Even their daughters had made a friend at the Farmers' Market. Skye was talking more every day—a fact Dave suddenly noticed but didn't mention. He knew if he said something, his words would quickly be interpreted by Monica as evidence of his lack of presence in the girls' lives.

They parked and tucked Skye into her stroller, then walked to the market. Fresh breezes off Lake Erie fluttered the canopies and the bright tablecloths of dozens of vendors who lined each side of a long pavilion. The scents of their wares wafted on the breeze. Summer fruits and vegetables were stacked high on tables marked with handmade signs. For the next hour or so, they browsed the displays of fresh blackberries, sunflowers, greens, and oddities such as purple potatoes. Monica selected a plastic bag of nasturtium and salad greens. They picked up bright heirloom tomatoes, tasted cheese samples, and the girls stained their dresses with berry juice popsicles.

After they looked at everything, bought loaves of bread from the Italians, and pastries from the Hungarian lady, they at last made their way to the Weaver stand. The Weavers and their driver, Mel, were there rain or shine with a refrigerated truck full of produce from their gardens, orchards, and a few neighboring farms.

Aden Weaver, the Amish vegetable guy, was a calm presence in the middle of the city, in the middle of the week. Around Aden, Dave somehow felt more himself. They didn't talk about much other than the weather and vegetables, but Aden was the rock Dave wished he could be—strong, grounded, gentle. He was gentler than any surgeon Dave had ever met. But even at that, Dave knew Aden sometimes butchered hogs. For some reason, the idea of that seemed worse to him than wielding a scalpel.

His girls loved Ellie, Aden Weaver's ten-year-old daughter. She always had something to show them—a funny twisted carrot with two legs, a purple tomato, or the perfect star found in a cut apple. Monica preferred Aden's fruits and vegetables above all the other vendors.

Aden greeted them jovially. His broad smile and thick black beard were a welcome sight.

"Well, hello! The Woodruff family! You'd better step up. The zucchini is going fast." Today he was unusually talkative, as if he'd had an infusion of caffeine from the cappuccino truck. Dave smiled at the passing thought of his Amish farmer friend drinking a cappuccino.

"Kylie! How's my friend Kylie today?" Ellie was ready for the doctor's two little girls. Kylie jumped from one foot to the other and Ellie grasped both her hands and whirled her around. Skye reached out, eager for her turn. Meanwhile, Monica filled a box with fresh vegetables and selected a flat of strawberries. Ellie answered Monica's vegetable questions and told her about a recent infestation of Japanese beetles. She admired Skye's sunbonnet and showed them a flower doll she'd made. Its head was a Shasta daisy with a petunia bonnet. The skirt was an upside-down daylily. Kylie danced it up and down the table, singing a made-up song.

Aden quickly added up the bill in his head, and Dave handed over the total. Aden veered away from the weather and began telling Dave about a benefit auction in Amish Country. From a hidden pocket in his black denim vest, he drew out a colorful flyer promoting this important upcoming event. "Hey! This is just the thing for you, Doctor! It's the Children's Relief Auction. Let me give you this." Aden handed Dave the flyer covered with pictures of handmade quilts, wooden rocking chairs, and plates piled high with food.

"What is this?" Dave asked. He studied the flyer, noticing the slice of yummy-looking pie topped with ice cream.

"We do this every year in Holmes County. It's our way of helping some of the Amish families who have big medical expenses. You probably know we don't have medical insurance."

Dave nodded. He'd heard about that from colleagues at Cleveland Regional Hospital where he was a surgeon.

"The church takes care of their expenses. To help, all the Amish groups get together and do this. It raises thousands of dollars every year. Shopping for a good cause. And it's a lot of fun. A chance to get together and visit, give your little girls a pony ride, eat good food . . ."

"Say no more. You had me at 'good food!'" Dave said. He tucked the flyer in his shirt pocket.

"It's in a couple of weeks. Hope you can make it," said Aden.

"This sounds great! Don't you think so, Hun?"

Monica nodded. "Yes! It does! That would be something different for us."

Aden handed another flyer to Monica. "It's mostly Amish who go to it. But we get more *Englischers* every year. I think you'd like the quilts and the handmade furniture."

"I'm sure we would," said Dave. "And we're overdue for a weekend getaway. Monica has been saying we should visit Amish Country this summer." Dave picked up Skye and put her back in the stroller. It was about time to head back to the car.

"If the auction is on Saturday, maybe we will come down there on Friday." Dave tucked the flyer into the pocket of his shirt. He felt a sense of satisfaction. He'd arranged for more family time without being prompted by Monica or a marriage counselor. Now to find a cozy bed and breakfast. They could get out of the city; it was a short trip—just a couple of hours away.

"If you come on Friday, you should come over to Valley View and visit our farm. We're right in that same area, not far from Mt. Hope where they have the auction. I could show you around our place, the gardens, the strawberry patch, and, of course, the orchard. The grafts we did last year are coming along. We're going to have some good apples later."

Grafts? Dave questioned that comment on the way back to Briarwood. How would you graft a tree? He was intrigued. He was more familiar with bone grafts and skin grafts.

CHAPTER 9

Susan Troyer

Just before noon on Monday, Susan was pushing a hand cultivator through the garden rows. *Maemm* still insisted on using the old implement to protect the young plants. When Susan stopped at the end of a row, she spied Ben Keim, who was bounding towards her across the pasture. He skidded to a stop and leaned against the fence to catch his breath.

"Whoa! What's the big rush?" Susan asked. She propped the old cultivator against the fence and swiped her sweaty, sore hands over her skirt.

"Aaron sent me over. We had an idea about this weekend. It's the Children's Relief Auction, remember?" Ben asked.

"How can I forget? Leah and I are scheduled to help Fannie set up the needlework tables Friday afternoon. She asked us long ago," Susan said. She'd been looking forward to a break from the garden, which was taking up most of her time lately.

"Yeah, I thought so," said Ben. "Aaron and I will help put up the tents. My Uncle Sam is in charge, and he wants us there Friday afternoon, too. He said we could stay over at his place afterward. Should be fun and he's right in Mt. Hope. Real close to the auction grounds."

"I guess we'll see you there then," said Susan.

"Aaron said I should ask if you and Leah want to ride bikes over to Mt. Hope with the two of us on Friday morning. Make a day of it," Ben said. "And a night of it," he added.

"Sounds fun," Susan said. "I'm not sure what Leah will say. Anymore, I have trouble getting her to do things. I'll ask her at dinnertime. See what she says."

"Okay, let me know. Tell her it was Aaron's idea. I think he might have his eye on her. But don't tell her that," Ben cautioned.

Susan wasn't sure if he was joking. Maybe he was. Maybe not. "Check with me tomorrow," said Susan. "Leah likes to ride. It would be good for her to get away. She's such a homebody."

When Ben left, Susan trudged back to the house to wash up. *Maybe she'll quit moping around if we do this.* But Susan had a sinking feeling Leah would balk at the plan. Ever since Leah had finished eighth grade, her last year of school, she'd begged off going places, even to young people's singing and volleyball—things everyone else their age looked forward to. If she wasn't escaping to the pages of library books, she escaped to the *Dawdi haus*. She and *Dawdi* seemed to share a special bond that Susan didn't.

Susan resented their closeness. One time she asked Leah about it. "What do the two of you talk about?"

"Oh, nothing much. Just what he will have for supper tonight or how *Mommi* used to do things. Sometimes he talks about his aches and pains, that sort of thing." *Mommi*, their grandmother, had died a year ago. *Dawdi* never mentioned her when Susan was around.

He likes her more than me. I'm sure he feels sorry for her because of her crooked back. The instant she had the thought she felt guilty. It was ridiculous to be jealous of Leah who was fragile, almost a cripple. Susan was sure she would marry and have children, but Leah would probably stay single and care for their parents in their old age. Maybe Leah suspected this future, too.

But she acts like an old woman and she's not even eighteen. Susan waited to bring up the bike ride until after dinner when the two sisters stood at the sink doing dishes while *Maemm* put the leftovers away and tidied the kitchen. Susan filled the sink with hot water, while Leah found a clean dishtowel. "Ben came over to the garden just before dinner," Susan said. "He said Aaron had an idea."

"What kind of idea?" Leah asked.

"Ben asked if we wanted to ride bikes to Mt. Hope with him and Aaron on Friday morning. They are helping put up the tents for the Children's Relief Auction," Susan said. "We can all stay overnight at his Uncle Sam's place. They live right in Mt. Hope."

"We can't. We're supposed to help Fannie, remember?" said Leah.

"Yes. But can't you see? That's perfect. We need to be there, too, so we can ride over there with Aaron and Ben," Susan said. From the corner of her eye, she saw Leah's frown as she concentrated on drying the biggest crockery mixing bowl.

"I'd rather not," said Leah. Her short answer sounded final.

"Why not? And, hey, don't let on that you know, but a little bird told me Aaron wants to ride with you." Out of the corner of her eye, she saw Leah blush at this suggestion.

"*Shtobb tsidda!* Don't tease like that. You know Fannie needs us to help load Hank's van. We can ride with Hank."

Leah and I used to be close, and she liked my ideas. What happened to her?

Susan wasn't giving up. "Ben said Aaron wants both of us to come. Otherwise, I'd just go myself," Susan said.

Maemm paused in wiping down the table. "I think you should go, Leah. It will be good for you to get exercise and fresh air. You're in the house so much lately. Someone else will help Fannie. And Hank can even bring your overnight bags in the car."

Susan jumped in before Leah could disagree again. "Okay then, it's all settled. I'll tell Ben tomorrow." She stole a look at her sister who was hanging the dishtowel to dry. Leah looked upset, but not enough to challenge *Maemm*.

After resting a bit, Susan went back to the garden to finish pulling weeds. *Maemm* brought a dozen tomato cages from the garden shed. The two worked silently, pushing them in the ground around the young plants. Susan thought of Leah who was still in the house sweeping the floors and shaking rugs. Once again, she'd gotten the easy chores.

"I'm glad Leah agreed to go with you and the Keim boys," said *Maemm*. "I worry about her. You know how it is."

Susan did indeed know. *Maybe you worry too much. You treat her so special.* But, at least for once, *Maemm* had told Leah she should go.

"I'm glad, too," said Susan. "I was afraid she wouldn't go." It was hard to understand this sister-friend and their confusing relationship now that they'd grown up. They still lived under the same roof—even shared the same bedroom—but *Gott* seemed to be sending them in different directions. Susan was excited they were both old enough to go to the youth group together. It was a time to have fun and socialize before they settled down and became grown-ups. But Leah behaved as if she was already settled, yet she was only seventeen.

Susan ruminated: *If only we could be close like we used to be at school.* At least now she had Friday to look forward to. *We will finally do something together, the way sisters are supposed to. We can wear our matching dresses. We'll look and act like sisters for once.*

How had their childhood passed so quickly? Susan wasn't quite ready to be all grown up.

But Leah didn't seem to mind it at all.

CHAPTER 10

Leah Troyer

The Friday before the Children's Relief Auction was less hot and humid than earlier in the week. Leah and her sister were awake before dawn doing their morning chores. *Maemm* had gotten up at four to mix another batch of bread. Her cinnamon bread was always the first to sell at the auction bake sale. She used an old recipe from her Maryland cousins. The odor of cinnamon bread came to be associated with the Children's Relief Auction, the way molasses cookies made Leah think of Christmas or whoopie pies made her think of the first day of school.

Leah and Susan packed clean dresses, their nightgowns, and toiletries into their duffel bags. Leah packed more things since she'd be going to help Aunt Lydia after the auction. Susan insisted they wear their matching deep purple dresses, and they wore their new tennis shoes and short socks.

Before going on the bikes, they had to take their bags and a dozen loaves of *Maemm's* bread to Fannie's. Hank would deliver it to the auction grounds along with all the handmade things Fannie had collected from her shop and all the neighbors.

"I wish we didn't have to spend the whole day helping Fannie tomorrow," said Leah. She dreaded standing in one place behind those tables for hours; it made her back hurt.

"She always gives us time off for dinner, at least," said Susan in her aunt's defense.

"Well, she should have a lot more girls to help," said Leah. "And have shorter shifts."

"I guess you don't like selling stuff," Susan said. "You're not so much for being around people."

"What makes you think that?" Leah asked. "I suppose you love standing there in the heat for hours on end, answering questions and making small talk?"

"I think it's kind of fun to pitch in and be able to help a good cause. If it weren't for the Children's Relief Auction, certain families would be in debt because of their big medical bills," Susan reminded.

Leah knew she had a point. She just resented that Susan had arranged an entire two-day event filled with a bike ride, an overnight stay, and too many people. As usual, Susan made the plans and expected her older sister to go along with everything. And Susan always got her way.

Leah dreaded all of it. She dreaded the long bike ride, the hordes of people determined to find out which family she belonged to, the stares, the pity, the glances away. *Are they trying to figure out how I'm related to the other crooked-backed people walking around here? Susan has no idea how hard this is for me. Why can't she understand?*

At Cozy Corner Quilt Shop, Fannie and Hank were carrying boxes and storage bins to the back of his van. Fannie had outdone herself stocking up the needlework tables with merchandise this year. Leah noted her aunt's flushed face and the trivial banter between Fannie and her driver, Hank. They sounded like old friends but suddenly got quiet and serious when they noticed they were being observed.

"*Maemm* sent us here with her bread. And we brought our overnight bags," said Susan. "Can you take these in the car?"

"Well, sure. We'll make room," Hank said in a jolly tone. "What are you ladies up to? Looks like you're going on vacation to Mt. Hope."

"No, we don't take vacations. But we are going on a long bike ride today. We're riding to Mt. Hope with the Keim brothers," Leah said.

"That's about twelve miles, isn't it? Maybe fifteen," said Hank.

Leah nodded. She didn't let on how much she dreaded the ride.

"How are you going to make it up the Boonetown Hill?" Hank asked.

Leah was worried about that very thing. Hank's question only reminded her of all the reservations she had about this trip.

As if reading her mind, Susan chimed in. "Oh, we are going to have a great time!"

"Be safe," Hank said in a fatherly tone. "There might be a lot of traffic today."

He's a nice man. I can see why Fannie likes him.

As they walked back up the hill to the house, they ran into Ben and Aaron, already on their bikes. Ben had a red plastic milk crate bungeed to the rack over his fender. Inside was a garbage bag that presumably held their clothes for the overnight stay. The girls ran the rest of the way to the house and said a quick goodbye to *Maemm*. Their little brothers watched enviously as Leah and Susan got on their bikes and coasted down to the road. Adam was behind on his scooter, but only to the end of the lane where he watched. Aaron and Ben joined the girls and the four set off at a steady pace. For a while, the boys kept back, and the girls took the lead, but after a time they rearranged. Ben rode alongside Susan when there was no traffic behind them. He teased her about being slow on the hills. Aaron rode beside Leah, and they gradually fell further behind. At Salt Creek, midway through the trip, the Keim brothers announced a surprise lunch stop at the Heifer Creamery.

"Of course, there will be food at Mt. Hope, and supper will be at Sam and Edna's, but this is our treat," said Ben. Aaron held the door as they entered and walked to the counter to order. Leah waited to hear what Susan ordered and then ordered the same thing. Then they found a booth and the girls slid in first. Ben took the spot beside Susan, leaving Aaron to sit next to Leah. She felt sweaty and nervous with him so close to her. She sipped the cool sweet tea.

After lunch, Aaron rode with Leah the rest of the way. They didn't talk much and the rhythmic pedaling gave way to contemplation. *How did I ever let Susan talk me into this long ride? They probably just asked me because I'm older and thought I'd feel left out. I'm barely making it up this hill, slowing Aaron down. I'm so ashamed.* If it bothered Aaron, he didn't let on. By now, their two companions were far ahead. Leah pushed harder but her legs were giving out. She was panting.

"Let's take a break," Aaron said. They were in the middle of the long Boonetown Hill.

He pities me. Bike riders don't stop to rest in the middle of a long hill. Everyone knows it's even harder if you do that. Susan and Ben had dismounted at the top of the hill and were taking a water break. They waited and watched as Leah and Aaron rested and then trundled up. *Aaron is so nice. He didn't have to stay with me.*

Then in no time, all the dark thoughts were whooshed away as they flew down the other side of the hill. Leah's *kapp* strings tickled her cheeks. Her full skirt flared in the wind. She felt exhilarated. She'd accomplished something that a few hours ago she hadn't thought possible. They braked and skidded to a stop. Resting briefly at the entrance to the Mt. Hope auction grounds, they took in the hive of activity in front of them. One large tent had already been erected. Aaron and Ben were late to their job. They dropped their bikes near an overgrown shrub and the boys simultaneously pulled red hankies from their pockets to wipe the sweat from their faces.

Leah took a deep breath. *I did it! For a while there I wasn't sure I would make it. But here I am.*

"We'll see you girls later," Aaron said. He stuffed the hanky back into his pocket and smiled at Leah. His blue eyes met hers and lingered as if to congratulate her.

"See ya," said Susan. "Come by the needlework table when you can. Fannie will make us stay all evening if you don't come and rescue us."

"Sure thing," said Ben.

The rest of the afternoon the girls helped Fannie set up the table and arrange displays of embroidered pillows, crocheted throws, baby quilts, potholders, and dishtowels. Susan quickly set to work unloading all the heavy bins from Hank's van. "Get over here and help me," she commanded. "Hank has better things to do than wait around for us to unload."

But Leah saw that Hank seemed in no great hurry to leave. She ignored Susan. Her younger sister might have gotten her way and coaxed her into that long, hot bike ride, but Leah drew the line at following her orders now.

"This tent is going to ruin our sales," Fannie complained. "Look at the way the colors of these things are all wrong when the sun shines through the tent."

Susan disagreed—of course. "I think it's just fine. No one cares about that."

That was Susan's way. She always had to have the last word.

CHAPTER 11

Leah Troyer

T he next morning, a buttery, vinegary scent of barbequed chicken wafted across the auction grounds. They did a brisk business as they greeted customers and sold their wares.

The morning went fast. "You girls can take a break now," said Fannie. "Go enjoy some time with your family."

Just then, *Maemm* and *Daett* walked over with their aunt and uncle, Aden and Lydia Weaver. Leah and Susan stepped out from behind the tables. Leah's body ached from yesterday's bike ride and the lumpy bed the previous night. Her legs hurt from standing in one spot most of the morning.

"I'd say it's time for some dinner," Uncle Aden said. "Let's go get in line."

As they walked toward the food tent, an *Englischer* family caught up with them. Aden clapped the man on the back. "Come and meet more of the *freindshaft*," he said. "Here's some of my wife's family. These are our nieces, Leah and Susan Troyer. And this is Dr. Dave Woodruff and his wife, Monica."

Leah looked sidewise and shyly whispered hello, echoing Susan's more convincing greeting.

The doctor's wife, Monica, had a quilt wrapped in plastic draped over her arm.

"I see these folks every week at the Lakewood Farmers' Market in Cleveland," Aden said. Then he turned to the *Englischers*. "You might as well join us. Are you ready for dinner?"

Daett, Aden, and Dr. Dave walked shoulder to shoulder toward the food tent. The doctor pushed a stroller. Monica walked with Leah, Susan, and the older women. Ellie Weaver, Aden's eldest daughter, held the hand of the youngest Woodruff child. Trailing behind her were the three Weaver cousins and Leah's three younger brothers.

The food line moved quickly and soon everyone was seated at one of the long tables. Leah felt relieved when she ended up at the far end, near the men. At least she could avoid all the women's chatter and eat her meal. She bit into the salty, tender chicken, realizing how hungry she was. Then she noticed that the doctor's little girl had settled in beside her. The doctor's wife, Monica, looked in her direction from further down the table.

"Oh, dear," said Monica. "Is she bothering you?"

"It's no trouble," Leah said. "I'm used to helping *kinnah.*" She wiped her fingers on a napkin and punched a straw into the little girl's chocolate milk. She opened the plastic utensils.

Across the table from her, the doctor put a chicken drumstick on his daughter's plate.

"Thanks for helping," he said.

"I help with my little brothers all the time at home," Leah said. She felt embarrassed talking to a stranger, but the doctor leaned forward and continued.

"This is Skye. She's our youngest," he said. "And that one is Kylie." He gestured toward their other child. "She's great friends with Ellie ever since we met her at the farmers' market."

"Those are different names," Leah said, then blushed at her silly comment.

"I suppose so," the doctor said. "And what is your name again?"

"I'm Leah Troyer." She wished she could ignore him and

eat her food. The doctor didn't seem to notice. She looked down at her plate.

"Did Aden Weaver say you are his niece?" the doctor asked.

"Yes, he is our uncle. *Maemm* and his wife, Lydia, are sisters."

"I can see the resemblance," he said. "I'd say Lydia is the youngest."

"Yes. She's eight years younger than *Maemm*." Leah relaxed a bit. "I'm going to help Aunt Lydia after the auction. I'll take care of the children while she works in the garden."

"I'm sure Lydia can use your help." The doctor smiled at her and continued, "And what about you? Which one is older, you or your sister?"

"I'm the oldest. I'm seventeen and Susan's sixteen."

Skye pushed her plate away, twisted on the bench, and left to sit beside her mother.

"I see. Let me ask you something, Leah," the doctor's tone was suddenly more serious.

He bent closer and looked straight at her.

Leah felt nervous. *What if I don't know the answer? Why is he talking to me so much?*

The doctor drank his lemonade and Leah noticed his delicate hands, so different from the rough, calloused hands of the men and boys she knew.

"I don't want to embarrass you, but I can't help noticing that you have severe scoliosis. That's a hard thing to live with, isn't it?" His voice dropped as he said this part as if he didn't want anyone else to overhear him. There was kindness in the doctor's simple words that touched her.

"Yes," she said. She didn't dare look at him. In her family, they rarely talked openly about scoliosis.

"As you probably heard your uncle say, I'm a doctor. I'm an orthopedic spine surgeon at Cleveland General Hospital."

Leah swallowed and looked down at her plate of food she'd barely tasted.

"I'm not sure what you know about your condition. I hope you know scoliosis can be corrected with surgery," he said.

Leah glanced up and his gray-blue eyes met hers. She looked down at her plate again. "I don't know. My parents . . ." Her voice was shaking. *Why does he keep looking at me? Surgery? What is he talking about?*

"I understand. I mean, I think I understand," the doctor corrected himself.

"*Maemm* took me to the chiropractor sometimes when I was younger. We didn't think it helped much," Leah said.

"Probably not," he said. "I'm going to talk with them this afternoon, if that's okay with you. What do you think?"

Leah nodded nervously. It was a whole new idea. No one had ever mentioned surgery for her back. Her stomach flip-flopped as she grasped at the hope he suggested. The moment passed.

"Looks like I need a refill," the doctor said in a cheery tone. "Can I get you more lemonade?"

"No, thanks," Leah said.

He stood and picked up his plate. Somehow, he'd managed to consume his chicken dinner while they'd talked. Leah stayed where she was and ate her food now that no one was talking to her. The doctor got his refill and, to Leah's relief, found a place to sit near his wife and girls. She finished her food and went back to the needlework tent. Susan and Fannie were sitting on chairs behind the table. Fannie was eating a piece of cherry pie topped with melting ice cream.

"Look at how much we sold!" she exclaimed. "I just counted the money. We made almost $500."

For the next couple of hours, the three of them took turns minding the table and wandering around the auction grounds, where they caught up with friends and relatives they hadn't seen in a while.

At three o'clock, men and boys appeared and began folding up chairs. Tractors and wagons arrived to haul things away. Vendors packed up their remaining wares and prepared to leave. Fannie was putting unsold items into a plastic bin when *Maemm* and *Daett* came walking quickly toward Leah. The doctor, Dave Woodruff, was with them.

"Can you spare Leah right now?" *Maemm* asked Fannie.

"Sure," said Fannie. "We're pretty much done here, I think. You can go, Leah."

Leah followed as *Daett* led them to a picnic table under a tree away from the auction cleanup. Her insides were quaking. She knew this would be an important conversation.

Daett motioned for everyone to sit down. "We were talking to the doctor about you this afternoon," he said "Were your ears burning?" He kept his tone light and smiled at her.

Leah felt flip-flops in her stomach for the second time today. The look on her parents' faces signaled an important conversation was about to begin. *Please,* Gott. *Help me.* The prayer in her heart surprised her. Suddenly she knew how much she wanted to believe things could change.

Once they were settled, *Maemm* said, "Doctor, can you go ahead and explain it to her?"

"Leah and I did talk a little bit at lunch today," said Dave. "But not in detail."

He turned and looked into her eyes again as he had earlier when they were eating. Leah felt less nervous this time. Dr. Dave spoke so kindly. And *Maemm* and *Daett* were with her now.

"Since I'm a spine surgeon, I am very aware of your condition. It struck me the moment I saw you. I felt it was only right for me to talk with your parents. I wonder if you would consider having corrective surgery. The birth defect you have is known as 'idiopathic scoliosis.' The cause is unknown, although it may have a genetic basis."

Leah nodded.

"There's some on my side among our cousins' families," said *Maemm.*

"I'm not surprised to hear that," said Dr. Dave. "It may be more prevalent in communities like the Amish where intermarriage between families goes back a few generations, although we can't be sure of this."

Leah and her parents nodded as the doctor continued his explanation.

"Idiopathic scoliosis causes the spine to curve sideways and sometimes outward as well. The result is uneven shoulders and a waistline that is higher on one side than the other. It causes the person to lean slightly to one side," the doctor said. "It also causes a hump on one side of the back, which you've probably noticed on Leah. Without correction, it could cause problems with internal organs as she grows older."

"We notice it when we fit her dresses," said *Maemm.* "We used to go to the chiropractor, but then we quit going. Maybe we should have kept it up."

"Unfortunately," said the doctor, "that isn't the answer when the problem is as severe as Leah's. But it *can* be corrected with surgery. I've done quite a few of these surgeries and I'd like to suggest you consider surgery to correct your daughter's disability. When it's as severe as it is in Leah's case, the risk of long-term disability is significant. It's the least I can do for the niece of my good friend, Aden Weaver," the doctor said.

The butterflies in Leah's stomach started up again. She looked at the doctor. She thought about her long talks with *Dawdi*. The doctor's kindness reminded her of *Dawdi*.

What will Maemm *and* Daett *say? Will they agree to it?*

Daett spoke up first. "I'm sure you mean well, doctor. But we know people who have this, and they get along all right. We think it's just the way *Gott* made our Leah."

Leah's heart sank. *Daett* had a stubborn streak that could make things difficult.

"I don't know anyone who had surgery for it," *Daett* said. He tapped his fingers nervously on the tabletop as he spoke.

Maemm added, "Some of the older ones have a few health issues, but it's probably just aging, like everyone." She was careful about how she disagreed. "What do you think about all this?" *Maemm* cast a searching look in Leah's direction.

"I keep wishing there was a cure for me," Leah said. *We haven't spoken of this ever. Now this.*

"If it's just about making her look better, that's not so important to our people," *Daett* said. "Scripture says: 'Man looketh on the outside, but the Lord looketh on the heart.' Why should we do this if this is how *Gott* made her?" *Daett* asked.

Leah's heart sank. *Why does he have to think this way? Our people have surgery when a doctor says they need it.* She'd tried to accept her problem. *But . . . can't* Gott *use the doctor to help me? Could it even be* Gott's *will that we met this doctor today?*

Leah felt the doctor's eyes on her. He spoke slowly. "I know this is kind of sudden, but I wonder if you'd consider letting Leah come to Cleveland General Hospital for some testing and evaluation.

If she's a candidate for surgery, which I suspect she is, I'm prepared to do the surgery at no cost. I hate to see someone suffering from scoliosis when I know I could help her. What do you think about that idea, Leah?"

Leah's heart pounded in her chest. *How can this be happening?* Her feeling of disbelief was like the night of the fire. It didn't seem real. She looked at her parents. *Maemm's* eyes were brimming with tears. *Daett's* face was hard to read. But his words suggested he wasn't ready to consider it. *Is he afraid for me?* They sat under the tree in silence. Leah waited. She held her breath.

"What do you think, Leah?" *Daett* spoke slowly.

Leah wasn't used to anyone asking her what she thought, least of all her *Daett*. "I don't know . . ." She felt everyone's eyes on her as she struggled to speak the thoughts that were swirling around in her head. She was nervous, excited, and confused all at once. "I could at least get the tests, I suppose," she said. "I would like to stand up straight and be able to work like everyone else." She knew her parents felt bad about her condition and tried to protect her. Especially *Maemm*.

Maemm dabbed at her eyes and smiled. *Daett* picked up his straw hat from the table and put it back on as if the conversation was over. "We don't want to be beholden to anyone," said *Daett*.

Leah knew the church often helped with medical expenses. That's what the Children's Relief Auction was all about. Maybe the Children's Relief Committee would pay if *Daett* didn't want to accept the doctor's gift.

"I understand," said the doctor. "I'm sure we can work it out somehow if you are open to at least *considering* corrective surgery."

Maemm nodded in agreement. *Daett* nodded his head too, but he stroked his beard. A sign he wasn't quite sure.

"I was thinking about something else this afternoon," said Dr. Dave. "Skye, our youngest daughter, seemed to like Leah when we were sitting together at lunch. I've been telling Monica, my wife, that we should hire a summer nanny. She needs a break from those girls. Maybe Leah could come back to Cleveland with us tonight. It would be difficult for me to get back here anytime soon, but we're here now. She could get the tests in the next couple of weeks and try out as our nanny. Would you consider that?" Dave looked back and forth between Leah and her parents. The question hung in the air.

"I think we'd be open to having her stay with us for longer. For the summer, perhaps," said the doctor.

Leah was dumbfounded at this suggestion. *Me, a nanny? What will Susan think when she hears this?*

"Leah, would you be interested in being our nanny?"

Would they agree to such a thing? "I think I could do that. Unless *Maemm* still wants me to help Lydia." Leah wanted to respect her parents' wishes on the matter. But she liked the idea of being an *Englischer's* nanny for the summer. That would be even better than caring for the Weaver cousins.

"I don't see much harm in her at least having the tests if you could arrange it," said *Daett*. "If she'd be a help to you and your wife in return, I think we can spare her for a little."

Leah let out a sigh of relief. Throughout the conversation, she'd never been certain how *Daett* would answer.

Maemm seemed pleased that *Daett* agreed. "She was planning to go home with Lydia and help her, but I'm sure Lydia will understand. This is so important for Leah," said *Maemm*. "I think if Leah wants to have the tests and help with the children for a couple of weeks that would be fine. We should at least find out if surgery is a possibility. You've made such a generous offer."

Leah knew both her parents worried about her future even though they never said it straight out. They must want her to get help, now that they knew it was possible to correct her crooked back with surgery.

Leah's parents talked to the doctor about the details and exchanged phone numbers. They finally stood but kept talking together under the big shade tree. Leah felt a surge of anticipation, along with nervousness about all the changes ahead.

"All right. I need to get back to Monica and the girls," the doctor said. "I'll go get the car. We had to park way out in a hayfield because we got here so late. I'll meet you near here as soon as I can."

After he left, *Maemm* wiped her eyes again and *Daett* handed her a handkerchief from his pocket. He looked at Leah and her mother.

"We have to find Aunt Lydia," Leah said. "And I need my bag from Hank Kratzer's van."

After the strange events of the last hour, it was a relief to have simple things to do.

CHAPTER 12

Susan Troyer

The following week, Fannie left with Hank while Susan was still hanging out the last load of wash for *Maemm*. After gathering her sewing into a plastic bag, Susan yelled up the stairs, "I'm going now. Time to open for Fannie!"

Susan walked across the yard and then took the shortcut path to Cozy Corner Quilt Shop. She retrieved the key that was under the white-painted stone beside the plastic urn trailing sweet potato vines near the shop door. She unlocked the door, took the key for the cashbox from its nail beneath the curtained counter, unlocked the box, and replaced both keys to their hiding places. She counted the cash, placed all the bills in order, and wrote their amount on the slip as Fannie required.

There was a note on the counter. "Susan—went to Farmerstown. Looking for toys & such. Don't forget to sweep and dust." Susan did the chores. She was glad for the quiet. It gave her time to think.

The longer Leah was gone, the more Susan felt a confusing mixture of emotions. She was jealous that Leah was a nanny for an *Englischer* family while she was stuck working for Fannie. With Leah gone, Susan had to do double the work at home. She was ashamed of her negative thoughts. And yet she was also happy for her sister. *She's going to have a much better life if this surgery fixes her back.* She shook off her worries and resolved to be a better sister.

Susan swept the stoop and the concrete steppingstones leading up to the door. After a quick swipe of the windows with cleaning
spray, and a flick of the feather duster over the tops of quilts hanging
from their wooden holders, all the opening chores were done.

Susan carried her half-sewed dress to the back room and
cleared off a space on the table to work on the pleated skirt. She
needed uninterrupted time to fold and pin, but she wasn't in the
mood to sew. Already the air was close and warm in the tiny,
crowded back room.

Susan had carefully measured and pinned only two pleats
when the sleigh bells on the screen door signaled a customer had entered the shop. It was a neighbor, for sure, since there was no sound
of a car or horse. With a sigh, Susan pushed aside the curtain to
find a slightly sweaty Aaron smiling at her as he stepped across the
threshold.

"May I help you, sir?" Susan spoke in her best fake shopkeeper
voice.

"I don't know. Do you have . . ."—Aaron took her bait and
played along—". . . a fancy dish towel, Clover salve? My achin' back!
I need my Yoder's Elixir to get me through this day!" He clutched the
items to his chest and then slapped them onto the counter.

His grin broadened to a real smile. His wheat-colored hair
stuck to him where it was sweaty under his hat band. His bluer-than-
blue eyes held hers for a moment.

Susan grabbed a bag, stuffed the items inside, and tossed it towards Aaron. He caught it and then grabbed Fannie's stool, scraping
it across the floor until he could tip it to rest on two legs, his back
against the wall.

"Why aren't you at the shop?" Susan asked. "Your *Daett* needs
your help, I dare say."

"We're on break, waiting for the lumberyard truck. That's my signal. Until then, I'm here shopping at my favorite store." Aaron surveyed the small window facing the road where there wasn't any traffic except for a cart pulled by a pony, carrying three small boys.

"Heard anything from Leah?" Aaron asked. Susan wasn't fooled by the casual tone in his voice. It was the whole reason he'd walked down two lanes to jingle the screen door on Fannie's shop.

"The family hears from her almost every day. *Maemm* calls her sometimes," Susan assured him. "And just this morning she said she was going to start a circle letter for her. I think she already passed it on to some Troyer relatives or I'd say you could add to it." This was Susan's chance to evaluate Aaron's interest in Leah.

"Circle letters are for the old folks," Aaron said. "But, sure! I'd write to her. But I need her address."

Susan wrote Leah's address on a piece of scrap paper and handed it to him. He folded it and tucked it inside his hat band. "Here's some paper." Susan grabbed a bright pink flyer advertising a charity auction and flipped it to the blank side. "What do you want to tell Leah? Go!"

Susan scrawled the date at the top of the page. Underneath it, she wrote, "Dear Leah," before passing it across the counter to Aaron. Again, Aaron played along with Susan and began writing in his fine penmanship, adding extra flourishes on the ends of words. From her vantage, Susan couldn't see what he was writing, but it seemed he had a lot to say. This would be a different letter for Leah to open when she got the mail in Cleveland.

Aaron thrust his masterpiece under Susan's nose. "How's this for a letter?" he asked.

Susan read the letter aloud. "Dear Leah, how are you? I am fine. The weather is hot, and it looks like rain. How is life in the big city of Cleveland? Are you staying out of trouble?"

"Really, Aaron? That's your idea of a good letter?" Susan looked up from the pink page and waved it in the air between them. "What would Mr. Miller say if he saw such a lame letter? But I have to say, you do have nice handwriting."

Mr. Miller, their sixth-grade teacher, assigned the students to write letters describing their activities and adding interesting details with vivid descriptions. He wouldn't have liked Aaron's dull, boring letter. They both knew that much.

"Yes, you should send her a letter. I know she'd like to hear from you," Susan said.

"I'll do that," Aaron said. "I sure will do that, if it helps your sister get back to Benville any sooner."

I knew it! He's sweet on her. Susan just grinned at him. "I know what you mean. I miss her, too. We all do, *Dawdi,* too. He might even miss her the most. Or is it you that misses her most?" Susan threw that out hoping he'd admit what she now suspected.

Aaron slammed the front legs of the stool onto the floor. His face reddened. "What makes you think that? I'm just trying to help. That's all."

That blush and his attempt at distraction was a sure sign Aaron was interested in dating Leah someday. She hoped Aaron would write a real letter, expressing his feelings. Her sister was so homesick. Letters from home would surely help.

"Get your letter in the mail tomorrow morning," Susan said. "Write a Mr. Miller letter—you know, one that makes her smile when she reads it. By the time *Maemm's* circle letter gets passed around to all the Troyers, Leah could be back home. But we younger people can make sure she gets letters from us."

Just then a large flatbed truck turned into the K&T shop lane and groaned its way up the hill.

"Okay! Time out is over. Back to work! See you tomorrow, Susan."

"Don't forget! Write a good letter!" Susan shouted over the roar of the truck's engine. "A Mr. Miller letter!" She waved the pink paper in his direction. Aaron nodded as he slapped his hat on and let the screen door slam behind him.

Susan ate the bologna sandwich she'd brought for lunch and then made space on the small counter. She found a notebook and tore out a couple of pages.

Dear Leah,

I'm at Fannie's store today waiting on customers. I mean waiting for customers. It's been a slow week (again!). I finished sewing two dresses while I'm here minding the store. Fannie is out with Hank. I think they went to Farmerstown today to pick up something she ordered.

It sounds like you're having a good time with the doctor's children. I can't imagine what it's like to have a whole room filled with toys. You must like watching them play. Or maybe you're playing with them, too. I hope you're not working too hard, ha ha!

It would be different to have a dishwasher. I don't know if I'd want one. Think of all the good talks we'd miss if we didn't do the dishes together. Since you left, Maemm has made Andy dry dishes. He's mad about it and won't talk to me, but too bad. Maemm told him if he's mad, he's just going to have to get glad again. She put together a package for you. Aden will bring it on Saturday with the produce truck.

This morning, Aaron Keim came over and was asking about you. I gave him your address because I'm sure that's what

his visit was all about. Maybe he'll write to you. I tried to make
it easy for him. Hope you don't mind.

The K&T will be rebuilt soon. They're going to completely
replace the burned part. I think Daett *said we can expect over*
a hundred men will come to work on it. I'll be helping with the
food. It's going to take a lot of pie for that crowd. We'll bake a
couple of cakes, too. It's going to be a fun day and we'll be glad
the shop is up and running again. Before then there's a lot to
clean up. And Daett *said they won't be caught up on all the*
furniture orders until next year because of the fire.

That's all for now. Write soon!
Yours Truly,

Susan reread every word of her letter. When she got to the
end she paused to reflect. *I should tell her I miss her. Because I do.* She
erased *That's all for now* and changed it to *I miss you, Leah.*

Mr. Miller liked to sign letters with "Yours truly," but that
didn't seem right this time. She erased it and wrote *With love, Susan.*

CHAPTER 13

Leah Troyer

L eah sat scrunched between the bulky car seat and the plastic booster seat where the two girls dozed, holding onto their worn stuffed animals. The couple in the front seat of the Woodruff's SUV, Leah learned, had spent the previous night at one of the Amish Country B&Bs. Hours later, the sun was going down as Dave Woodruff drove onto the expressway ramp that would take them to Cleveland. Everyone was quiet.

Leah felt tired, too, but napping was out of the question. Random thoughts churned through her mind: *Wish I could have said goodbye to* Dawdi. *What will he think? What is happening to me?* But then his words flitted through her tired mind, snatches of Bible verses about vines and gardens and seasons—comforting thoughts. Strangely, she was not afraid of what was to come. *Gott* had placed her here in this car with these people—Uncle Aden's friends. She imagined herself snug between the car seats, in the palm of *Gott's* hand. She felt strong—as if she could deal with anything.

That first week in Cleveland went by quickly. There was no time to get homesick. Life in the Woodruffs' home in Shaker Heights was far different from her home in Benville. Rather than the whole family eating together, the children ate their meals at a child-sized table in the corner of the kitchen. They ate kid's food—small bits of cut-up fresh fruit and vegetables. They had juice boxes and tiny crackers for snacks. After breakfast, they sat watching television in their pajamas. At home, everyone got dressed as soon as they got out of bed, and most mornings the whole family gathered around the table for breakfast and a morning prayer.

Monica gave Leah a list of morning chores. Like at home, she swept the floors, took care of the dishes, and looked after the children. She also picked up dozens of plastic toys each day. The toys talked and sang and lit up and moved across the floor, powered by batteries. Leah had no problem spending time with Kylie and Skye. Together, they learned what all the toys could do. She even fixed a couple of them by replacing the batteries so they could enjoy them again.

On the afternoons when the girls were in preschool, Monica took Leah to Cleveland General Hospital for her appointments. Leah was glad Monica was there to guide her through the unfamiliar experiences and help her find her way around the huge hospital that covered an entire city block. Monica expertly made her way down busy city streets. They had access to the doctor's parking deck and a staff elevator. Monica led the way to the offices where Leah had her testing and evaluation.

On Friday, Leah was picking up toys and clutter in the family room when Monica came from the kitchen and held out her phone. "It's your mother. She wants to talk to you," she said.

Leah took Monica's iPhone. "Hello?" she said tentatively. Was something wrong at home?

"Leah!" *Maemm* greeted her. She sounded excited.

"*Maemm*, you called me!" She sank into a soft white leather chair. It was strange to hear *Maemm's* voice on the phone.

"Yes. We exchanged contact information at the auction before you left. She said I could call. We thought we might hear from you. Are you okay?"

Guilty feelings rose inside Leah's chest. Was it so easy to forget Benville now that she was living here?

"What have you been doing? We wonder so much about you. When you didn't call, we thought maybe you'd sent us a letter. Did you write us yet?"

Leah swallowed, aware of her lapse. Of course, *Maemm* had been worrying about her. And she knew how Leah liked to write. In school, she had even exchanged letters with Amish pen pals from other states.

"Sorry, I've been busy going to appointments, and Monica didn't have any stamps," Leah said. "Can you send me stamps when you write? Do you have the address?"

"Yes. We have it along with phone numbers," *Maemm* said. "You can call in the evenings. *Daett* brings the shop phone home after work. We like to hear your voice."

Leah felt nervous talking on Monica's cell phone, knowing its owner was just around the corner chopping vegetables and listening. Leah switched to talking in *Deutsch.* "You sound far away. What's happening there this week?"

Maemm talked about the garden and about *Daett's* meeting with the neighbor men to plan for rebuilding K&T. *Maemm* and Fannie were planning to make six pies each for the frolic when the men came to rebuild. They hoped it was enough and would make a couple of cakes just in case they needed them. Susan went to the youth group's volleyball tournament last night with Ben and Aaron. It was good for her to get out. She'd been working a lot at home, plus helping Fannie.

Leah told *Maemm* a little more about her first visit to the clinic. She'd had an MRI and blood tests. They took three tubes of blood for tests. The MRI was scary, having to lie so still inside that big noisy tube. She'd closed her eyes until it was over. She didn't tell *Maemm* about how she almost passed out, or how it was hard to understand the hospital volunteer. She would tell her that later when Monica wasn't nearby.

There was a long silence while they tried to think what else to say.

"Okay, then. That's all," *Maemm* said. "You can call in the evenings. We miss you." Then *Maemm's* voice was gone. A surge of homesickness rose inside Leah as she handed the phone back to Monica.

"*Maemm* wondered why I didn't call before now. I guess I should have," Leah said. "It's a good thing we have a phone for business that we keep inside the house in the evening. Our neighbors still have a *phone haus* instead of a cell phone. "

"I wasn't sure if Amish used cell phones," Monica said.

"Some don't," Leah said. "But most of the families in Benville have a cell phone for their furniture building businesses."

"I was so surprised when she called that I forgot to tell her things. I'm going to write a letter. *Maemm* would like that, I think," Leah said.

"Letter writing is a lost art," Monica said with a sigh. "That's a good idea. Sometimes writing a letter is even better than a phone call. But remember, you can call whenever you want," Monica added. "I think I have an old phone of mine around here. I'll get it activated for you. We can put it on our plan, so you have one while you're here with us."

"Thank you. That would be good," Leah said. "Do you have some paper, and a pencil or pen?"

Monica went to the family room computer desk and opened the printer tray. She handed Leah a stack of white pages. "It doesn't have lines, but there's always plenty of paper here," she said. She reached into a drawer and came up with a handful of pens and pencils, even some colored pencils.

"I'll get stamps for you tomorrow. I didn't even think of getting you a phone until just now. You should have said something. Don't be shy if you need something."

"Thank you," Leah said. "I'd like that."

After lunch, Leah walked outside into the hot summer afternoon. She climbed the stairs to her room above the garage and turned off the air conditioning. It was too cold. Then she opened the window and sat down at the little desk that was perfectly placed under the window.

She spread out a couple of blank pages and examined all the pens, settling on an extra fine point.

She gazed out to the wide lawn with its clusters of river birch surrounded by vines, and farther back a row of weeping hemlock and blue spruce trees. There was so much to write. She decided to write to her sister first.

Dear Susan,

You can't imagine what it's like here in Cleveland. The Woodruff house is larger than ours and older, too. They have three bedrooms in the main part, but they gave me another one above the garage. Monica calls it the carriage house. It has its own bathroom and a window seat. Also, a little desk under the window.

I went to Cleveland General Hospital already on Monday after I got here. I had an MRI at the hospital. Scary! But the people there are nice. It was a noisy machine, so they gave me headphones and told me I could listen to music. I didn't know what to pick, so the nurse put on Beatles songs. Even so, I could still hear the machine.

The Woodruffs *are trying to make me feel at home, but everything is different. I try to help a little with the children and cleaning up after supper. The doctor,* Dave, *is teaching me how to load the dishwasher. They like the way I clean and tell me I'm "a natural" at being a nanny. It's not very hard because the girls have so many toys and they are so cute.*

Monica *took me with her to* Trader Joe's. *It's a grocery store but there are two rows of natural supplements like Healthy Corner back home. I didn't even know what some of the food was in the deli section. Did you know people eat grass? It's wheatgrass growing right there in a glass case.* Daett *would sure laugh about that, wouldn't he?*

Maemm *says they will soon rebuild K&T. Do you know when? I hope I can be home for it, but I don't know. I might be here longer than we thought.*

Leah took a break to watch a finch in the bird bath. What was happening now back home? In her mind, she pictured the front porch, the boys chasing Toby around in the yard in the evening. They all seemed so far away just now. Leah locked down at the letter and a tear fell onto the page. She wiped it and the ink smudged.

Maemm *called me today. She said you went to the youth group. I hope you had fun. Did they have homemade ice cream? Are you still happy about working at Fannie's? I miss everyone. Tell* Dawdi *I said "Hi" and tell him to write to me. You too!*

Yours Truly, Leah.

CHAPTER 14

Fannie Troyer

"I need to make some plans," Fannie said. She and Henry were driving again, the stretch of curvy road after Valley View where the fields lifted away from the ditches and drifts of elderberry grew wild. They were in bloom, heralding a season of pie, a winter of jelly.

"What sort of plans?" Henry asked.

"Secret sisters," Fannie answered.

"You have a sister?"

"No. It's something we do with a group of friends. They call us the 'old girls,' the 'leftover blessings.'" Fannie glimpsed a perfect flower garden as they drove past a farmhouse. Bright zinnias were surrounded by burgundy and lime-green coleus that gave way to a border of white alyssum. "Single women and widows. We get together every month. It's my turn to plan."

"What do the secret sisters do when they get together?" Henry asked. "Or is that a secret?"

"We go out to eat, maybe have a picnic, or quilt if someone has one ready," Fannie said. "The secret part is that we draw names at the beginning of the year and then come up with surprises for that person every so often. We remember birthdays, sneak a box of candy into our sister's buggy after church, and send them a Valentine's card. Then we also have surprises that are 'just for anyhow.'"

"That sounds fun," said Henry.

"I'm in charge of planning something in two weeks and I don't have any ideas. I should do something special for Elva. It's my secret sister's birthday on that very day." Fannie looked sidewise at Henry. "I just can't think of anything good."

"Oh no! Your secret's out!" Henry said with a twinkle in his eye. "Maybe I can help. Tell me, what does Elva like?"

How did that happen? All these years of secret sisters and I haven't told a soul, and now it came out first thing. "You can keep secrets, can't you, Henry?" Fannie asked.

"Sure, I won't tell." Henry said with a wink. "And call me Hank. Everyone does."

Fannie ignored that. He was Henry to her. But she was impressed with his offer to help. Men never cared much about women's little outings, craft projects, and such. "Let's see, she's one for lots of flowers—the difficult ones like gladiolus, dahlias, and delphiniums."

"Difficult ones?" Henry asked.

"Flowers that are hard to grow and take too much work. I can't possibly surprise her with a bouquet or a garden book. She already has a whole shelf of garden books," said Fannie.

The van hummed and the air conditioning cooled the space between Henry and Fannie.

He kept his eyes on the road, slowing for a horse and wagon, then speeding around it.

"You're sneaky," Fannie teased.

"Only trying to assist."

"Now you have to help! Any ideas on what we can do? Where could we go?"

"Have you ever been to the arboretum? There should be an abundance of flowers there to enjoy," Henry said.

"Years ago, but not lately." Fannie's eyes crinkled with her smile.

"Well, then, that's perfect! What time do you want to pick everyone up?"

Was Henry volunteering to drive them? "Let's see . . . it's on a Friday, you know. We should probably leave by 5:00. How far is it?" Fannie asked. "I'm not sure your van can hold all of us. Maybe we need two drivers."

"I'd say we can get there in a half hour," Henry replied. "You'll still have plenty of daylight to walk through the gardens and get back before too late."

"We can have a picnic supper. That is just the thing! Henry, you are always surprising me," Fannie exclaimed.

"I have to say, Fannie, I've never in my life heard the words secret and surprise so often until I moved here. I think of your people as serious and sober, but you have so much fun together."

"I don't know what to say about that," Fannie said.

"You do have so many social times that involve eating, though. I will say that for you." He gave a second wink.

The van made another turn and now they were just south of Benville. Soon they'd be back at the quilt shop and Henry would be on his way. Fannie lapsed into silence, mentally planning the details of the picnic and plotting about which sister would bring which dish. Fannie herself would bring the sandwiches, but maybe Bertha would be willing to do the cake.

Otherwise, Elva might suspect Fannie.

Then again, if Fannie brought it, Elva might think her secret sister was someone else. She might think it was obvious if Fannie assigned someone else to bring the cake. It would have to be a hummingbird cake. That was a given. Maybe no one had to know who brought the cake. In any case, there would have to be a cake for Elva.

"I wonder, do you think we could get ice cream to go with the birthday cake? Could we keep it frozen that long?"

"I can pick up ice cream at the Circle-K while you ladies stroll through the arboretum. I can even set out your food."

Henry was such a gentleman. *What would the sisters think about a man setting out the food? I've got to be careful; everyone talks. They'll wonder about me—us.* Fannie felt a brief embarrassment at her thoughts—embarrassment all her own making.

"That's nice of you, Henry, but I wouldn't put you to any trouble. It will be more than enough if you just drive us to the arboretum and then pick up the ice cream. I would have never thought of going there. That's just perfect."

At suppertime on the day of the picnic, a soft breeze cooled the air. Everything had gone as planned. Once the second car arrived with the rest of the women, Fannie claimed a picnic table under a tree near the driveway. She spread a large plastic cloth on it and the women carried their picnic baskets over before they wandered off to look at the plants. They walked down the paths in clusters of two and three, admiring the colorful summer flowers and studying the name plates and markers. Elva fell in step beside Fannie.

"How is it going with your niece?" she asked.

"Which one?" Fannie countered.

"I was thinking of Leah, the one with the crooked back. She's in Cleveland, isn't she? Is she having surgery or not? I didn't hear what they decided."

"Poor Leah! We hope it won't be too much longer. She's having tests and so on."

"Oh, my!" said Elva. "What's taking so long?"

"I think it's money. My brother's family, Leah's *Daett,* has had a rough time of it financially, with the shop fire and all. The doctor isn't charging for the surgery itself, but there are other expenses, I'm sure. Albert and Elma just can't afford all that right now. Albert is stubborn. Doesn't want to turn in his hospital bills to the Children's Relief Committee. But it's hard to say no to such a good gift." After she said this, she realized she shouldn't talk so much. Albert wouldn't like her saying the family was in need. Or that he was stubborn. But it was the truth.

"I should think so," said Elva. "Surely the Children's Relief Fund would help. That's for such things, don't you think?"

"*Yah!* Anna Maust came in the other day and wondered why Albert and Elma let Leah go up to Cleveland. I said, 'Poor Leah can't work in the garden . . . is just hiding away in her room reading . . . not mixing with the young people. Her back's already so crooked, like those Troyer cousins. She'll end up an invalid for the rest of her life, lots of health problems later. . .' that sort of thing," Fannie said. "I just told her it's good for Leah to get help."

They'd stopped in front of a colorful planting of butterfly milkweed and other pollinators. Monarch butterflies flitted from flower to flower. Elva and Fannie were quiet as they watched them and then read the information on the sign. But they already knew everything it said from reading *Birds and Blooms.*

Elva read faster. "I didn't know she was that bad," she said, coming back to the subject of Leah. "I do pray that everything will work out for poor Leah."

"I hope Albert speaks up for once," Fannie said. "There's no shame in needing help with medical expenses. She needs that surgery, according to the doctor. Albert should forget his pride and think about helping his girl have a better life." *Oh no. Now I'm talking out of school again. What's the matter with me anyhow?*

"*Yah,*" Elva nodded.

Fannie continued walking down the path and Elva fell in step. "Now Susan, Leah's younger sister, she's been such a help to me this summer," Fannie said. "I'm able to get away a little and look for some new crafts to sell. Getting ready for when tourists come through this fall." Fannie smiled, thinking of the times she and Henry drove through the countryside enjoying the beauty of summer. Her mind rested on the comforts of his friendly ways, his winks and teasing, and the feeling of freedom as they listened to music. She felt like a young girl again. *He's such a comfortable friend. We* are *just friends, aren't we?*

"I don't know how you do it all," Elva said. "The older I get, the more I have days I can't do much. Have you had tourist business this summer?"

"No. That's mostly in leaf season," said Fannie. "Susan's helping me rearrange and clean. The store should do better this coming fall." Both women knew the struggle. It was embarrassing to need financial aid from the church, but single women sometimes did.

The two women drifted among plants, touching leaves, smelling flowers, and admiring the well-kept beds lush with familiar and unusual plants. *This garden is like us. Something a little different.* Fannie thought about Elva, short and stocky. Her skin sagged and her hands were freckled with dark age spots. She lingered by a Japanese maple, admiring the crimson leaves. Life hadn't been kind to her. She'd been childless, widowed before she was twenty-five, cared for by relatives, and eventually became a caregiver for one of them.

Farther up the path was Bertha, whose husband died in a tragic buggy accident leaving her to raise three young children with the help of church and family. Ruby had suffered disfiguring burns in a house fire during her childhood and never married. Violet and Lena were inseparable twin sisters who cared for their aged father. They sold the handwoven rugs they made on ancient looms that had been in their family for generations.

"I need to go back and set up our picnic. Why don't you catch up with the others?" Fannie said. She motioned towards the group out ahead of them. Fannie turned around and went back to the picnic table. She began setting out the food. Henry arrived with a cooler filled with ice and two tubs of ice cream. "I thought about what you said the other day about your group," Henry said. "I wouldn't call you or any of your friends 'old girls' or 'leftover blessings.'"

Fannie blushed and busied herself with the tableware. She felt Henry's eyes on her. "It's just something people say," she said. She'd never figured out why she'd been left behind. *Do I talk too much? Am I too tall? Is it because of the mole on my face?*

"I know they say that. But I'd say I'm blessed to know you. I'm glad we're friends," Henry said.

"Me, too, Henry. Thanks for being my friend." Fannie's eyes met his and held a moment longer than usual. She wished she could invite him to join their dinner, but the others would wonder about that. "I'll save you a piece of cake for later," she said.

"Now, that's a leftover blessing," Henry said. "Enjoy your supper. I'll come back at eight to take you all home."

CHAPTER 15

Hank Kratzer

There hadn't been a plan to write—a retrospective blog, an immersive anthropological study, a literary exploration of alternative American culture, or even a review of Amish Country's Best for *Ohio Magazine*. No, there had only been a desire to escape Ohio University and surroundings steeped in life with Elaine. He missed her chatter, her laugh, her goodnight kiss after they'd shared a cup of tea and a butter cookie. Sadly, moving to Amish Country hadn't changed much. He still missed her. But he'd managed to start over without her.

Late afternoons, when he returned to his condo at Honey Run, the light-filled sunroom beckoned. His laptop sat there on the old writing desk that had been with him since the year he'd married Elaine. She'd bought it for him as a birthday gift. He sat down in front of it, pushing aside the bills and junk mail from organizations he once belonged to.

It was a habit, gravitating to the computer. But now he could legitimately avoid the university website. He didn't miss the stacks of awkward sophomoric prose praising the virtues of Emerson: "Ralph was a stand-up guy with a lot to say and he said it well. I would like to start by espousing . . ." (obviously a thesaurus word thrown in here) and so on. Thankfully that was all behind him. He glanced at the bookshelf and that old picture of them together in front of the Ferris wheel at Ocean City that first summer after graduation. If only Elaine could be here to enjoy this new life, a simple life.

Elaine probably wouldn't have wanted to live at Honey Run, miles from the library and mall. She would have hated dodging wagons and bicycles on the road. He couldn't quite imagine her shopping at the humble little stores that didn't stock feta cheese or low-fat sour cream. Life would have been different, had she survived to enjoy retirement with him. Most likely she'd have signed them up for a cruise on the Danube or arranged a cross-country tour to visit their old friends and that relative of hers who had retired to Sun City.

Hank looked at the urn on top of the bookshelf. *I'm so sorry, Elaine. I promise someday I'll take you to the Colorado Rockies and the Pacific Ocean. It will happen. Someday.* The microwave dinged and Hank retrieved his frozen dinner. He tore off the wrapper and ate quickly, eager to get to the waiting black raspberry pie Fannie had managed to hide all day. He poked his fork through the delicate flaky crust that gave way to seedy, syrupy goodness. She'd handed it to him as she slid out of the front seat that afternoon.

Earlier that afternoon, he'd held it, his mouth watering while she gathered her purchases at the end of their trip. "Thanks again, Henry." *Why won't she call me Hank?* "Can you open the back? Remember? I put my plants back there."

Hank had lifted Fannie's tray of sad-looking bargain plants. They left a trail of pine bark and peat on the previously pristine interior. But he said nothing.

"If I pinch these back and get them planted tonight, they will still grow. Late bloomers are always a bargain I can't pass up," said Fannie. "I'm a late bloomer myself."

Hank smiled at her self-awareness. As she hurried toward her house, he climbed back into the van. It had been a long day. He was tired.

Mornings began early. The Amish were early. They were often on the road before 8:00 and home by 5:00. Evenings were his to do as he wished. He was old-school and didn't stream entertainment. His television viewing was just the local station giving the weather and news of murders and theft in Cleveland.

Hank savored the pie and set his plate in the sink. He brewed a decaf in the Keurig and opened the laptop.

Retrospective: An Amish Country Meditation

When one moves to Amish Country after a lifetime in academia, the adjustments one makes are at once familiar and dissimilar. I will try to tease out some of the important elements (is there a better word for "elements"? Note to self: check thesaurus). Hank reread the title and the sentence. His anemic introduction didn't convey what was happening to him. It was as dull and ignorant as his former students' writing.

He persevered, laying words down, knowing that he was writing complete garbage. But he felt at home with his fingers on the keyboard, trying to capture the essence of life among the Amish. In his mind, he was writing for an astute journal—the *Humanities Monthly* or maybe *Ethno-Conversations*. As such, he couldn't mention Fannie as an actual person, just a construct of a Fannie (who had somehow hidden a piece of pie from him for an entire afternoon, or had she bought it at that relatives' farm market where they'd stopped?).

The dullness of his prose nearly put him to sleep; however, the sweetness of the pie may have also been a factor. Hank saved the garbage writing to a flash drive and moved to his recliner. He switched on Channel 3 News and serendipitously learned about a Cleveland hospital doing a study of birth defects among the Amish. He thought of Fannie's niece, Leah. He'd have to tell Fannie about this tomorrow—wait, tomorrow? He wasn't driving her tomorrow. Nevertheless, she was on his mind. If not tomorrow, later this week. Hank closed his eyes and muted the TV during commercials for pharmaceuticals and vehicles. His mind wandered.

Had any regular person—say a guy like himself—ever joined the Amish after having another life? What would he have to give up if he were to become Amish? His TV, for sure. The dishwasher, movies, his collegiate robe, hood, and title—no big deal. He wouldn't be able to speak the language—or would he? Already, he could understand bits and pieces. He was good with languages. And television bored him. Tomorrow night, instead of writing the stuffy journal article, he'd start a blog—or maybe just one of those private journals you can write online. He could call it "Living Amish, One Day at a Time." Something like that.

He started writing it in his head. *I'm learning a lot about the Amish while driving Miss Fannie. For instance, it is possible to spend an entire day looking for the best wooden marble game. You can enjoy thrift shopping even when you're Amish, and if you go to the right places they will even have a rack of Plain dresses, but it's more enjoyable to look at the glass dishes and kitchen gadgets. It's surprising what some people give away. And when you drive Fannie somewhere, who knows when you will be asked to stop and drink from a tin cup at an artesian well or identify a moth with blue and orange wings or hear about the time she and her brothers hid in a cave no one knew about and ended up missing a ride in the open buggy—she called it a "hack"—to get ice cream. You will come away from the day believing in your heart that straggly dry marigolds are late bloomers that still have a great deal of life left in them.*

Leah Troyer

L eah woke up at seven on Saturday morning. Everything was quiet. It was far too early to get up here in Cleveland, even though at home everyone had been up for at least two hours. She picked up the thick folder of pages and medical brochures from Cleveland General Hospital. She'd been avoiding reading what was inside. One look at the models of the human spine and the brief explanation by an intern had made her stomach feel sick. And this was more of the same. But staff at the hospital had recommended that she thoroughly read everything in the folder. *Why did I agree to come here? I don't want to do this. Dawdi, do you miss me?* Leah whispered. Her heart fluttered.

There was no answer, just silence.

Just then a bright sunbeam shined through the window. Outside, birds raised a ruckus. A soft breeze lifted the linen curtains. Leah took a deep breath of the fresh morning air. It was as if *Gott* had whispered reassurance to her from the world beyond this room. She was *Gott's maydel, Gott's* daughter. She propped herself up in bed and took another deep breath. She opened a colorful brochure and studied the drawings of crooked backs. Leah read about percentages of curvature and shivered at the mention of rods, bone grafts, and fusion.

It was all new to her. In the eighth grade, her Amish school had studied health—the importance of washing hands and getting fresh air. They'd had a visitor who talked to them about safety around machinery and while driving horses. But she had little knowledge about how bones and muscles worked. As she looked at the pictures, she recalled Mr. Miller's words about the human body. "Scripture says 'we are fearfully and wonderfully made.'" He'd explained that the word "fearful" meant something like "awesome" or "with great wisdom."

Leah opened another fold in the brochure and read the next page. "The surgery for scoliosis involves spinal fusion. The curved vertebrae are realigned and fused so that they heal into a single, solid bone. Curvature is significantly improved using the tools and technology available today, preventing long-term disability and disfigurement." Leah studied the pictures and drawings. She hitched the pillows higher behind her, sitting up a bit straighter. She thought about the bones in her own body. Twisting slightly, she traced her fingers down her spine. She felt the knobs and indentations through her thin summer nightgown.

She read a page about the various types of scoliosis and wondered which type she had. She read about long-term pain and disability that could happen. She stared intently at pictures of crooked backs and read about possible damage to internal organs. The pages in the folder had paragraphs of questions and answers. There were questions she'd never thought of, but she read each one, along with the answers. The more she read, the stronger she felt.

She set the messy pages and brochures on the bedside table. *Enough of this for now.* She lay back, closed her eyes, and tried to remember how *Dawdi* looked, his crinkly smile, his watery blue eyes, and his clean-shaved upper lip and long white beard. She missed her morning visits with him. She thought about the future when she would stand straight, be pain-free, and even have a straight hemline without a fuss. Then she pictured that fine day before she arrived in Cleveland when she had ridden her bike with Aaron, Susan, and Ben. It was the day she first understood that she could do hard things. Aaron's steady voice behind her gave her courage that day as she struggled to make the hill. It had prepared her for this. If she held onto these thoughts of home, she could make it through the next hard thing that lay ahead of her.

Leah dozed off again. She felt grateful she could sleep in on a Saturday under a blanket in the comfort of this large room she had all to herself. Her fingers curled around the cool bed sheets. A feeling of peace wafted across her like the breeze from her open window. She relaxed, giving way to welcome rest.

Suddenly she was wide awake again. Leah sat straight up in bed, alarmed by loud noises coming through the oak floorboards. The carriage house seemed to shake with the thunderous booming, snatches of amplified sounds. It started, stopped, and started up again. *What was happening?* It sounded like the Swartzentruber youths' buggies of Wayne County when Amish teens cranked up the music on their radios and paraded down country roads at all hours. Here in Cleveland, it was nearly 9 a.m. and something was happening in the garage. Leah heard men's voices. Music randomly started and stopped. She'd overslept. Leah leaped from her bed and got dressed. She ran down the stairs and across the lawn to the patio where she entered the kitchen through a sliding door.

Dr. Dave looked amused when Leah rushed into the kitchen. "Did those boys wake you up? Monica's nephew and his bandmates are having a Saturday practice. Seems they've signed up to perform at Buckeye Christian Praise Expo."

Leah had no idea what he was talking about. She stood there gazing at the sight in front of her.

Dave grimaced. "Don't tell me Monica forgot to tell you about this. I'm so sorry. Monica must have forgotten to tell you about the band coming over to practice. We'll be sure to give you fair warning next time."

Dave was wearing a goofy apron and brandishing a spatula as he juggled a griddle covered in pancakes and two skillets—a round one filled with sausage links and a square one lined with strips of bacon. Monica wasn't there. Kylie and Skye, in their Disney princess pajamas, chased one another around the kitchen island and through the doorway into the family room. The countertop was splattered with pancake batter and a puddle of spilled orange juice.

"Can I help?" Leah asked without so much as a second thought.

"Sure! Here! Watch the bacon for me, will you?"

Leah took the spatula and lowered the heat on the bacon. She automatically reached for the dishcloth and wiped up the spilled juice with her other hand.

"Monica went off somewhere this morning with her girl-friends. Starbucks, Chapel Hill Mall, a matinee where a new chick flick is showing . . . you know . . ." Dave said.

No, I don't. Leah rescued a burning piece of bacon. *Who is going to eat all this, anyway?*

Dr. Dave expertly flipped the pancakes and reached for plates. "Skye, Kylie, stop running and get over here. Pancakes are ready!" The girls stopped in front of their dad who handed them each a plate. "Back, back, back," he said, motioning with the spatula for them to back up.

The girls obeyed. They seemed to know the drill and held out their plates as Dr. Dave flipped a pancake to each one, making sure it hit the mark. The girls squealed, then climbed onto the tall stools. Leah scooped the rest of the bacon and sausage onto an extra plate and Dave stacked a pile of pancakes on two more plates. They joined the girls on the stools at the counter.

He bowed his head slightly. "God's neat, let's eat!" he said.

Leah reached for the maple syrup in front of her. Dave slathered butter on his stack and then did the same for the girls. The room got quiet as everyone devoured breakfast. She felt at home there, and as she reached for seconds of bacon and sausage Leah realized just how hungry she was.

After they'd eaten most of the food, Dave and Leah cleared it away and wiped down the countertop. "Let's go see what's going on in the garage, maybe have a quick house concert," Dave said.

Everyone trooped out to the third bay of the garage. Dave stepped through the door and greeted the band. They'd spread themselves out in the area just below Leah's bedroom. Now the noises she heard made sense. Leah followed with Kylie and Skye holding her two hands.

"Let me introduce you to the Corner Stones, the best Christian rock band in Northeast Ohio," said Dave. "This is my nephew Alec Wilson, lead singer, and . . .?" Dave gestured to the three other band members who were entangled in electrical cords, instruments, microphones, and portable speakers.

"Hi! Welcome! Didn't know you had a visitor, Dave." Alec gave Leah a once-over.

She was used to stares because of her back and her Amish clothes. This felt like more. She blushed and looked down, fussed with her *kapp* strings, and avoided his gaze.

"This is Leah Troyer from Holmes County. She's our new nanny. I think you woke her up this morning." Dave gestured to the ceiling. "She's staying in the guest room."

"Oops! Sorry 'bout that!" Alec finally stopped staring at Leah. He strummed his guitar and then went back to tuning it.

"Let's hear some music," Dave said. He took folding chairs from their storage hooks on the garage wall. "Have a seat!" The girls and Leah settled into the chairs. Dave braced himself against the wall. The lead singer counted out the tempo and sound erupted, bouncing off the walls.

"Awesome! God is awesome! High above the earth! Our God! Our God!" The song blared on for what seemed like minutes. Their singing continued between long stretches of guitar, keyboard, drum, and cymbals crashing. Leah sat still in her folding chair and clasped her hands in her lap. The sound was loud, but she didn't hold her hands over her ears like Kylie and Skye did. She felt her toes tapping inside her shoes while the girls clapped in time with the drummer whose hair kept falling into his eyes.

Kylie stood up and pranced around in time to the music, trailing a scarf she'd found in a pocket on her chair. Skye jumped up and did her own dance, bobbing her head in time to the beat. She mimicked the drummer who had to jerk his head to see. The song went on and on with no break in the ear-splitting beat. Leah couldn't make out many of the words they were singing. The song ended abruptly with a final cymbal crash. Leah realized she'd been holding her breath. It was all so different, and too loud. But the song gave her a rush of excitement she'd never felt singing hymns with the young people at home.

"That's some show you guys gave there," Dr. Dave said. "What's this I hear about your upcoming gig?"

"Thanks for letting us use your garage. We're tuning up for the Christian Praise Expo. We're opening for Disciple—the featured band this year. Good band. Solid message. Between us, we've got all their albums. But, hey! I never introduced you to the guys. We'll make it an intro practice."

Alec struck a pose and said: "Hi, everyone! I'm Alec Wilson with the Corner Stones." He gestured towards the drummer who brushed a mop of hair out of his eyes. "And this is Jed Akers!" The drummer flipped his drumsticks and tapped out a quick cadence. "Jennings Morgan, our backup singer. And, on bass guitar, we have McGwire Powers. Let's praise the Lord!"

"Look guys, thanks for the entertainment," Dave said. "I need to get these girls dressed and ready for the day—what's left of it! Carry on." Dave grabbed the girls' hands and led them out of the garage. Leah stood, ready to follow.

Dave turned to Leah. "You have the day off, Leah. We'll see you before dinner. Remember, it's date night for Monica and me—pizza for you and the girls." With this parting shot, Dave grabbed the girls' hands and headed back to the house.

"Hey! We're about to wrap here," Alec said, flashing a smile in Leah's direction. "Then we're gonna grab coffee at Dunkin' Donuts." He included her in the general statement to the band guys. Leah wasn't hungry after all those pancakes, but there was no mistaking Alec's invitation. Jed looked up from folding the legs of the keyboard stand. "Look, Alec, me and the guys here are heading over to Grace to set up for church tomorrow. You'll have to go without us this time."

"Okay. Then it's just me and the Amish girl. What's your name again?" Alec asked without a hint of embarrassment.

"Leah Troyer." She stood there bewildered, not knowing how to refuse.

Jed, Jennings, and McGwire started tearing down the sound system and Alec put the instruments back in their cases. He tossed a heavy looped cord to Leah as if she was part of the team. She barely caught it; it felt like a loop of rope—horse tack.

She hung back, then followed the guys to the van parked in front of the garage, the cord still looped on her arm. Jed grabbed things in what seemed to be a pre-determined order and stowed everything in the cargo bay of the scruffy black Ford Explorer. The guys hopped in, McGwire behind the wheel. They took off, leaving Leah and Alec standing in the bright morning sun, awkwardly alone, but together.

CHAPTER 17

Susan Troyer

S usan treadled away on Fannie's ancient sewing machine in the back room behind the curtain that served as a door. The place was steaming hot and there was barely room to turn around, let alone try on the pale blue knit dress, the second one she'd made this summer. Before setting the sleeve, she had to try it on and make sure the side seams were snug enough, but not too tight.

Susan slipped out of her old, everyday brown dress that was a little looser than she liked. She stood in the corner away from the window and dropped the brown dress to the floor, then quickly stepped into the blue polyester one. She twisted slightly and tugged at the fabric under her arms, looking for straight pins to mark the alteration.

The bell jingled on the shop door. Susan froze. *Oh no! What now? I can't greet a customer in a half-made dress!*

"Just a minute, I'll be right with you." Quickly, Susan stepped out of the blue dress and back into the brown one.

"Take your time. I'm in no hurry." The voice on the other side of the curtain was not what she expected. *How long had it been since a man darkened the door of this shop? Well, maybe Fannie's beau, Hank Kratzer. But this isn't Hank.*

"Is that you, Ben?" Susan tucked a strand of blonde hair into her *kapp* and pushed aside the curtain, leaving the blue dress in a puddle on the floor. Her face was flushed from the exertion of changing in such a hurry.

"What are you doing back there? Snooping through Fannie's treasures?" Ben liked to tease.

"I was sewing a dress. No one has been in here all day and now you show up. Fannie is still off in Sugar Creek or somewhere looking for more bargains she can overprice and let sit around here collecting dust."

Ben laughed at Susan's description. He picked up a mesh bag filled with plain wooden blocks.

"Here's a bag of chopped-up table legs. What's her price on this? Twenty-five dollars? Are you kidding me? But someday an *Englischer* woman will think she got a bargain. A good old-fashioned toy for her grandchildren."

"But when? 'Someday' is right. In the meantime, I have something to dust when business is slow," joked Susan. "Seriously, I have no idea when Fannie will get back. Sometimes she's gone all day."

"How can she afford to pay a driver for the entire day?" asked Ben. "Maybe they aren't driving the whole time," he said slyly.

"Well, I noticed she's started tweezing her chin hairs," Susan said. "And she has a tube of pink lip balm under the counter." She lifted the evidence and pulled off the cap.

"What do you mean 'tweezing her chin hairs?' You think Fannie's gone fancy on us?" Susan dodged that one but responded with, "I saw them sharing Kettle Korn from the same tub at the Children's Relief Auction."

"And a hot pretzel, too," Ben reminded her.

"Fannie seems comfortable around him. But I never know what to expect out of her." Susan tried to pass off her recent worrisome thoughts about her aunt. *What if Fannie is falling for Hank? What if he wants to marry Fannie? The church would never approve. What if he's just helping her out because she gives him pies?* But she didn't dare think like that. Fannie was settled. Her place in the community was fixed. She wasn't going anywhere.

"Maybe he doesn't charge her full price," Susan said. "I think they're just friends. Two lonely old people." Despite the jokes about her quirky elder, deep down Susan respected her aunt, who had her own business and didn't depend on the church to support her. Besides, Fannie had given her a job and gotten her out of the garden. "I know. It is unusual, though," Susan said.

"I say we hire a driver and follow them—maybe a Saturday," Ben said. "We don't know what she does behind our backs. I wouldn't be surprised if ole Henry is taking her out for a steak and a beer."

Susan burst out laughing. "Ben. Stop it! You know she doesn't drink beer! She *is* going to Black Steer with the Troyer cousins on Saturday to celebrate all the July birthdays. We could follow them. I don't know if Hank is driving, but I can find out."

Susan liked Ben's idea. She was up for a night out. Besides, it would give her something interesting to write to Leah. "So, if you didn't come here to buy table leg blocks? What brings you here?"

"Aaron sent me over. We were wondering . . . I mean, Aaron was asking me what you heard from Leah. It's been a while since she went up to Cleveland. Did you hear from her yet? We just wondered."

"Hmmm." Susan put her hand on her hip and feigned confusion. "Aaron is wondering about Leah, is he? Well, we get letters every day or so. I think she's homesick. She's having tests at the hospital and in between she is caring for the doctor's children. She's alone a lot, even so. Just waiting for the next step. And we haven't heard from the doctor. If you ask me, she could've stayed here and just had a driver take her up there to do the tests. Why did *Maemm* and *Daett* let her stay up there?" Her voice had an edge that surprised her.

It bothered Susan that Leah was having such a good time with the doctor's little children. Her letters had the names Kylie and Skye on every other line. Leah used to complain about looking after their younger brothers, but now she was a nanny who doted on the doctor's two little girls. Her letters were full of interesting stories, while Susan's seemed dull in comparison.

"I wish she hadn't gone. I miss her," Susan said.

"It sure did happen fast," Ben said.

"Right. Suddenly, everything changed. I'm just glad it's not me. I'd be scared to have surgery on my back and just as scared to be up there by myself. I hope everything works out," Susan said.

"Ask Aaron if he knows a boy with a car. Maybe you could ask Amos Maust. He has a car now, doesn't he? I'll get the scoop on Fannie's plans, and we can go to the Black Steer on Saturday and spy on Fannie. I don't have a July birthday, but I sure need a night out!" Susan said. She fanned her flushed face with a supply catalog lying on Fannie's counter.

"Okay, consider it done," said Ben. "I'd better get back to the shop. We've been cleaning and sorting. Getting ready for the frolic when they put up the new building. My *Daett* will be wondering why it took me so long just to get the mail."

"I'd better get busy, too," Susan said. "Fannie will check to see if I've dusted the counters and swept the porch. She expects nothing less than perfection."

"Isn't that the truth," said Ben. The bell jingled and he was on his way. Susan grabbed the broom and swept the thread and scraps off the floor.

Fannie arrived back at the shop just as Susan was counting the cash. No one besides Ben had been into the store, but she still counted the money, as her aunt required.

Through the screen door, Susan heard Fannie say goodbye to

Hank. Once inside, Fannie exclaimed, "My, but it's hot. I'm spoiled with Henry's air conditioning. How did you do today? Any customers?"

"Sorry, no. But I'm ready to set the sleeves in my blue dress. I'm going to wear it Saturday, I think." *Careful now. Don't give away our plan.*

"Do the young people have something going on Saturday?" Fannie liked keeping track of her nieces' plans.

"Oh, nothing special." Susan ducked behind the curtain to collect her unfinished dress and evade Fannie's question. "But you do, I think. Isn't this the week the Troyer cousins are going to the Black Steer? *Daett* and *Maemm* can't go. There's still so much cleanup after the fire at K&T." Susan returned to the counter.

"I know. Everyone understands. Six o'clock is too early for them, I guess. Saturday is your Uncle Paul Troyer's birthday. And mine is on July 17, so I thought I'd go anyways. They hired a van to pick everyone up."

"Oh, I was thinking maybe Hank would take you," Susan said.

Fannie's eyes lit up as she considered Susan's suggestion. "You know, that's a good idea. It's just me going from Benville. I'm so far out of the way. The rest are all over near Valley View. I could just get Henry to take me to the Black Steer."

"That's a good idea," said Susan. She suppressed a giggle and rearranged the dress, again avoiding Fannie's gaze. "Okay, I'm going now. *Maemm* needs me to help get supper on. I do everything now that Leah's not here."

"You must miss your sister," Fannie said. "We all do."

"Yes. I hope we have another letter from her today. It's like she's writing a story for us." She did like Leah's letters and the occasional phone call. But she was also getting tired of all the fuss over Leah all the time.

CHAPTER 18

Leah Troyer

Alec whipped a ring of keys from his pocket and spun them on his index finger. "Ready to go?" Leah had missed her chance to refuse the donut offer. She felt sick inside. *Dave, how could you let this happen?*

Alec led her to his beat-up nondescript green hatchback, which only increased her apprehension. "Leah, I'd like you to meet Tinkerbell. Tinkerbell, meet Leah. Take us to the donuts!" He flung open the passenger door that let out a nasty screech. As if to ease her anxiety, Alec made an elaborate show of gentlemanly behavior, even giving a slight bow.

Leah settled into the frayed, sagging seat. She reached for the seat belt and pulled it across her body, buckling herself securely. She'd never been alone in a car with a boy, let alone an *Englischer* she had just met. *What am I doing? What would* Maemm *think?* She could imagine *Maemm's* frown, the way she'd shake her head. But when she looked over at Alec, he seemed completely harmless. He was about the same age as Aaron back home. *What are you all doing today? Do you miss me?*

Alec started Tinkerbell and headed for the street. "Me and the guys, we like this Dunkin'. Usually go before practice but didn't make it today. It's just a few streets over." Suddenly, Leah realized she should have grabbed her purse. She didn't have money for donuts. Or for any sort of emergency.

"I forgot my purse. Can we go back?"

"No worries, lady. This is on me," Alec said. They drove through Shaker Heights listening to Christian rock music that boomed from the speakers. It was far too loud. When they reached McKinley Street, he maneuvered into the turn lane and waited for the green arrow. It was a busy city street lined with fast food places, office buildings, and storefronts. Traffic swirled past them. Leah fidgeted, running her fingers over the snagged seat cover. Alec didn't notice her nervousness. Of course, Leah didn't have a driver's license, but she knew traffic rules and had used them when driving a buggy. She'd never negotiated a turn lane with the buggy, though. She'd never been on roads as busy as these Cleveland streets.

"Here we are!" Alec's voice brought her out of her buggy-driving daydream. She opened the heavy car door and it screeched again. "Sorry. I need to get that thing fixed. There's something wrong with the hinge." He was already out of the car and heading for the door of the donut shop.

Alec's blond hair was long, like Aaron's. His eyes were blue, but not cobalt, like Aaron's. Alec was more outgoing than Aaron. A little unpredictable. He walked fast, as if he'd forgotten her, not at all like Aaron who stayed close and knew she moved slower than others. Leah caught up with Alec. He was holding the door and seemed to be in a hurry. The sweet overtone of fried dough made Leah think of *Maemm's* donut-making day during apple cider season.

As they stood in line, Leah noticed people staring at them. Leah wished she could disappear. *How did I let this happen?* It felt like everyone's eyes were on her white *kapp,* the plain homemade pink dress, and the bulky white running shoes. Or were they studying her crooked back? Alec seemed unaware of the stares.

He touched her arm, bringing her back to the moment. "What do you want?" he asked, pointing to the large trays behind the counter. She pulled away and then focused on the rows and rows of donuts. "I don't know. I'm not very hungry. What do you like?" Leah dodged. "I'll take what you're having." Her stomach fluttered again at the thought of standing here with an *Englischer* boy. *It's like a date. I shouldn't have come here.*

"Wait a minute. You don't know what I'm going to order. How do you know you'll like it?" Alec asked.

Leah shifted onto her stronger leg and studied the signs posted just below the display of donuts in front of her. One of the labels caught her eye. "Boston Kreme," she declared in a surprisingly strong voice, even to her ears.

"Boston Kreme? What's that?" It was Alec's turn to be taken off guard.

"Don't tell me you never had Boston cream pie," Leah said. "Fannie always brings Boston cream pie to the Troyer reunion. She's famous for it."

"Boston Kreme it is," said Alec. "I'm in! If it's good enough for Fannie, it's good enough for me."

Alec ordered the donuts and two iced vanilla chai lattes. He carried their tray to a booth in the furthest corner of the dining area and placed it on the table between them. Leah had no idea what a chai latte was, but she didn't let on. She was still basking in her moment of victory with the Boston Kreme decision.

Leah soon forgot to be self-conscious. She forgot she was an Amish girl who looked out of place in a Cleveland suburb. She sipped the spicy, milky chai and forgot to feel awkward with Alec. She watched him lick his fingers just like every Amish boy would do. She forgot she wasn't hungry and nibbled on the sweet, filled donut.

"So," Alec launched into what seemed like an important conversation, "tell me about your religion. What's your Sunday church service like?" His voice sounded earnest as if his question was all-important. Leah looked down, shy again.

"I don't know . . . we sing, from the *Ausbund*. We have a sermon. Well, we have two sermons. One sermon is in English; the other one is in Pennsylvania Dutch. The minister reads the Scripture in German and then explains it to us. I don't understand German well, but *Dawdi* does. And we learn about the Bible with our family, too."

"Wait," Alec broke in. "What's the *Ausbund?* Who is *Dawdi?*"

"The *Ausbund* is our songbook. The Amish have used the same songs for generations. *Dawdi,* he's my grandfather. He says his great-great-great-grandfathers and even before them sang these same songs."

"Wow! That's crazy. Me and the guys in the band, we're all about the new songs. 'Sing a new song to the Lord.' That's what it says in the Bible somewhere, maybe in the psalms."

Leah nodded. She wasn't sure his new songs were an improvement.

"So tell me more. I'm into learning about other religions," Alec said.

Leah paused, trying to think how to explain something she'd done her whole life. "The sermon is long. Sometimes they preach about every important story in the whole Bible, all in one sermon. Then after another sermon we sing again." Her answer sounded feeble. She wasn't expecting to talk about this. *Although lately nothing much is what I expect it to be. Including these delicious Boston Kreme donuts and chai with an* Englischer *boy.*

"Why did you ask me about church? Is it because of how I dress?" Leah knew people were curious about the Amish religion, but she had never had anyone ask about it before.

Whenever she'd asked about something at home, her parents and grandparents always said the same thing: "It's just our way."

Alec gripped his chai in both hands. "I like your dress and that thing you wear on your head," he said.

Leah blushed. "It's called a *kapp*. We're Christians just like you are. It's our faith. Being Amish is a lifestyle choice Christians make."

"Whatever," Alec said. "I don't pay much attention to clothes. It's what's on the inside that counts." Leah nodded. She agreed with this at least. But she felt trapped sitting here trying to explain things she'd never put into words before.

"But are you saved?" Alec didn't wait for her answer but forged ahead. "I came to a saving knowledge of Jesus Christ when I was eleven years old. I was baptized in the Cuyahoga River on Easter Sunday, five years ago, and have been a believer ever since. Are you a believer? Are the Amish believers?"

Leah looked down at her half-eaten donut. It seemed that her answer mattered a great deal to Alec. *Why do we have to talk about this?* She wanted to be agreeable, but she didn't quite know how to answer. "We believe in God and Jesus, like you do. Someday I will be baptized, too," Leah said. "The bishop pours water on your head. That's when we join the church."

Just then an employee stopped by their table. He broke into the awkward conversation, saving Leah from having to respond to Alec's strange questions. "Is everything okay here? Can I get either of you anything else?" They both shook their heads and the server moved on.

Alec drummed his fingers on the table and then crumpled the tissue on the tray into a ball. Alec shifted the conversation to his band, the music they were working up for the Expo, and a long, detailed explanation about the other band members' involvement at Grace Church, which he only attended for special youth group activities. Leah listened attentively, happy to hear about Alec's life instead of answering questions about her own.

"You could come with us sometime," Alec said. "You totally could come to one of the youth rallies or a lockdown some night." Leah took a last sip of the sweet chai to avoid a response. She didn't know what a lockdown was, but it didn't sound like fun to her. When they'd finished their donuts, Alec swept up the empty cups and napkins and threw them in the trash.

In the parking lot, Leah spotted Alec's car parked a bit crookedly under a crabapple tree.

For the first time, she noticed the bumper sticker on Tinkerbell. It proclaimed, "Jesus Is the Answer." Alec came around to her side and opened the damaged door for her. "Yep! I gotta fix this thing," he said as he gave it a kick. He slid behind the wheel.

"I noticed your bumper sticker on Tinkerbell. It says, 'Jesus Is the Answer,'" Leah said.

She suddenly felt comfortable making a little joke. "So, if 'Jesus Is the Answer.' What's the question?" She threw a bright smile in the direction of Alec.

A look of surprise crossed his face when he realized she'd made a joke. Alec started the car and Leah waited for him to respond. He threw it in reverse. "Don't you agree? Jesus is the answer to everything. Every question you've ever had. Everything you aren't sure about. Jesus knows us better than we know ourselves." He sounded confident and strong. Like he meant it. Like it was part of him.

Leah admired the way he talked about his faith. He took her question seriously. She hadn't thought of Jesus in quite that way before. For her, Jesus was someone she followed, an example of how *Gott* wanted her to live. But she wanted to think more about what he said. He was right. And life was so full of questions. This whole day had been strange—hearing the band's loud music, riding with an *Englisher* boy, eating Boston Kreme donuts, and talking with Alec about Jesus and about being Amish.

On the way home, Alec took another route. They passed a park. He pointed out a couple of churches and a favorite Italian restaurant. Before long, they were back at the Woodruffs' house. Alec pulled up in front of the garage.

"Wait," Alec commanded. "I'll get you. That door."

Leah waited and he came around. He leaned over and she caught a whiff of aftershave mingled with vanilla. Something was appealing about Alec, despite his strange questions and loud music. *He's different from Aaron. With Aaron, I know what to expect.*

"Thank you for taking me," Leah said. "I liked the chai."

"No problem," said Alec. "See you around."

CHAPTER 19

Aaron Keim

A aron had been dragged into Ben and Susan's plan to spy on Susan's aunt. "Spying? What are you talking about?" Aaron asked Ben.

"Fannie asked Hank to take her to the Black Steer for the Troyer cousins' birthday dinner, as if they were having a date. Imagine two old people like them getting together." Ben laughed at his little joke. "What does that man see in her, anyway? According to Susan, we're going to find out what's going on between those two."

"Count me out," Aaron said. He was planning to work with his new buggy horse this weekend. He'd been daydreaming of taking Leah for a ride after she was back from Cleveland. "Hank's a good guy," Aaron replied, "but I think Susan's imagining things. Unless she just wants to have dinner out with you." Aaron snapped Ben's suspender from behind and Ben jumped in surprise. "She's trying to get *your* attention. And it's working. Look at you in your best shirt and new shoes."

"We're just friends and you know it. I'm not ready for dating," said Ben.

Aaron judged that Ben was right about that. Despite misgivings, Aaron decided to humor his brother. But his heart wasn't in it. So far, no one suspected that he and Leah had become close. They'd been writing every day or two. Aaron surreptitiously slipped a letter into the mailbox when no one was around. He wrote at odd moments—a sentence here, a paragraph there. He and Leah had begun to share their hopes and dreams. It was easier to express such feelings on paper. If she were here tonight, she would sit beside him. That would make it so much more fun. And he wouldn't care how many people knew he was falling in love.

He turned his attention back to Ben. "You're getting all slicked up for Susan. But she isn't going to look your way but once this evening. She just used you because you're friends with Amos—to ask him to take us in his car." Amos Maust, the bishop's son, was Ben's hunting buddy. He had a driver's license and a car. "I don't know why you'd include Amos," Aaron said. "He's a wild child if there ever was one."

"It was Susan's idea," Ben said. "Not mine."

It bothered Aaron that Ben spent time with Amos. He had an obnoxious habit of smoking long, skinny, brown-wrapped cigarettes their *Daett* called "rattails." "Why would a nice girl like Susan want him with our group?"

Ben ignored his brother's put-down. "We're all just friends and you know it. Why can't we go out for a steak, friends from the district? No harm in that, is there?" Ben asked. "It might keep Amos out of trouble if we included him more often."

Aaron buttoned his blue shirt and straightened the collar. "There. I hear Amos coming down the lane. His rattletrap needs an exhaust job. I'm ashamed to ride anywhere in that thing." Aaron peered out the window and watched the car careen down the gravel lane.

When they got to the car, Aaron saw that Susan and Ruthie, her best friend, were already in the back seat. Aaron claimed the front and Ben squeezed in the back beside Susan. Amos was smoking but put it out when Aaron and Ben got in the car. His red and gray Ohio State ball cap looked new. He'd turned it backward. The bill grazed his long curly blond hair that trailed onto his plaid shirt collar. Amos turned the music down a notch. "Where we headed, and what's our mission?" he asked. He shifted his smoke to the other hand and dropped it on the gravel.

"Black Steer Restaurant," answered Ben.

"Black Steer? Really? That's an old folks' place. Why not the Hitchin' Post Bar & Grill? They have live music on Saturday night."

"Susan planned this. Tell him, Susan."

Aaron thought Ruthie seemed a little nervous. As far as he knew, this was the first time she'd been out on a Saturday night in a car with a group of young people.

"It's 'cause of Aunt Fannie . . ." Susan seemed to be at a loss for words.

"Aww! I knew it. Aunt Fannie wants you to eat with a bunch of old people at the Black Steer," Amos said with disdain.

"No, it's not like that. We are *spying* on Fannie and her driver." Susan emphasized the word as if to make it sound exciting. "We think they are . . ."

"An item!" Ben shouted over the din of the car radio. "We think Fannie and ole Hanky Doodle are . . ." His voice drifted off. Aaron waited, wondering how his brother would explain the relationship Susan and Ben thought existed between the *Englischer* and Fannie.

"So, are they having, like, a date at the Black Steer, or what? Is that why we're going there? To *spy* on them? Where are your *Englischer* outfits? She's going to notice you right away. You know Fannie. She notices everything," said Amos.

"I didn't think of that. I figured she wouldn't see us walk in. She's with the younger Troyer cousins, so I'm sure she'll be busy talking and eating by the time we get there."

"Nah, Hanky Doodle's probably hangin' out at the bar."

Amos made Aaron nervous. He was overly interested in alcohol. Everyone knew it. Susan was foolish to ask him to drive. They all were, for riding with him. But it was too late now.

"Don't be stupid, Amos. Hank doesn't drink. I predict he's going to be sitting right beside Fannie the whole time." Susan raised her voice for emphasis as she came to the end of her pronouncement. Aaron had another round of misgivings as he listened to the ridiculous chatter. He was the oldest one here. He should have talked them out of this childish game. But it was too late. They were at the restaurant now.

As the five Amish young people entered the Black Steer, Aaron inhaled the mingled odors of meat and melted cheese, an aroma not completely enticing. He stepped forward as the group's leader. "We need a table for five," he said to the host.

"Sure, right this way. I have a four-top back here in the corner. We can add a chair at one end."

Aaron followed the greeter, and the others went single file behind them. After they were seated, Ben turned to Susan. "See who you're looking for?"

She scanned the room looking for the Troyer cousins. "That's them. Over there." She pointed her chin in the direction of a group of Amish people seated on the other side of a long half-wall. A bedraggled hanging philodendron and galvanized tubs of fake geraniums partially obscured the view. Dusty leather chaps hung from the top of the divider, and enormous aqua and white cowboy boots sat heel-to-heel on the divider's ledge.

Aaron took a quick look, then averted his eyes.

"Well, at least you're in a good spot for your *spying*," Amos said sarcastically.

Susan scowled at him and then turned to study the Troyer contingent. "That's Fannie with her back to us," she stage-whispered.

The older Amish group was busy buttering their bread and sipping Mountain Dew. They hadn't so much as looked up when the young people entered the room.

"Is that her in the purple dress?" Ben asked. "Who's that beside her?"

Aaron looked across the room. It was easy to spot their neighbor Fannie. On each side of her was a bald man wearing suspenders, one in a plain light blue shirt, the other wearing a white shirt. Both were short-sleeved. "What do you think, Susan, is one of those guys Fannie's Hank?" Aaron asked. Now that he was here, he was glad he'd come. It was good to get out and do something, get his mind off Leah for a while, although he still wished she could have come along.

Ben elbowed Susan. "Amos said to check the bar. Hank might be over there." Despite her earlier judgment, she looked in that direction. Only one couple was sitting there sipping tall glasses of beer.

Then the older Amish group started laughing. But none of the young people had been able to overhear the joke.

"Susan, I don't think there's anything, or anyone, to spy on," Aaron said. "Those guys all look like Troyers to me."

"I'm going to check it out. I'll be back." Susan got up and wandered off. Aaron watched her as she headed toward the restroom. The server brought everyone their drinks.

Soon Susan returned. "You're right," she said. "I didn't see Hank. 'Course it was kind of hard to spy without being noticed." She nervously fiddled with her napkin. Everyone glanced toward the older group again. Susan appeared to be tallying up the presence of her uncles. "I think they're all accounted for. But there are so many of them it's hard to keep them all straight in my mind sometimes. Hank probably dropped Fannie off and left," she said.

"Susan, I think you have an overactive imagination," Ben said.

Susan gave him an elbow and made a show of studying the menu.

"I'm having Surf and Turf. Gotta' live a little," Ben announced.

Aaron studied the menu and hoped the conjecture about Fannie and Hank was over. Amos looked up from the menu and addressed Susan. "You've wasted a perfectly good Saturday night. I'm tellin' you the Hitchin' Post Bar has the best burgers ever. Let's go. I'm in. Are you?"

Aaron gave him a piercing look. "We're here now. We've got a good table in the corner. Let's just stay here and order," he said. His voice held the weight of authority and finality. Amos looked irritated but didn't argue.

"I'll buy you a steak, okay?" Aaron said.

Amos frowned. Then nodded ever so slightly.

The rest of the meal was uneventful except that Ben discovered he didn't like the blackened shrimp on his Surf 'n Turf. He passed it around and everyone got a taste. When the server brought the check, Aaron picked it up and produced bills from his pocket. He calculated the tip as his *Daett* had taught him. "You guys can pay me your share later," he said. "No need to make this harder than it has to be."

They wandered back out into the parking lot and stood in the warm evening, waiting while Amos smoked another rattail. The aromas of the Black Steer and other nearby restaurants mingled in the summer air. The girls and Ben tried to figure out what they owed Aaron for their dinners and rummaged in handbags and pockets to find the correct change. Diners continued to stream out of the restaurant as Ben told a story about losing his hat when he rode in a convertible. When he went back for it later, it had been half-eaten by a goat. The way Ben told the story made it so much funnier, of course. Aaron watched Susan, who laughed so hard she claimed her sides hurt. It wasn't the laughter, but something about Susan reminded him of Leah. Or maybe when he looked at her sister he just wanted to think about Leah, as he'd been doing this entire evening. None of the young people standing there had any idea how much he missed Leah, his girl. None of them had even mentioned her name.

The group was still in the parking lot, leaning against Amos' old clunker, when the older group of Troyer cousins left the restaurant and headed for a white van waiting on the other side of the restaurant. Aaron, standing on the edge of his little group, watched as Fannie, in her purple dress, walked close to a man wearing suspenders and a summer straw hat. Aaron saw the two split off from the rest at the corner of the building. The couple made their way to Hank's blue minivan. Aaron watched while the others talked and laughed among themselves, but he said nothing about seeing Fannie with Hank.

Life was strange, sometimes. You had to wonder. Could there be something romantic going on between those two?

Soon the group was back in the car. Hank's van was probably out ahead of them on the road, headed back to Benville, just like they were. Aaron started another letter to Leah in his mind. *Dearest Leah, I was thinking of you all evening, wishing you were here. We young people went to Black Steer for supper. Your Aunt Fannie was there with the Troyer cousins. Susan will tell you about it. She said we were spying on Fannie and Hank, that driver she favors. He was with them, sitting right beside Fannie. He was dressed just like the Amish men with suspenders and a straw hat. Can you keep a secret? I'm the only spy who saw them together afterward. And he looked just like one of the Troyers.*

CHAPTER 20

Leah Troyer

*D*ear Susan, Guess what? I'm sitting here all alone in my attic. It's a little after 6:00 in the morning. When I looked out the window of the "carriage house," as Monica calls it, the first thing I saw was a few hummingbirds flitting around the huge Rose of Sharon—it's grown up to the second-story window—bigger than Fannie's. Monica told me hummingbirds are a sign of love. They remind me of Benville and the people I love back home. Here I am watching birds, and you are already helping Maemm hang out the laundry on this Monday morning.

There's not much to tell you about my upcoming surgery. It seems I'm completely in the dark about what comes next. I don't know why Dr. Dave doesn't set a date. I asked him once and he said he didn't know. Why not? I've been here for weeks already and have had two or three appointments at the hospital with X-rays and measurements of my back. They said all the tests were completed.

At the hospital, everyone is so nice to me. I like my nanny job. Kylie and Skye are so cute, and they are attached to me. Monica said I can bake cookies with them whenever I want, so I'm going to try that this week.

Monica's nephew, Alec, is part of a rock band. The four guys practice in the empty part of the garage that's right below *me. Alec sings and plays the guitar. It's terribly loud. The first week I was here, Dave made me sit and listen to them for a couple of songs. They sing Christian songs and write their music. It's so different from the way we sing in our youth group. I went to a coffee shop with Alec after their band practice. He was trying to be nice to me. Maybe I should have said no, but I didn't know what to do and just went along with it. Shhh! Don't tell anyone at home.* Maemm *wouldn't like it if she knew. I had a chai latte (bet you don't know what that is). And I introduced him to Boston Kreme, which comes in donuts. He was friendly and asked lots of questions about the Amish, so it was okay.*

Nothing here is like at home. Keep writing those letters. And call me sometimes. I want to know everything that is going on there. I miss everyone so much. How are Ben and Aaron? Been on any bike rides with them? I keep thinking about our ride to Mt. Hope. That was so much fun! I heard the furniture shop is repaired. Are they working there again now? Did Aunt Lydia say yet when the baby's due? I will be so glad when this is over and I'm home again. Your sister, Leah

Leah looked up from her desk and sighed, letting out a long wave of homesickness. She imagined the trumpet vine climbing up the side of the porch that led between their house and *Dawdi's*. She pictured him filling the hummingbird feeder and walking back to his rocker. Next time she would write *him* a letter. He would be so happy to hear from her. But not now; it was almost time for breakfast and Monica would expect her in the kitchen.

When she got there, Dave was rummaging in the refrigerator. He was usually at the hospital long before this. He closed the door and greeted Leah. "Good morning!" He had bowls lined up on the countertop and started spooning yogurt onto fresh raspberries and blueberries.

"Good morning." Leah stood there, wondering what to do.

Monica loaded a tray with orange juice and a French press of coffee, ready to take it to the patio. "Good morning, sweetheart," she said. Her voice sounded slightly annoyed despite her endearment. "Could you be a darling and get the girls up? They don't need baths; just have them wash up and put on the outfits I have laid out on the dresser. Dave will get their breakfast stuff out in a minute."

"Why is Dr. Dave home? This is Monday, isn't it?" Leah asked. She knew he usually had an early Monday morning meeting. Monica had complained about it more than once.

"Oh, you must have forgotten. It's July 4th. Dave's off today thank goodness! Get the girls ready and then we have a surprise—I should say *Dave* has a surprise." Leah waited, thinking Monica would let her know about the day's activities, but she said nothing more.

Leah had completely forgotten it was a holiday. The Amish didn't make much of July 4th—Independence Day—although the shop would probably be closed. *Maemm* and *Daett* would stay up a little later and go with Leah's brothers and Susan to watch fireworks from their pasture field with the rest of Benville, but otherwise, it was just another day. Monday in July meant checking for early sweet corn in the patch and picking the ripe raspberries and blackberries. Leah's mouth watered thinking of cobbler and roasting ears and the steamy kitchen filled with all that extra heat. To her, it was preferable to yogurt at the Woodruff house where it was sometimes so cold from the air conditioning that the windows fogged up.

The moment Leah appeared in their bedroom, Kylie jumped out of bed and emitted a shrill scream. "Boo!" yelled Skye as she jumped out of the closet. Kylie belatedly ran to hide behind her massive almost-empty toy box. Toys were strewn from one side of the room to the other. Leah stepped carefully over a wooden Noah's ark and bent to pick up several animals scattered about the jungle of a nursery.

"Let's get dressed, okay?" Leah looked at Kylie, faking sternness, but Kylie ran to the bed and jumped on it. "That isn't a trampoline, little girl. Get off that bed and put these on. Wash your face and hands. There's a surprise after breakfast."

Kylie and Skye now gave Leah their full attention. "What surprise? What kind of surprise?" asked Kylie.

"'Prise!" echoed Skye.

"I don't know," Leah answered. "It's a surprise for me, too. Now put on these clothes, will you?" Leah held out the tiny undies and helped Skye into a dress that looked more like a Halloween costume than something to wear all day—although it was red, white, and blue with star sequins sewed all over the skirt—probably chosen for the July 4th holiday. Kylie's outfit was also red, white, and blue but was a pair of short leggings with a ruffled stars and stripes top.

"What's the surprise? What?"

The questions didn't stop and the more she responded with "I don't know," the more curious she became herself. *What could Dave and Monica be planning?* "Let's get breakfast," Leah said. She dipped a comb under the faucet and pulled Kylie's hair back with a hair tie and barrettes from the children's bathroom. "Let's go find out, okay?" After making a quick effort to get the toys back in the toy box, she marshaled the two down the stairs. Leah carried the girls' cereal outside and settled them at their child-sized picnic table.

"I fixed you a dish of yogurt and berries. It's inside," Dr. Dave said.

Leah went inside and found the bowl and a coffee mug. She topped the yogurt with a generous helping of granola from a bag on the counter, then joined the family on the patio. The girls were finally quiet, eating their cereal and drinking from juice boxes. The sounds of nature surrounded them as they all sat eating in silence for a few moments, taking in the warmth of the season and the communion of family.

Leah once again thought about the strange circumstances that had brought her to this little family group. One minute she'd been selling potholders for Fannie and then she had joined the Woodruffs and was on her way to Cleveland. She felt grown up sitting here with Dave and Monica and being trusted as a nanny to Kylie and Skye. She was even starting to feel at home with this family. But it was all so different from the routines in the Troyer home. Sometimes she felt she was living in another country, another world.

How can this be, Aaron? How did I get here? What am I doing here? Her daydream took her again to the confidant who was always close in her mind. Aaron on his bicycle beside her, slow and steady, urging her on, telling her to keep looking at the top of Boonetown Hill as they climbed and ignore the pavement under her wheels. His advice was just what she needed that day. He was the most understanding man she'd ever met. She hoped he understood why she was here.

Leah's thoughts were interrupted as Dave stood up and turned toward the girls. "May I have your attention, everyone," he said. A smile played around his eyes. The girls stopped talking and watched him. "If everyone is ready, I have a surprise."

"We've been waiting long enough," Monica said impatiently. "What's up?"

"I've decided we're going to Benville today. I need to get signatures on Leah's paperwork. I've been holding a surgery date open on my calendar. And I thought Leah might appreciate seeing her family."

Monica's face was hard to read. But Leah was happy about going home to see her family.

"Aren't you getting a little homesick, Leah?" Dave asked.

"It will be nice to see everyone," Leah said. Her heart pounded at the thought of seeing her family, even if only for the day. *But what if they wouldn't let her come back to Cleveland? What if her parents had changed their minds?* She wanted to have the surgery. It still seemed so far from being a reality.

Leah finished her breakfast and helped clear the patio table. Her thoughts again turned toward home as she loaded the dishwasher. Dave might have called it a surprise for *this* family, but it would also be a big surprise for the Troyer family when Leah showed up with no warning before noon.

CHAPTER 21

Leah Troyer

L eah sat beside Skye in the middle seat of the van. Skye was strapped securely into a monstrous car seat with a bright print liner. She was fussing as usual; she hated being confined. But for once her mood didn't bother Leah. She would soon be back in Benville. Even if only for a visit. *Maemm* and *Daett* and the rest would be so glad to see her.

Leah felt a surge of hope. Soon her long wait would be over, she'd have the surgery, and be home for good. As they drove out of the city, Dave reviewed the reason for this visit.

"Leah, you're just seventeen years old, so we need to get a parent's signature on this folder of documents, just like we did before you had the tests at the hospital." Dave pointed to the manila packet tucked beside the driver's seat. He caught her eye in the rearview mirror and continued. "I'm holding open August fifteenth on my calendar. Does that sound like a good date to you?"

Leah felt a flutter of anxiety when he said this. A calendar date made it more real. "Any time you want is okay with me. I'm sure my family will come to the hospital, no matter when it is," Leah answered. It felt peculiar to be looking at his face in the mirror and see him looking back at her.

"I'll bet you can't wait to visit your family," Monica turned toward Leah. "I'm guessing you've been a little homesick, haven't you?"

"I do miss them," Leah answered. "But I like helping you with the girls. It makes the time go faster." Sometimes she still couldn't believe she was a live-in nanny. She didn't know any other Amish girls who had ever done that.

"I want to see Benville, the town you call home," Monica said. "We never got to see where you live. This trip is long overdue."

"Benville isn't a town," Leah said. "More of a crossroads with a couple of stores."

"I guess you can tell Dave how to get there," Monica said.

"I've got your address on these papers," Dave said. "I put it in the GPS."

Leah didn't know if she'd ever get used to having a strange voice in the car giving directions. Monica didn't like it either, so Dave had turned off the sound. Leah looked at the map on the screen. GPS saved Leah from having to give directions herself and that was a good thing. She had no idea how to get from Shaker Heights to Benville.

"We can fill your folks in on everything when we talk today," Dave said.

"I told them about getting the tests and MRI," Leah said. "In one of my letters."

"There was never much question in my mind that you were a candidate for surgery," Dave said. "But now we have proof after these scans and X-rays."

Leah shivered at the word "surgery." She tried to hide the wobbly feelings in her stomach. Once again, she fought back the nerves that surfaced whenever she thought of the ordeal ahead of her. She sometimes almost managed to forget it until someone started talking about it like Dave was now.

"Will your parents even be home today?" Monica sounded a little annoyed. Maybe she wasn't as happy as Leah was about the surprise road trip. Or maybe she didn't like talking about surgery on a holiday. "What do the Amish do to celebrate Independence Day?" Monica asked.

Leah hesitated, not sure how to answer. "We don't celebrate this holiday with a church service or anything," Leah said. "But the shops close and we watch the fireworks. In Benville, we can watch from the pasture field. It's just another day. No one makes much of it or flies a flag. *Dawdi* says our citizenship is in heaven, not in this world."

Monica looked puzzled. "That's a different way of thinking," she said.

Leah remembered *Dawdi's* lesson from last year when she'd asked why he didn't go with them to watch the fireworks. There were so many things she'd learned from *Dawdi*. It would be good to see him today. "The Fourth of July is just a day for visiting and catching up around home in Benville," Leah said.

Dave turned onto a smaller road. "Might as well take the scenic route today, don't you think?" he asked.

"You'd better hope Kylie doesn't get car sick in the back seat," Monica said. "If she does, you're cleaning up the mess."

Monica sounded provoked. But that happened sometimes. Leah had been with this family long enough to pick up on the occasional tension between Monica and Dave. Amish couples usually didn't let their bad feelings show much if others were around.

Dave turned on the radio and they listened to a patriotic music program on WKSU.

Everyone got quiet and the girls fell asleep. Leah stared at the back of Monica's head, wondering why she wanted to wear her hair like that. She'd called it a messy bun, which seemed funny but a good description. Leah thought of her long hair that was simply coiled under her *kapp,* or sometimes a headscarf, and fastened with a barrette.

Soon the landscape claimed Leah's undivided attention. The scenic route took them past horse farms and a llama farm. Large rolling hayfields were dotted with round bales waiting to be loaded and stored in barns and sheds. White fences and pastures were interspersed with homes of every style as they traveled through Medina County where the roadsides were thick with wild carrot and asters. It looked a lot like Amish Country, without the buggies and furniture shops.

Just like in Holmes County, some people here left patches of wild milkweed growing. The milkweed fed the Monarchs that spent time in Ohio during July and August. Children and adults in their yards and driveways shot hoops or played catch. They passed a small park where cars lined the street. Softball and baseball games were underway. Cars in the roadway were towing boats or campers or they had their bicycles with them as they headed for a trail somewhere.

Leah tapped her toes gently in time with the music. She was wearing the new Skechers Monica had gotten at the mall. The music made her feel happy, despite the tension circling between Dave and Monica.

After Wooster, familiar sights came into view as they made their way to the township road leading to Benville. Leah's heart raced at the thought of seeing *Maemm* and *Daett,* Susan, and her little brothers. As they got closer, Dave kept checking the GPS screen for the route. Today everything familiar looked new to Leah. She noticed small things, the colorful flower beds, laundry hanging limply on the wash lines, and empty schoolyards because it was summer.

A strange mixture of anxiety and excitement tumbled in Leah's tummy. It was easy to understand the anticipation. She'd soon see her whole family again. But this other feeling was different, a sinking, scary feeling she couldn't ignore but didn't understand.

Dave finally pulled up in front of the Troyers' home. Leah unfastened her seatbelt. Monica opened the car door and released Kylie from her booster seat. Leah got out and stretched, leaving Monica to deal with Skye who was still asleep in the car seat. After the air-conditioned car, the heat already felt oppressive even though it was only midmorning.

Three pairs of bare feet came running toward Leah, their too-short denim pants flapping at their ankles. Jake, Andy, and Adam had each grown taller in the weeks she'd been gone. Toby, the yellow lab, sniffed the hem of her skirt. The boys halted just in front of Leah and looked at her as if they'd seen a ghost. Everyone stood there not knowing what to say. Leah breathed in the sweet scent of home, a mixture of corn, clover, and *Maemm's* pink petunias.

"Leah! You came home!" Jake said. They stared at their sister.

"We didn't know you were coming," Andy said. "You surprised us."

"*Yah*, it is a surprise, isn't it?"

The boys nodded, suddenly shy, then each gave her a quick hug. Leah hugged them back.

Skye, who was still sleeping in Monica's arms, woke up and began wailing.

Everyone finally headed for the house looking for *Maemm*. Where was she? In the garden? She had surely heard the car and seen them drive in. Leah led the way to the porch where the petunias she'd watered in May now trailed onto the railing. The screen door opened, and Fannie stood there in purple flip-flops, fanning herself with a colorful folded paper fan.

Maemm wasn't beside her. *Why was Fannie at their house in the middle of the day? Why wasn't she at her shop?*

"Oh, it's you!" Fannie greeted them unceremoniously. Her face was flushed from the heat. "What are you doing here today?"

"It's a holiday, so we came to see everybody," Leah said.

"Oh, my! We surely weren't expecting you. You should have called. But it's nice you came," Fannie said.

Leah was confused. "But . . . why are *you* here?" Leah asked back. "Where's *Maemm?*" At the sight of home and her brothers, Leah's strange feelings had gone away. Now they'd come back. Something wasn't right.

"Your parents had to go to Millersburg a couple hours ago. And now you're here visiting. My goodness! Is everything okay?"

"Everything's fine. Don't you worry," Dr. Dave answered. "You might remember us from the auction. We just thought since it was a holiday we'd come for a little visit."

"Oh, yes! With all the excitement this morning I almost forgot it's the Fourth of July. Let's go sit under that shade tree," Fannie said, gesturing to a spreading maple in the yard. "My but it's hot today." She fanned her face again. Several lawn chairs were arranged in a circle under the tree, almost as if someone had known they were coming.

"I brought documents for Leah's parents to sign before her surgery." He lifted the binder held together with elastic bands.

"Why did *Maemm* and *Daett* go to Millersburg?" Leah asked. She felt sick inside.

Millersburg wasn't a place her parents went to very often. Unless it was to the hospital.

"They went with the emergency squad. I don't know when they'll be back." Fannie fanned herself with her apron. "Albert asked me to look after the little ones—wouldn't you know on a holiday when I could expect tourists to stop at the shop? But family comes first."

Then, as an afterthought: "Susan even went with them, or she could have helped out here."

Leah stood dumbfounded. *The squad? The ambulance? Something bad must have happened.* "What happened, Fannie? Who needed the squad?"

"Well, your *Maemm* went over to check with *Dawdi* this morning. He wasn't sitting on his porch like he usually does . . ."

No! Not Dawdi! Leah's breath came in shaky bursts. Her heart pounded in her ears.

Fannie continued with her story. "She found him still in bed and he wasn't breathing good at all—he was kind of gasping for air—so she ran to the shop, and they called. They came right away and took him to Millersburg Hospital." Fannie's words came out in a rush. She looked worried.

"*Dawdi's* in the hospital?" Leah asked in disbelief. "No! Not now!" The blood drained from her face and the weight of fear dropped from her chest to her stomach. The memory was vivid. Two years ago, *Mommi* had died at that same hospital. Leah's eyes filled with tears. She wiped at them with the back of her hand.

Dave and Monica's faces held concern as they looked in Leah's direction. And Fannie's teary eyes met Leah's.

"*Dawdi's* going to be okay," Fannie said. "Don't you worry, Leah. I'm sure he's in good hands."

CHAPTER 22

Dave Woodruff

L eah's Aunt Fannie gestured to a large maple tree in the front yard where lawn chairs were clustered in a circle under the leafy branches. "Let's go sit. Albert and Elma might be here soon. I don't know."

Fannie led them to a circle of well-made outdoor seating under a tree. The yellow lab followed them. Dave sat down and trained his eye on the white house with its colorful hanging baskets spaced across the front. He saw the large vegetable garden beside the house and the flowers. Flowers everywhere. *So this is Leah's home.*

After they were seated, life moved in slow motion. But his brain remained focused on the day's errand. He had to get the surgery consent forms signed.

Monica guided the girls to the child-sized chairs. Fannie went inside to get cold lemonade and sugar cookies. When she returned, she sat down in the remaining chair.

"Do you think the Troyers will be home soon?" Dave asked as he accepted the cold glass and declined the cookie. Life had skidded and slowed to a snail's pace. He'd been thrown into Amish time. Lemonade and cookies were now the priority. "I know you weren't expecting us. We came on a whim, hoping to get Albert and Elma's signatures on Leah's hospital paperwork."

"I don't know when they'll be back," Fannie said. "They went down to the hospital in Millersburg to sit with *Dawdi*. He was admitted this morning for tests."

"What do you think is wrong? Will he be okay?" Leah asked.

"I don't know. He's been more tired lately." Fannie looked at Leah's stricken face and continued, "It's probably nothing. This hot weather is hard on the old people."

Dave glanced at Leah who looked as if she would burst into tears at any moment.

"I'm so sorry to hear that," Dave said. "It's good they are having it checked out." He chose his words carefully, conscious of Leah's feelings. *She's far more worried about her* Dawdi *than she is about this paperwork.*

Leah stood up. "I'm going inside. I want to get things from my room." Her voice shook and Dave saw a couple of tears. She needed time alone. Monica, distracted by Leah's sadness, seemed oblivious to Dave's distress. She looked relaxed as she took in the scene of flower gardens and hanging baskets at the edge of the porch roof. They were lush and full, the only color on an otherwise white frame house.

From across the circle, Dave admired his wife, the woman he'd fallen in love with years ago. Now he saw her as if for the first time. She was still the same Monica, as beautiful as ever. Her trim figure folded into the chair, her fresh bright-colored sundress was picture-perfect, and her flawless skin glowed in the warmth of midsummer. A feeling of love rose inside him. Why did he so often take her for granted? He breathed in the flower-scented air and tried to slow his expectations to the rhythm of this time and place.

"You've got a beautiful home here," Dave said.

"My place is over there," Fannie said, pointing in the direction of her house and the nearby quilt shop. "They wanted me to keep an eye on these boys while they were gone, so I closed my shop for the day. I planned to stay open on the holiday. I thought tourists might come through today. I'm needed here though, I guess."

They sat in awkward silence.

"How's your weather been here?" Dave asked.

"It's been hot and humid. We've been watering the gardens a little. We need rain," Fannie said. "How has the weather been in Cleveland?"

"About the same as here, I think. I'm at the hospital in the air conditioning so much I almost don't notice the weather," Dave said. "What do you think, Monica? You're outside more than I am these days." He looked toward Monica, hoping to draw her into the conversation. Their eyes met and she smiled at him, that sweet smile, so genuine.

"I don't have near this many flowers. I've been watering my patio pots, though. Leah's been such a help in the house and with the girls lately, I have time to get outside," Monica said.

"I imagine Leah's a big help to you. She's such a responsible girl," Fannie said. "She's quiet, though. And quite the reader, too. But she can work. I know Elma misses having her here this summer. There's always so much to do this time of year," Fannie said.

"We're glad to have her at our place. We sure are," Dave said.

Just then Leah came from the house carrying a shopping bag that appeared to be stuffed with clothing. The dog and a couple of her brothers followed her as she walked across the grass and put the bag in the van before returning to her chair.

"That's quite a nice dog you've got there," Dave said to Leah. "What's his name? The girls want to know his name. Don't you Kylie?"

"His name is Toby," Leah said. "We got him from the dog shelter after our other dog got hit on the road."

Dave saw Monica wince at this matter-of-fact statement. He met her gaze and watched as she nervously redid her messy bun.

"Well, he looks like a good dog," Dave said. He reached out and patted Toby's head. The dog looked up at Leah like he remembered her. Then he took off across the yard, running.

Leah's brothers ran too, chasing Toby around the side of the house. Kylie ditched her sandals and followed them.

Dave cleared his throat and drummed his fingers nervously on the arm of his chair. He shifted to the edge of his chair. "Maybe we could go to Millersburg to get Albert and Elma's signatures," he said. He looked at Monica, hoping she understood his idea. *We need to find Albert and Elma and get those papers signed.*

"That's a good idea," Monica said. "And Leah might like to have a little visit with her grandfather before we go back to Cleveland."

Dave felt that tug in his heart again. Monica understood him. Knew what he was thinking. At least she did this time. *We need to get going. And soon.*

"Great idea. Do you want to see if we can catch up with your parents at the hospital, Leah? Maybe see if we can get you in to have a little visit with your grandfather?"

"That would be nice if you think we can go there." Leah brightened at the mention of seeing her parents and *Dawdi.*

Before they could get up and take their leave, a blue minivan pulled into the driveway. Fannie rose from her chair as the driver leaned out the window and greeted her. "Oh, my goodness! Henry Kratzer, what are you doing here? Isn't this a holiday for you?" She strode toward him as he got out of his car and made his way to Fannie and the group gathered under the old maple.

"I took a family to Charm for a reunion there. They're staying until after the fireworks. I thought you wanted me to drive you over to Fryburg. Maybe I was mistaken."

A look of dismay came over Fannie's face. "Oh, I completely forgot that in all the commotion with *Dawdi*," she said.

"I saw you all sitting here as I went by. Your Cozy Corner Shop is closed. Aren't you afraid you're going to lose your holiday customers?" His tone was light, but he wasn't teasing her.

Dave stood and walked over to shake hands and hopefully make a break for it. It was time to leave. "Good morning! I'm Dave Woodruff, Doctor Dave Woodruff. This is my wife, Monica, and our children, Skye, and Kylie—she's around here somewhere. We're down from Cleveland for the day."

"Hank Kratzer. Pleased to meet you. What brings you to Benville today—certainly not our Fourth of July parade?"

Fannie lifted the empty pitcher. "I'll go in and get more lemonade," she said. "You just stay put. I'll be right back." And she hurried off to the house.

Hank settled into an empty chair. Reluctantly, Dave sat down again. "So there's no parade in Benville?"

"No parade. But I wouldn't be surprised to find a picnic with some good food," Hank said. "I've been doing some reading. The Amish are Anabaptists who go way back to the 16th century when they protested the church-state relationship, including government conscription into the army. I suppose Independence Day and all it stands for is *verboten*," Hank said.

"Is that so? Well, you learn something new every day," said Dave. He slapped his knee and stood. "We were just ready to head out." Monica and Leah also stood, registering Dave's signal that it was time to go. "In any case, we aren't here for a holiday celebration, although I appreciate my day off from the hospital. I'm the surgical supervisor of my department at Cleveland General. We were hoping to talk to Leah's parents. I guess I shouldn't say more than that. HIPPA rules and all." Dave grinned and looked Hank in the eye.

"I guess you know Leah." Dave began to recall seeing this man at the Children's Relief Auction. "Leah's been our nanny for the summer. This is my wife, Monica."

"Oh, yes. I know Leah," Hank said. "Fannie's niece. Fannie always talks about 'Leah, up in Cleveland . . .' It worries her." He looked at Leah and smiled broadly. Leah blushed and dropped her eyes. "It's such a nice thing you're doing for Leah. I tell Fannie, 'Don't you worry. That girl is going to be just fine.'"

"The trouble is, Leah's parents aren't here," Dave continued. "I planned to review everything with them and get their signatures on these documents." He pointed at the fat folder on the ground beside his chair. "Grandpa Troyer had an emergency of some sort, and they took him to the hospital."

Fannie returned from the house with a full pitcher of lemonade. "I made some more. It's just from a powder mix but it will cool us off anyway," she apologized. She poured a fresh glass and handed it to Hank.

Dave glanced at his wife again, desperate to move on. Monica returned his look. "Thank you, but I think we've all had enough," she said. "Leah, can you go find Kylie and Skye?"

Leah nodded and headed for the house to round up the girls.

"Thanks for the cold drink. That hit the spot. And great cookies, too." Dave and Monica placed their glasses on the wide arms of the chairs where they'd been sitting. "We decided to go to Millersburg," Dave told Fannie. "I need to talk with Leah's parents before we go home."

Dave stepped closer and wrapped his arm around Monica's

bare shoulders. In the other arm, he held the bulging medical folder. Her skin felt warm and smooth.

"Kylie, sweetie, come here so Mommy can fix your hair. Put on your shoes. We need to get ready to go."

Dave started moving in the direction of the car. "We should see if we can find Albert and Elma at the hospital. I'll call the front desk and leave a message so they don't leave before we arrive."

"You need directions?" Hank asked. "It's about a half hour to get down there."

"I think we can find it," Dave said. "But thanks."

He turned to Fannie. "My wife and I are so grateful for your hospitality, but we need to be going." Dave patted the portfolio. "I wish we could stay longer. I'm sorry to bother Albert and Elma today, but duty calls. Hank says it's about a half-hour drive. I can easily GPS it," Dave said.

"Yes, of course! GPS is a wonderful thing. Hank surely appreciates it. I know that," Fannie said.

Hank smiled, then turned to Dave. "Just go out 212 until you come to a large farm with two blue silos. That's Township Road 18. Turn left and stay on it and you'll come out at Route 83 near the Gingerich produce stand. You can't miss it. I'm warning you now, don't let Monica see those beautiful hanging baskets or your car will be full of petunias on the way back to Cleveland."

"Well that certainly sounds easy enough," said Dave. "Come on, Woodruff family—all aboard! Leah let's go to Millersburg to see your grandfather and your parents. And get these papers signed. You are probably just what the doctor ordered for a day like today."

Leah grasped the hands of Kylie and Skye who looked with longing at the rambunctious dog and Leah's young brothers. "Bye, Fannie. It was good to see you," Leah said.

Dave got behind the wheel and saw Fannie and Hank still sitting under the tree. Time didn't matter much to the old folks. The two sat across from one another in the shade drinking lemonade. Toby sat at attention beside Hank, who was stroking his head. The three of them were the picture of contentment.

CHAPTER 23

Monica Woodruff

Monica was glad Leah would get to see her parents and her sick grandfather. Dave, intent on his driving, remained silent until they came to the two blue silos. "Here's the turn, I guess," he said. "Where can we get some lunch, Leah? Any suggestions?"

Monica's stomach rumbled. *Had Dave read her mind?*

"There is a little restaurant up the road," Leah said. "I've never eaten there, though." She paused. "There's a hotel on Main Street and some fast-food places out by Walmart."

"Are there any organic restaurants? Farm to table? Anything like that?" Monica asked.

"Uh, I don't know . . ."

As they approached Millersburg, Monica said, "Why don't I take the girls somewhere for lunch while you two go to the hospital?"

"That's a good idea," Dave said. "But are you sure?" He turned onto the street leading to the small county hospital.

"Yes, I'm sure," Monica said.

After life in the city, Millersburg was alien territory. Streets were winding, hills steep. Old brick buildings, now filled with antiques, hinted at long-ago shops where country people once bought clothing and hardware.

As they passed through town, Monica's thoughts wandered. She reflected on the way Dave had looked at her when they were sitting under the tree at Leah's home. Her heart softened toward him.

Out here in the country, away from their usual surroundings, her perspective on their life together had mellowed in the midsummer sun. She'd agreed to this errand and would see it through. Leah's parents were waiting at the hospital.

Monica was learning that life among the Amish was slower and simpler. And that wasn't a bad thing. It's just that everything took longer than expected. This errand they were on wasn't going as planned.

Dave had one thing on his mind. He needed to deal with those papers in his folder. He and Leah had work to do. Monica's sense of adventure kicked in, aided by the unfamiliar territory they'd just passed through. "Just pull into the parking lot. You and Leah can go in. I'm sure there's a hospital cafeteria where you can get something. I'm going to find us some food and a park. Millersburg has a park, doesn't it?" She looked in Leah's direction and then back to Dave. Leah looked unsure.

"Maybe down that road." She pointed away from the hospital.

"Just text me when you're ready to leave and I'll come back and pick you up," Monica said to Dave.

"Sounds like a plan," said Dave as he handed over the key fob.

Monica walked around the car and got into the driver's seat. She consulted her phone for directions to the park and turned onto an ancient brick-paved street that led to Park Street. The girls were sleeping in their car seats. She pulled up to a rustic fence and stopped. They'd need food—more than a granola bar and juice box—when they woke up. Ordinarily, she'd have packed a cooler with plenty of healthy food and drinks. But Dave had sprung his July 4th surprise trip on them, and she had no time to plan a picnic lunch. *Surprises aren't as fun when you're juggling medical errands and two toddlers. I'd have preferred to plan today. But here we are.*

Dave's surprises had made her fall in love with him—the dinner on a yacht at sunset when she had left the house in heels and a full-skirted sundress, the trip to an obscure inn on the Lake Michigan shore for steak and lobster, the outdoor concert complete with fancy boxed dinners.

Now she lived with Dr. Dave Woodruff who stayed at the hospital until 9 p.m. to surprise a low-risk patient with a post-op visit or accepted invitations to eat birthday cake with a group of surgical nurses or went to the hospital an hour early to read the chart of a young Amish girl whose surgery fee he'd waived on a whim.

That surprise decision he'd made in early June had taken some getting used to. She'd gone along with it. She liked having a nanny. And she was proud of Dave for stepping up to help Leah. Dave was still the unpredictable Dr. Dave she married—a man full of surprises, consumed by his career.

While she was pleased with her status in life and appreciated their lack of financial worries, she missed the fun times they used to have. Medical school loans were paid off and their income seemed to increase every year. But this good life came at a price. She'd felt more and more lonely and abandoned while Dave worked long hours in an emotionally draining career.

Monica sat staring at the park where huge trees shaded an elaborate, colorful playground that rivaled any in Cleveland. Her thoughts drifted to her discontent. Why did it cloud her happiness? Their home on Briarwood was all she'd ever dreamed of—a century Tudor with a large lot, trees, and a carriage house. What was not to like? Yet there were things she didn't like: her loss of a significant career and the feeling of being trapped, isolated, and lost in a city where meaningful relationships were hard to come by and everyone was always on the go. When had she last sat in a circle with others under a tree, sipping lemonade like they did today with Fannie? Was this something that only happened in the country, among the Amish?

Suddenly, an elderly man tapped his cane on her car window. Monica cracked the window an inch and glanced to see if the doors were locked. "Can I help you with something ma'am? You don't look like you're from around here." His voice was raspy, and his scraggly beard had gone mostly gray. He looked unkempt.

Monica's stomach clenched with fear. "I'm trying to figure out how to fill a couple of hours. I need to find a place to get lunch for my girls. My husband is at the hospital." *I shouldn't be talking to strangers. This is exactly what I tell the girls not to do. Good thing they're asleep.*

"At the hospital, eh? Hey, I hope everything is okay."

He seems nice enough. He's trying to be friendly. This isn't the city, after all. Still, Monica's instincts told her to be on guard. "Everything's okay. He's a doctor. He's looking for someone there." She put her finger on the window button, ready to end the conversation. "I need to get my girls some lunch before we tackle this playground," she said.

"Village Pizza is right around the corner." He pointed his cane in the general direction.

Monica shook her head.

"I'll tell you, then," Scraggly Beard said. "Front Street, right over there, and hang a right. You might like the Cuppa coffee shop. I hear they have good food, trendy stuff—wraps and paninis."

Monica nodded and pressed the window button. "Perfect." She mouthed her thanks and started the car. *Time to get out of here. Away from this guy. You can never be too careful.*

The man wandered off and Monica tapped the food icon on the Google Map. She pressed "Go" and backed away. Scraggly Beard sat on the park bench and leaned on his cane looking in the direction of distant rolling hills. Monica hoped he wouldn't be there long. He shouldn't be hanging around the playground. And he didn't look like someone who would know a panini from a cheeseburger. *I suppose looks can be deceiving. It's just that when you're out in the country like this, you don't know what to think, or who to trust.*

Monica found Cuppa and extracted the drowsy girls from the car. At the door, she stopped to read a poster "Fresh Local Food! Weaver's Produce *(Could that be the Aden and Lydia Weaver she and Dave knew?)* supplies all our fresh vegetables and seasonal fruits. Welcome!" Now she did feel welcome at the thought of Aden and Lydia, their beautiful farm, and gentle ways. She opened the door and entered the small shop.

Soon Monica was settled into a cozy booth, helping Kylie and Skye with their orange juice while they waited for the girls' grilled cheese sandwiches and Monica's beet and kale salad with local goat cheese.

The Amish barista delivered a tall latte for Monica, she'd topped it with a tower of whipped cream and a dusting of festive red, white, and blue sugar crystals. Monica swirled the cream, watching it dissolve into the coffee until gratitude surfaced, warming her heart and nourishing her soul in this land of abundant simplicity.

CHAPTER 24

Dave Woodruff

Dave and Leah connected with her parents in the hospital cafeteria. After the excitement of this unexpected visit was behind them, and Dave explained to Albert and Elma why they'd come, Leah asked if she could visit *Dawdi.*

Elma, who was paging through *Birds and Blooms,* offered to show Leah to his room. "I'll wait in the little waiting room up there while you visit him," she said. "It will do his heart good to see you."

Dave wanted to present the consent folders to Leah's father at once but knew there was no choice but to wait for Elma and Leah's return. To make conversation, he asked Albert about his furniture manufacturing business. "Leah said there was a fire at your shop this spring. I hope it didn't do too much damage," Dave said.

"We were able to get things put right fairly soon with the help of our church people," Albert said. "When everyone pitches in, the work goes fast."

Dave nodded. "Those Amish barn raisings are legendary. I imagine you had excellent help." Albert didn't respond, so Dave pushed on. "Until I visited Amish Country, I didn't realize how many small shops there are. Do you work together, or is each one independent?" He was trying to connect with this man. They had little in common other than their concern for Albert's daughter, Leah.

"Things are changing fast in the industry," Albert said. "We have a business model where small shops each manage a different piece of the whole. We're all in the Benville area and coordinate our work. We might soon need a warehouse and a centralized distribution center."

Albert continued talking about his business. Ordinarily, Dave would have enjoyed this chance to learn from the Amish entrepreneur, but he couldn't concentrate. Getting those surgery permissions signed was at the top of his mind. When the conversation lagged, he excused himself and took his time ordering a pastry and a cup of strong coffee. He opened small packets of sugar and two creamers, glancing at the door in the hope of seeing Leah and her mother. He wandered outside with his coffee, keeping an eye on the hallway just inside while he sipped the coffee and ate the jelly donut that would have to replace lunch for him.

It was a relief when he saw Leah and her mother pass the doorway on their way back to the cafeteria. He joined them and they made their way to the table in a corner where Leah's dad sat waiting for them. Leah's sister brought Leah a milkshake and then disappeared.

When they were settled, Dave got an update on *Dawdi* before he plunged in. "Now that we're all here, I'd like to go over everything with you today and make sure all your questions are answered." He opened his bulging folder. "Because Leah is still a minor, her parents' signatures are needed before surgery. There are also billing issues we need to discuss and, of course, the details of her surgery and recovery."

Dave continued, "As you, of course, are aware, Leah was probably born with a predisposition to idiopathic scoliosis, which can be a birth defect that progresses as a child grows. I think you said you know others who have scoliosis and probably some other genetic diseases that are more common among the Amish. I believe there's even a special clinic that is studying these, as well as providing treatment for some children.

"Be that as it may"—Dave shuffled the papers he'd removed from the folder until he found some colorful, illustrated leaflets—"this brochure explains the surgery I'm proposing for Leah. I'll give you a little time to look it over." He handed one to each of Leah's parents. Leah leaned in to read it along with her mother. "Leah's seen this brochure before, and I've thoroughly explained to her what we do to correct the curvature.

"Scoliosis causes the spine to curve sideways and sometimes outward as well; the result is uneven shoulders. The waistline is higher on one side than the other. It causes the patient to lean slightly to one side. In severe cases, there's a hump on one side of the back, like Leah has. It's what I immediately saw when I met her at the Children's Relief Auction."

Dave noticed the way Albert looked away from his daughter's face. The lines around his mouth betrayed his discomfort with discussing his daughter's body. He glanced toward his wife. "I know you mean well, doctor, but we know several children who have this, and it hasn't bothered them a bit. They haven't had surgery to correct it." Albert took a breath and continued. "I guess I'm not sure she needs this surgery. It's a big risk. She's healthy now, except for her spine problem." His voice held a severe tone that wasn't there when he'd talked about his woodshop.

Dave tried to find words to ease Leah's father's fears, to persuade Albert.

Elma's lips formed a tight line as if she had to prevent herself from saying the wrong thing.

Leah's hand went over her mouth as her father's words registered.

Frustration rose in Dave's chest, but he pushed it away in favor of a rational argument. "Mr. Troyer, I have done dozens of these surgeries, and while there are some risks, I can assure you that it's extremely rare to see anything but a positive result. I'm afraid I don't understand your hesitancy." Dave had a suspicion that it wasn't the medical risk as much as the financial risk that bothered Albert Troyer. Albert was likely now aware there would be added costs besides the surgery itself, which he was donating.

But the Amish had funds to help pay medical bills. Hadn't Aden Weaver told him that very thing when they were at the auction in May?

"In the end, it will be your own, and your wife's, decision—and, of course, I hope Leah here has a say in it, too. We do this to prevent future disability. Surely you understand the consequences of not correcting this. We're talking about damage to internal organs, eventual difficulty walking normally . . ." His voice increased in pitch. He took another breath. Then waited.

Leah stared at the empty tabletop. She twisted the ribbon of her *kapp*. Dave observed Leah's discomfort and his heart went out to her.

He turned towards Elma. "Do you have any questions about the procedure and the reasons for doing it?" *Please. Think of your daughter's future.*

"Are you sure these things will happen if she doesn't have surgery?" Elma asked. "We notice how crooked she is when we sew her dresses, so I know the things you're saying about her waist and shoulder are right. And she has a little limp sometimes when she's overly tired."

At least her mother understands the severity of Leah's condition.

"I try to give her easier jobs. Even then, I see how hard it can be for her. She never complains, though." Elma looked sidewise at

Leah. Dave could understand the deep worry lines on her forehead, signaling her fear that Albert would put his mistaken ideas and financial worries before Leah's needs. He suspected Elma knew better than to argue with Albert here in front of him, or probably any time, for that matter.

Dave renewed his efforts to explain. "Children do grow out of this, and sometimes, at younger ages, it can be corrected by wearing a brace. This is usually done between the ages of ten and sixteen. How old are you now, Leah?"

"Seventeen, almost eighteen."

Dave nodded. "Severe, untreated scoliosis, like the kind Leah has, can lead to heart and lung problems. When the spine isn't properly aligned, the organs may be overcrowded in the chest cavity. This can result in shortness of breath, greater risk of asthma, poor blood circulation, and more." As he spoke, Dave directed his words to Albert who had crossed his arms over his chest, as if to barricade himself from the truth.

"We've been to the chiropractor and that seemed to help her some. I guess you don't believe that's good enough then?" Albert's voice faltered.

"Maybe it did help her somewhat, Mr. Troyer, but it won't cure the problem. Surgery is the only way to correct Leah's condition."

Dave's calm, professional manner belied his inner turmoil. He had no idea he'd encounter resistance. After all, he'd gone out of his way to help. He cared about Leah. And Leah's parents had allowed her to come to Cleveland to be examined. *What could this man be thinking? He wouldn't let a crooked table leg out of his shop, but he would consider sending his daughter into the world with this kind of disfigurement.*

Maybe they needed a picture to help them understand. Dave opened a larger booklet to the center spread. He turned the pages, so they faced the three. "The indication for surgery is based on the curve magnitude as well as the child's—young person's—skeletal maturity." Dave looked at Leah with a smile and she gave a weak smile in return. "Curves that reach forty-five to fifty degrees are nearly always treated with surgery. If not treated, the curvature likely continues to progress throughout adulthood." With his finger, he traced the spine drawing in the brochure.

"Please understand, when someone chooses to have this surgery, it's not because they don't like their appearance. This is about basic health and future wellness," Dave said, keeping his tone calm and rational. In his head, an inner voice added, *Why would you let a child suffer disfigurement and be physically compromised for the rest of her life? Don't you care about her well-being?* Dave flipped to the page that illustrated the surgical procedure.

"Without the proposed surgery, we risk continued progression of the curvature. If surgery is indicated—and in Leah's case, I believe it is—it is best done before adulthood. Children— young people— are much better equipped to recover from surgery than adults are." Dave paused to let his words sink in. He looked from one to the next. Leah and her mother met his glance.

Albert's eyes remained on the picture.

"Leah is on the edge of adulthood, and this could influence her long-term health."

Elma's eyes brimmed with tears.

Dave took a deep dive into a description of the familiar procedure he'd executed at Cleveland General Hospital a few hundred times. "During the procedure, we use metal anchors with rods to help straighten the spine. The bones will fuse together," Dave explained. "This holds the patient in a much better overall position and prevents pulmonary—lung—problems down the road." He looked at Leah's face. She appeared stoic despite the graphic words and pictures.

"If she has this surgery, Leah will stand taller and straighter." Dave smiled at Leah, and she looked away nervously. Most of his young patients had similar reactions when the procedure was described to them. "These illustrations show the approximate location of the surgical repair Leah would undergo," Dave said.

"Would I feel the metal in me later on, after I'm healed?" Leah asked. "Does it stay in there or do the metal and screws come out later on?"

It was the first time Leah had entered this conversation. Dave was pleased. He knew she'd looked at all these pictures in the brochures and had read every word long before today. "If you're asking if you will have to undergo another surgery, the answer is 'no.' The bone and cartilage fuse to the rods as you heal. You will never know they're there after a few weeks." Dave smiled warmly to reassure Leah.

He continued. "You will need to limit some activities for a while. Mrs. Troyer, your boys might have to do the garden work this fall." He chuckled at his little joke and then went on, speaking directly to Leah. "After you undergo rehabilitation and are completely healed, you should be able to do anything you want to. How does that sound to you?"

"*Goot*, I think. It all depends on what *Maemm* and *Daett* decide." Leah twisted her *kapp* strings, a sign she wasn't comfortable being the center of attention. "Whatever my parents decide is okay. It's scary, but you are so kind to offer to help me."

"I'm glad to hear this, Leah. Now we have a little business left to take care of." Dave pulled a few more papers from the folder and placed a shiny blue Cleveland General Hospital pen on top of them. "I processed Leah's situation with our billing office. As I understand, the Amish don't have insurance and are always self-paid. The hospital has special rates for self-pay patients, and we also waive certain fees in a case like this one." He slowed, hoping his next words would have the desired impact. "Particularly, since I will be performing this surgery at no cost to you." The doctor picked up the pen and tapped it on the table. The Troyer family was silent.

"There will still be the cost of anesthesia and the anesthesiologist, hospital charges, medications, and miscellaneous fees. All of it reduced to accommodate self-pay. I've tried to come up with a ballpark figure, but it is certainly negotiable. You don't know how much I dislike talking about this. But it's necessary." Dave slid a page across the table that included an itemized list and a number on the bottom line. "We could set up a payment schedule for you that would consider your situation and income." He held the pen out to Albert, who didn't take it. Albert's face looked stern, even a bit angry at the mention of "income" and "payment schedule." He glared at Leah's mother, who met his eyes, then turned to Leah sitting next to her.

Dave put the pen down and looked from Albert to Elma. He waited.

Then Leah's father stroked his beard a couple of times and cleared his throat. All eyes were on Albert. "I will get back to you. I just can't tell you for sure right now. We need to discuss it first, think it over more."

Dave kept his professional exterior, but impatience pounded inside his chest. He tried to stay calm, to project friendship and acceptance. "I'll leave you to discuss it, and we can sign this whenever you're ready," he said calmly. "I'll give you time alone to talk it over." Dave stood, leaving the papers and pen on the table.

Albert shook his head. "I'm not ready to sign anything today. I need more time to talk it over. To think about all of this." His chair scraped the floor as he pushed back and stood. The others followed his lead. The papers and pen remained in the center of the table.

"Of course. It's a big step for your family. And for Leah." Dave picked up the papers that needed to be signed and handed them to Albert with the envelope. "When you're ready, go ahead and sign the pages on the lines that are marked and return them to me."

Dave looked at Leah's mother who wiped a tear from her cheek with a balled-up tissue. Then his eyes darted to Leah who stood between her parents. Her face was blank as if she had mentally left for somewhere else. *And why wouldn't she? This is so hard. To get her hopes up, only to be met with this indecision. What was I thinking?*

"I should check in with my wife and girls," Dave said. He pulled a cell phone from his pocket and picked up the extra brochures. Leah stood and looked at her parents and then at Dave.

They walked toward the door of the cafeteria. Dave fell back but not out of ear shot.

"You should go back to Cleveland with the doctor," Dave heard Albert say to Leah.

"You agreed to work for them this summer. No matter what happens, you need to keep your promise."

Leah responded. "I was thinking I should stay here. Because of *Dawdi*. But they might not like it if I didn't go back."

"You need to go," Leah's mother said. "We will call when we know more. I think *Dawdi* will be released later today. Susan can help with him at home just like she has been doing."

Dave stepped outside and phoned Monica while Leah said goodbye to her parents in the hospital lobby. He stuffed his anger.

"Monica. I'm done here if you want to come back and pick us up."

"Did you get everything taken care of?" Monica sounded happy. The day must have gone better for her than it had for him.

"I'll tell you all about it tonight." Maybe he'd feel a little calmer then. Right now, his blood was boiling. He couldn't let on to Leah, though. She needed to stay hopeful. And so did he.

CHAPTER 25

Susan Troyer

Susan dropped a two-gallon bucket of red beets on the porch. She'd been up at 6:00 and in the garden for at least an hour. *Maemm* thought it was best to garden early in the day while it was still cool, but on a day like today, the heat was already rising from the fields. The corn crackled and gave off its sweet aroma. Everything was perfumed with that peculiar scent of summer—a mixture of freshly mowed hay, corn coming into tassel, and an undertone of leaf mold. A pair of swallowtail butterflies darted in and out of the coneflowers. Susan was suddenly overcome with gratitude. Life was *goot! Dawdi* had been released from the hospital and was back home.

Her eyes went back to the bucket of beets that predicted the day's activities. *Maemm* had told her to pull the smaller ones. She would pickle whole beets today. The jars were already scalding in the kettle, while the clove, cinnamon, mustard seed, and other spices were simmering in their broth of sugar and vinegar. The pungent scent mixed with the fresher outdoor perfume. Having deposited the bucket on the steps for *Maemm* and washed up, Susan made her way to *Dawdi's* porch and tapped lightly on the screen door. He was leaning on his cane and trying to pour milk onto a bowl of crunchy rice cereal.

Susan stepped inside. "Don't you want something better than that for breakfast, *Dawdi?*" Susan asked.

"No. I'm not very hungry."

"Do you want some toast with grape jelly?" *Dawdi* always preferred jelly on his toast.

"How about a nice cup of coffee?"

"No toast today. But if you want to bring me some coffee, I'd take that."

Susan settled *Dawdi* in a chair at his small table by the window. "*Maemm* has a kettle on. I'll bring your coffee over in a minute," Susan said. "Don't go anywhere."

"No, I'm not going anywhere. Now where did I put my glasses?"

Susan found them and handed them to him with the newspaper, then went to fetch the coffee. She returned and pulled out a chair across from him. He stirred milk and sugar into the coffee and Susan waited to see what *Dawdi* would say. Sometimes he told her a joke, other times he told a story about when he was a boy, and once he'd talked of *Mommi* and heaven. She hoped it wasn't that today. She didn't want to think about death.

"I wonder what they will do about Leah," he said. "They put the girly in such a bad way if she thinks she has a chance to get help and then they refuse it."

"I don't understand, *Dawdi*. *Maemm* and *Daett* agreed to let her have the tests. I thought they wanted her to have the surgery. But *Daett* hasn't signed the doctor's papers yet. Why would he do that?"

"*Ach*, yes! We all want her to have surgery. *Daett,* too. It's about money and such."

"But the doctor said the surgery is free," said Susan. "What's the problem?"

"*Ach, vell*, the surgery is free. *Yah.* But there are other costs. At the hospital. No one considered that when she went to Cleveland."

Susan sat there taking in what she'd just heard. "I thought it was all worked out."

"It will be. We must have faith. And pray that *Daett* will agree to accept help. I suspect the committee will pay the extra costs from the Children's Relief Fund. Our family can't pay all that without help right now."

Susan thought of her family's recent troubles. First the fire and then *Dawdi* in the hospital. *Thank goodness he didn't have to stay long. Daett* said it would be next year before the shop caught up with all their orders. That meant his pay would be less for a few months.

"So do you think the Children's Relief Committee will pay it?" Until now, Susan hadn't realized there was a problem. *Daett* hadn't signed the papers. He probably didn't want to get help with the bill. But Leah was still in Cleveland. Waiting. Hoping. Susan was sure of that. "They *have* to agree to help, don't they?" There was desperation in her voice.

Dawdi was still talking about Leah, but Susan was only half-listening.

"We will pray for *Gott's* wisdom and guidance. And for patience. 'Man sows the fields, but God giveth the increase.'"

Susan tried to focus on what *Dawdi* was saying. Was the Relief Committee's decision like a field? Or was it that Leah was a field and the committee was a sower? Or was . . . It was all so confusing! "Well, I just want Leah to come home, and for things to go back to normal. I miss Leah," Susan said.

"We all miss Leah," said *Dawdi*. "But remember, things will be different for Leah after this. No matter what happens. And for you, too. Because you're her sister."

Once again, Susan wasn't sure what *Dawdi* meant. Whatever he meant, she'd think about that later.

"I hear that the committee meets this Friday," he said. "So at least we won't have to wait too long for their decision. Your *Daett* went over to talk with Abe Maust last evening. He's on the helping committee. I'm sure Abe will put in a good word."

Dawdi slurped up some milk from his bowl.

"It's not wise to let Leah stay up there in Cleveland too long," he said. "She's a *goot* girl, but temptations are everywhere, and earthly pleasures can lure her away. No one wants that. Her home and family are in Benville."

Dawdi had been ill, but his mind was still sharp. Susan understood his concern. She'd had the same thoughts. Susan wasn't sure Abe was the best advocate. She thought of the bishop's long sermons. They were delivered in *Deutsch* without a trace of humor. Abe always looked towards his wife, Anna, when someone asked him something. The young girls giggled about that in the kitchen when they were washing up dishes after church. Susan suspected Abe Maust didn't have a mind of his own. Leah's fate might depend more on Anna Maust's ideas than on the bishop's decision.

By evening, the quarts of pickled beets were lined up on the countertop and the kitchen was tidy. After she'd damp-mopped the floor, Susan sat at the kitchen table, finally ready to write the letter that had been writing itself in her head all day.

Dear Leah,

I've been busy lately. Thanks for your letters. We all look forward to them and often read them out loud after supper. Dawdi *came back home on Wednesday. He must cut down on salty food and take his pills at the same time every day. I took over your job of looking in on him, but I know he misses you.*

We are canning pickles and pickled red beets and more beans—always more beans. Daett seems irritable. I'm sure it's because he didn't sign those papers when the doctor came last week. After talking to Dawdi, I think I understand what happened. The doctor is donating his surgery, but there are other expenses no one knew were part of it. Daett needs to request money from the Children's Relief Fund and make sure they will help before he signs the papers. Everyone is praying for you. We should soon know what they decide because, according to Dawdi, their meeting is on Friday.

Leah, this is hard to say but easier to write in a letter. I'm so sorry for the way I acted before you went to Cleveland. It seemed like you didn't have time for me or to hear about school. You were always reading a book when I wanted us to have fun together. And since you left, I have been mad about the extra work. I think I'm jealous because you have a better job than me and maybe even a boyfriend. I hope you can forgive me. I only want the best for you. I hope and pray you can have the surgery and that you will be back home soon.

With LOVE, Susan

CHAPTER 26

Leah Troyer

After the brief and disappointing Benville trip on July 4th, Leah fell into despair. She hid it from the Woodruff family, but when she retreated to her room over the garage each afternoon, she wept. She was alone in this strange and unfamiliar world, mourning the loss of hope. Until now, she hadn't realized how invested she'd become in having the surgery that would straighten her spine. She had unwisely begun dreaming of life without disability. A life that included a loving husband, children, a home to care for, and her rightful place in the Benville community.

Alec, Monica's charming nephew, only added to her confused feelings. Each Saturday the band opened the overhead door and set up in the garage below her room. She tried to avoid them by getting up early and going to the house for breakfast. She hoped the Woodruffs would include her in their family time. But each Saturday, Dave and Monica urged her to take the day off. "You've been such a help around here," Monica would say. "You need some time off. Why don't you find something to read and take it easy today?"

When Leah walked back to her loft retreat, Alec was waiting for her. He motioned for the band to take a break and tuned his guitar until Leah entered the garage. Then he pulled her into a conversation.

"Have a seat, Lady Leah," he'd say. "We need a live audience. Could you just listen to this bridge and tell us if my voice is balanced with the backup guitar?" His crooked grin lit up his face. His voice was playful and appealing.

"Sorry, I don't know anything about music," Leah responded.

"You don't have to. Just tell me if you can hear my voice and if you can understand the words," Alec said.

He pulled a lawn chair from its hook on the wall, opened it, and placed it in a corner. He motioned for her to sit, and she complied, reluctant to refuse when he so obviously wanted her there. She watched and listened as Alec sang his part, humming along under her breath. The music was becoming familiar to her, and she was enjoying it more all the time, even though it was awfully loud.

"So can you hear me above the guys playing?" Alec asked.

"I can hear you," Leah answered. "It sounds good . . . I think."

Alec had an easy way that was so different from most of the boys at home. He was the band leader with a charming personality and offhand manner. He included Leah as if it was the most natural thing in the world for an Amish girl to critique a Christian rock band.

And the pounding rhythms of the Corner Stones offered an escape from Leah's ever-present questions and relentless disappointment. Why had *Daett* refused to sign the consent forms? Leah sat in the low-slung folding chair and continued to listen, lost in the throbbing rhythms. She listened until the band wrapped for the morning, then pitched in and helped pack up their gear.

After the other guys left, Alec hung around. He closed the overhead door and led Leah outside by placing his hand on the small of her back. She shivered at his touch. They leaned against the stone wall beside the carriage house and Alec turned on the charm, giving her a wide smile that showed his straight, sparkling white teeth. "Dunkin' again today?" he asked.

Leah was prepared this time.

"I don't think so, not today."

It would have been so easy to accept his invitation, but Leah knew these small steps into Alec's world could take her to a life she didn't want, away from her family and community. Oh, yes, she could become more independent, able to make her own decisions about things like what she wore, boyfriends, and surgery. She could have conveniences and be on her own.

But she had too much to lose—family, community, the security of belonging.

Alec pulled his keys from a pocket and turned towards Tinkerbell. "It's your loss," he said. He tossed his head and threw his guitar case in the backseat. He got behind the wheel and waved. "See ya' next week if not before," he said. "Have a good one!"

Leah climbed the steps to her room. She sat at her desk where white sheets of paper lay, waiting. Somehow writing letters helped her think. The rhythm of the pen sweeping across the paper was a comfort to her.

Dear Susan,

I keep wondering about Dawdi. *How is he getting along?* Maemm *called to let me know he came home. Please tell him I'm asking about him and praying for him. Maybe that will cheer him up a little. Be sure he has* Maemm's *grape jelly on his toast. He always wants that with his breakfast. I know you will look after him while I'm gone.*

Expressing her feelings in a letter was easier than in person sometimes. Her people showed love by their actions. But she was far away now. There wasn't much Leah could do for *Dawdi,* except to pray.

*I'm praying that he will get stronger. Do you know any-
thing more about his heart failure? Is that very serious?*

Leah felt tears welling up in her eyes. She brushed them away.
Despite the question in her letter, she knew the truth, what they'd
said about *Dawdi's* illness. Heart failure. The words said it all. Leah
didn't want Susan to worry about her or *Dawdi*. She needed a cheer-
ful tone in this letter.

*Monica keeps me busy here, but it isn't like at home with
Maemm. On Tuesday Monica told me to clean the girls' room.
You have never seen so many toys and games as they have here.
And clothes! I had fun hanging up all their little outfits and
arranging their hair bows on the dresser. I cleaned their bathroom. (They have their own bathroom!) Monica thanked me
so much, it was embarrassing. She said it had never been that
clean before. I even washed the windows.*

Leah stopped writing and remembered that day early in the
summer when she'd washed the windows and cleaned the porch back
at home. That day, she had no idea she'd spend her entire summer in
Cleveland living a far different life.

*Later, we ate lunch at the Zoo. The Cleveland Zoo is won-
derful! It was fun, but it was hot. We spent an hour in the
aquarium building looking at the big, colorful fish because it
was cooler there. I read all the signs about the different fish.
I can't remember all of them, but one is called Toby the Giant Gourami! You know why I remember that name—it's like
our dog. That fish is almost the same size and color as Toby.*

We watched the zookeepers feed the sharks. They are also huge and have scary-looking teeth. There is so much to learn here in Cleveland. Before we went home, we took Kylie and Skye to the petting zoo where they have baby animals for children to play with. Kylie loved petting the sheep and miniature horses. Skye was a little afraid of the animals, though.

Leah looked up from her letter. She considered writing about *Daett's* refusal to sign those papers. Dr. Dave had taken them all the way to Benville and then to Millersburg. All for nothing. The pain of that moment was always lurking just below the surface of her thoughts. It made her feel sick.

I wish I was home with you instead of here. Hopefully, this summer will go fast. It looks like I might not have surgery after all. Unless Daett *changes his mind and signs the consent. I miss you all so much.*

Love, Leah

Leah placed the letter in an envelope and rehearsed the words she should have said that day. "I'd rather just stay in Benville if I'm not having the surgery. Is that okay?"

But *Daett* had talked about a promise she'd made to be the Woodruffs' nanny. She hadn't thought of it as a promise. It was just a convenience so she could be close to the hospital for the testing. Everyone agreed it was just for a couple of weeks. But now it had turned into a job for the whole summer. Why did *Daett* insist she come back to Cleveland? She wanted to be home in Benville. With her family. Close to Aaron. Why was *Daett* so stubborn? Was there another reason? Might he still agree to go ahead with the surgery?

Leah gazed out the window at the shady lawn, the patio with its umbrella, and the fence at the back of the Woodruff property. She did enjoy her peaceful home above the carriage house. It was so quiet here (except when the band practiced). Gratitude nudged out homesickness. *Gott* had placed her here, whether it was to have the surgery, to care for the little girls, or to help her appreciate her own home and community. Maybe there was a plan she didn't understand, a path she didn't yet know.

Leah liked writing letters to the people at home. It was one of the special things about being here. She'd felt a new connection to her family when she read their letters to her. And when she wrote to them, especially to Aaron. She had practiced keeping her letters interesting and full of details, the way Mr. Miller had taught them to write. Susan could learn about a life she wasn't part of, just by reading what Leah wrote. It was a gift she could give her sister. And to the others. And her sister was giving a similar gift back, keeping Leah connected to her home.

CHAPTER 27

Susan Troyer

I t was early August and again this morning Susan sat with *Dawdi* while he ate his breakfast. He poked his fork at his scrambled egg whites and nibbled a piece of toast. Since he'd been in the hospital, he seemed feeble and never ventured far beyond his porch. "*Ach!* I'm not worth much these days, I'm afraid." *Dawdi* slumped in his chair.

"That's not true at all, *Dawdi!* No matter what, you're the one we all depend on. For your prayers," she added quickly.

"*Ach, vell,* I do pray that Leah will be made well and have a quick recovery. We know *Gott* provides for us in everything. 'All things work together for the good, for those who love the Lord.'" *Dawdi's* watery blue eyes held the kind of faith Susan admired but didn't completely understand. She thought about questioning his belief that all would "work together for good." *What about* Mommi *and the way she died so suddenly right there in the hospital? What about the fact that Leah was born with a crooked back that caused pain and suffering? Where was the good in those things?*

"Maybe . . . I want to believe you're right," Susan said. "Everyone asks about Leah. They don't always say it, but I know they're praying."

"I daresay you've been missing Leah's help at home," *Dawdi* said. "Before, she did the inside work, while you helped in your *Maemm's* garden. Now you are doing all of it, helping in the garden, doing the house chores, and taking care of *me* along with everything else. And even helping Fannie."

Susan nodded. It was nice of *Dawdi* to notice. No one else seemed to. She sat across from him, soaking up this indirect praise.

"You know, *you* are part of the working together for good," said *Dawdi.*

"Me?"

"*Ach, yah,*" he said. "It's everyone doing their part. That's how our community works. It's about looking around for ways to help and then doing whatever we see that needs doing. Showing we care by our actions."

"Like helping Fannie at the auction, which raises money to help families in need?" Susan asked. "Or the frolic to rebuild K&T?"

"Yes. The community provides for its own," *Dawdi* said. "And you're part of the community."

"I've gone to auctions and such my whole life. Until now, I just thought of them as a good time. But I see what you mean," Susan said. "They aren't just for fun."

"*Nay.* Not *just* for fun. There's a purpose for them."

Dawdi finished breakfast and Susan washed his dishes. "Do you want to sit on the porch this morning, or would you rather be in here?" she asked.

"I'll stay here for now. Can you fetch my reading glasses and Bible before you go, girly?"

Susan settled *Dawdi* in his rocking chair near the window and placed a glass of water on a folding tray beside him. A glance out his window assured her that the long day at the Cozy Corner Quilt Shop was about to begin. Hank's van was already parked, and Fannie was looking at the *Dawdi haus* watching for Susan.

Susan stepped outside and waved to let Fannie know she was on her way. She hurried across the front porch, down the flight of steps, across the yard, and down the lane.

Fannie stood in the doorway of the shop waiting to give instructions. "I thought today I'd have you rearrange all the quilts and make sure they're dusted good," she said. "We need to move things around from time to time."

It didn't seem necessary to Susan, but it was useless to argue with Fannie who already had her little black purse in hand. Her crisp *kapp* looked new and fresh.

Hank was leaning against his van as the local radio announcer gave the price of hay and soybeans. Susan noticed his straw hat—one like many of the Amish men wore—clutched in his hand. He wiped the sweat from his forehead and Susan noticed how much, from the side, he looked like her Troyer uncles. If he was wearing black suspenders it might be hard to tell the difference. All of a sudden, Susan wondered if Hank might have been sitting beside Fannie at the restaurant when they tried to spy on them. How had she been so blind?

Fannie and Hank drove off leaving Susan to contemplate the huge quilts, attached securely to hinged rods near the ceiling. They creaked as she moved them sideways looking at each beautiful pattern—Dresden plate, broken dishes, flying geese, Ohio star, flower garden, and others she couldn't name. She admired the tiny stitches and intricate designs, really noticing the beauty of each one. Dust floated from the top of the display, making her sneeze. Yes, it was time to clean.

Susan retrieved the ladder, cleaning cloths, and a long-handled duster from the back room. The dusting was simple. Rearranging was another matter. She dreaded removing the heavy quilts clamped to the display rods, but Fannie had specifically told her to move them. As she swiped at a large spider web in the darkest corner, she heard someone whistling a tune off-key. Curious, she leaned over and bent to look out the window. The next thing she knew, the ladder was tipping precariously to the side. Susan grabbed onto one of the hinged rods that held a king-sized double wedding ring quilt. At that exact moment, the screen door jingled, and the whistler let out a final shrill note before shouting, "Hang on, Susan! I'm coming!"

Ben rushed to her aid, righting the ladder, and guiding her feet back onto a step. He grabbed her around the waist in a bear hug, and Susan regained her balance. Her fear turned to laughter as Ben let go and she stepped to the floor.

"This isn't a one-person job. What was Fannie thinking?"

"What are you trying to do?" Ben asked.

"I'm supposed to rearrange all these quilts. By myself," Susan said.

"Maybe I can help. Let me give you a hand." Ben moved the ladder far into the display and lifted a flower garden quilt, still attached to its rod. His muscles bulged under his thin short-sleeved summer shirt. "Here. Take this," he commanded. Susan reached for the quilt and a puff of dust filtered down.

As they worked together, Susan and Ben found a rhythm. Quilts were handed down, dusted, and placed in a new location.

"So is Leah having the surgery soon? Do you know when?"

Susan couldn't tell if he'd heard the news already, or if he truly didn't know. "I don't know the exact date, but it's going to be this month. *Daett* talked to someone on the committee, and they will help if it's more than we can pay. I'm pretty sure he finally signed those papers. I'm so ready for her to get back home. I miss her."

"And I know someone else who is ready for her to be back, too," said Ben.

"Who? *Dawdi?*"

"I was thinking of someone younger," said Ben. He wiggled his eyebrows.

"Aaron?"

"Yep! He doesn't like her being up there in Cleveland. And he's worried about her surgery, but it's more than that. He's sweet on her. I wouldn't be surprised if he was dating her by the end of the year. I think he writes to her almost every day."

"Well! That's some great news," Susan said. She'd suspected this ever since the bike ride. Aaron had been so attentive to Leah that day.

"I'm just going by things I've observed," Ben said. "When we bring up the subject of Leah, he gets quiet and goes red in the face. Then next thing you know he walks off for no reason." Ben turned to Susan as he stood on the ladder. He held up his hand as if to stop her questions. "That's all I'm saying right now."

Ben turned back to the quilts, putting an end to his revelations. He lifted the red and blue tumbling block quilt and Susan handed him one appliqued with bright tulips and green leaves.

More dust floated into the humid summer air of the shop.

"What was Fannie thinking?" Susan asked. "On the display rods, these quilts are so heavy."

"Oh, she thinks quite well," Ben quipped. "She probably guessed I'd be stopping by, and you'd get me to help. She saw my *Daett* leave for town in the buggy. She knows everything."

"Everything?" Susan asked.

"Well, almost everything," said Ben.

"But do we know everything about her?" Susan continued, answering her own question. "I don't think so. This morning Hank was wearing an Amish straw hat and I got to thinking he looked just like our Troyer uncles."

"Really? That's something!" said Ben. "So maybe he *was* at the Black Steer with Fannie."

"Maybe he *was*," said Susan. They looked at each other and shrugged. It was anyone's guess.

The morning passed quickly. When they finished, the room felt fresh and spacious.

"I had no idea the rods could be lifted off the hinges like that. Fannie is going to be so pleased. Just dusting and putting them in a different order makes them look brand new. Should I tell her you helped?" Susan asked.

"That's probably what she had in mind all along. You don't pull the wool over Fannie's eyes," said Ben.

"True. Yet sometimes I think she might be doing it to us."

"Of course she is. She's Fannie." Ben headed for the door. "Don't go anywhere. I'm coming back with some watermelon."

"I'll be here. When you get back, we should talk about planning a homecoming for Leah. Maybe an ice cream supper. There might not be too much time left to plan it. She's going to be back home before we know it." Susan felt a surge of excitement at the thought of planning a party.

"Right! We can have it the week when church meets in the K&T shop. Things will already be set up."

"That would be perfect!" Susan said. "She will be home by then, I'm sure."

Ben took off up the hill whistling his off-key tune. Susan brushed feathery dust from her face, trying not to smudge her *kapp*. *Thank goodness that job is over with. Thank goodness for Ben.*

CHAPTER 28

Leah Troyer

As the hot summer days advanced, Leah found her place in the order of things in the Woodruff household. Her homesickness was less intense than it had been, in part because she became lost in good books during her free time. Letter writing had also eased her loneliness. Or perhaps it was the letters that came. Letters from Aaron. Almost every day or two there was a new letter to add to the pretty box on her little writing desk. Their conversations on paper were a great source of hope, no matter what else happened. Like *Dawdi's* letters, Aaron reminded her of *Gott's* care, despite disappointment and not knowing the future.

As for reading, early during her stay, Monica had pulled down a set of classics packaged in matching bindings, encased in a cardboard holder. "Dave's mother gave us these last Christmas. They're far too advanced for my little girls. What was she thinking? You might as well enjoy them." And so Leah leaned into her love of reading.

Sometimes when something happened, she formed the words in her mind as if she were writing her own story. *Leah sat at the child-sized table with the little girl, encouraging her to eat her dinner. "After dinner, we can play in the yard," she told her. "We'll pick a bouquet and bring it to your mother."* Someday she might become a real writer and write for an Amish paper, a column in the *Budget*, the Amish newspaper. For now, though, she was content just being a letter writer.

On a Friday evening in late July Monica threw her arms around Dave as he lounged in his favorite outdoor chair. "We need to take advantage of having a nanny this summer," she said. "Let's have a morning coffee date. Maybe make a little stop at the West Side Market."

"Great idea! I think I can manage that tomorrow," Dave said. "How early? Eight? Nine? My schedule is open all day for once."

"Not too early. I might want to sleep in." Monica hugged Dave's shoulders. "Although Leah's been here long enough that I have no qualms about leaving her here with the girls for the entire morning." She smiled at Leah who was sitting nearby, a book in her lap. "I know we usually give you the day off, but could you help out, just this one time?" They were so careful not to take her for granted.

"Sure. I'll take good care of them. They're no trouble at all," Leah said.

"We'll be back by nap time. You'll still have a little time off before dinner," Monica assured her.

For her part, Leah welcomed an excuse to avoid Alec and the Corner Stones band. She preferred to stay busy and enjoyed caring for Kylie and Skye. After Leah had tidied the kitchen and folded a basket of laundry, the girls splashed in their plastic swimming pool, dancing to the beat of the band practicing in the garage across the driveway. Leah sat nearby watching them and listening to the now familiar songs. She tapped her toes and quietly sang the words she knew by heart. Later, when she'd showered and dressed them, Leah read to Kylie and Skye until lunchtime. It was nap time, but Dave and Monica were still not home; they must be enjoying themselves. Leah lay down with the children in Skye's bed until the girls fell asleep. Then she tiptoed out.

Now Leah sat in a wicker chair in the sunroom immersed in the adventures of *Heidi*, the young girl who had trudged up the mountain with her mean Aunt Dete to be left alone in the Alm Uncle's attic where she cried herself to sleep. The story had a ring of familiarity, at least the part about sleeping in an attic and living with strangers. Reading *Heidi* made Leah hungry for bread and cheese. She'd skipped lunch for herself, but now she put the book aside and went to the kitchen where she cut a thick slice of Italian bread and a generous slab from a wedge of baby Swiss cheese from Amish Country. She put it on a plate and warmed the open-faced sandwich in the microwave until the cheese bubbled. She ate it while she continued reading.

Dave and Monica finally arrived home midafternoon, loaded down with bags and apologies for their lateness.

"It's okay," Leah reassured them. "We had a good time, and the girls are still napping."

"Well, now you can go take a little nap yourself," Dave said. "You earned it."

"Looks like you found another book to read," Monica said. "You're off for the rest of the afternoon. Dave's grilling tonight. We have a good meal planned. See you at 6:00." And with that, Leah was dismissed from the house and on her own for the rest of the afternoon. She crossed the driveway, climbed the steps to her room over the carriage house, and lay down on the bed thinking she would read. Soon she was sleeping. A little before six, Leah awakened from her nap. She made her way to the house and joined Monica in the kitchen.

"Leah, honey, could you pull those two tubs of salad from the fridge?" she asked.

Monica opened a clear container holding a small cake decorated with chocolate rosettes. She slid it onto a glass plate. Leah thought of weekend summer suppers at home. At home, on weekdays, supper was simple because the big meal was dinner, served at noon.

But on Friday or Saturday night, *Maemm* usually invited *Dawdi* and Aunt Fannie for supper. Then there would be roast beef, mashed potatoes, sweet corn, and fresh applesauce made with apples from the old yellow transparent tree out back. There was always pie or a fluffy dessert. Usually, Leah or Susan chose the dessert recipe from one of the Amish cookbooks on the kitchen shelf beside the stove. In Benville, the family ate their pie or marshmallow fluff indoors at the table. Later, the older ones moved to the porch and the children played in the yard.

In Cleveland, the Woodruff family often cooked and ate outdoors. Leah liked being outside even if it meant carrying things out of the kitchen as they did this Saturday evening. Dave grilled hamburgers and hotdogs along with a dozen ears of corn. They ate it buttered and salted, along with the salads Monica had bought that morning at West Side Market. When it was time for dessert, Monica returned to the kitchen and brought out a tray with the fancy cake and three cups of coffee.

"It's a little hot to drink coffee, but I think we're going to need it with this. Leah, have you ever had cheesecake?" she asked.

"No, I don't think so," Leah answered.

"This is one of our favorites—made by an Italian woman who sells them at West Side," Dave said. He cut generous slices for each of them and passed the plates to Leah and Monica. The cake was like nothing Leah had ever tasted—sweet, heavy, and rich with a base of sweet graham cracker crust. That part was much like some of the desserts they made at home.

The cheesecake melted in her mouth and blended wonderfully with Monica's dark coffee. Leah savored each forkful. Dave and Monica grew silent, each one taking small bites of the cheesecake and sipping the strong coffee. It was a satisfying conclusion to another summertime cookout.

They watched the girls running around the lawn trying to catch lightning bugs. Monica had given them little screen houses from an educational toy set and Kylie and Skye finally succeeded in capturing one or two. At home, Leah's brothers were much better at catching them. This time of the evening, they would be gathering them by the handful and trapping them in Mason jars. The thought of them made her smile. A picture formed in her mind: Andy and Adam careening around the yard, Toby leaping at them from behind.

Finally, Dave broke the silence. "Well," he said calmly, "it's all settled. Leah, your surgery will be a week from this coming Friday, August 15, at 9:00 a.m. Just as I'd hoped. How does that sound?"

Leah lifted her head. Her fork remained suspended in midair. She was speechless for a moment and then placed the fork and its contents back on her plate. Just then Skye let out a scream and came running over to show Leah a brown moth that was clinging to her shirt. Leah examined it and told her it was just a miller—nothing to worry about.

But the interruption gave Leah a moment to take in Dave's announcement. She could hardly believe what she'd just heard. *How did this happen?* Daett *must have had a change of heart.* The question was set aside, and a mixture of happiness and fear washed over her as she took in the importance of this new development.

"I was waiting until we had dessert to tell you. We could call this a celebration dinner for you—for all of us, really," Dave said. "After all, it's the whole reason you're here this summer. For a while there I had my doubts about whether this day would ever come."

"I can hardly believe it!" Leah exclaimed. "I still don't understand why he didn't sign the papers when we took them to Benville. Maybe he was too worried about *Dawdi.*"

As the news washed over her, Leah felt tears well up in her eyes. She brushed them away.

Monica noticed and tried to help. "Of course, you're a little anxious about this surgery. We know it's scary for you, but you're a strong girl," she said.

Dave chimed in. "I can assure you, around the country hundreds of young boys and girls have this surgery every year. It's life changing. Trust me, this is the best time to do it. While you're still young and healthy. If you wait, it could be too late."

Both he and Monica interpreted her tears as fear. But they were tears of happiness and gratitude. "I'm just happy," Leah said. "And thankful, to both of you." Her voice was wobbly with emotion.

"So, cheers!" Dave raised his coffee cup and clinked with Monica's cup. They shared a meaningful glance. They were trying to ease her overwhelmed feelings. Leah didn't raise her coffee cup. But she took a sip as they did, swallowing the rich brew and allowing herself to accept the gift she'd just received. *How had this all happened?*

Dave sensed her questions. "As you know, Monica and I went to West Side Market this morning—where we got these salads and cheesecake. While we were there, I got a phone call from your father. He told me he'd signed the papers and offered to send a driver up to Cleveland with the package. We could have done it electronically, but I guess this was easier for him. Who am I to argue with your dad? I've been waiting for those documents." Dave's voice held an edge of excitement that Leah couldn't ignore.

"I gave him the address of the Cleveland General outpatient clinic. That's south of here. Hank Kratzer, the driver we met on July

Fourth, was waiting there when we drove into the empty parking lot. No problem finding him. The place was closed since it was Saturday. He handed me a brown manila envelope with the hospital logo in the corner. Said everything was signed and ready to go." Dave slammed his hand on the table, a gesture of finality after days of waiting.

"I thanked him. Oh, I thanked him for sure," Dave continued. "I gave him a little extra tip for his trouble. He's a good man." Dave gestured toward the house. "I have that packet inside, on the desk. We're all set now." He sounded as if he'd been given a Christmas present.

"Monica and I made a quick stop at the Lakewood Farmer's Market on our way back. It's peak season so it's open on Saturday, too," Dave said. "Where did you think that candy onion came from?" Dave gestured towards the giant, thin sliced white onion that had topped their burgers. It was truly as sweet as candy. Leah thought about Aden and Lydia's large garden and the truck patch they'd made in a field. Some of her cousins regularly ate cucumber and onion sandwiches on butter bread for supper during the hot summer. Even though she was nearly finished with dessert, Leah's mouth watered just looking at that plate of remaining candy onion slices.

"Aden already knew your dad had signed the papers. Good news travels fast, I guess. He said to tell you he wishes you well."

"So he said the Children's Relief Fund is helping to pay some of the hospital bills," Monica chimed in. "Is that the same as the auction we went to in June?"

"Yes," Leah said. "I think they have a committee that decides who needs help with expenses and such. When I went to that auction last spring, I never thought the committee would help *me*. It's good you and Aden are friends, or this might never have happened." Gratitude swelled inside Leah's chest at the way all things had worked together. For the good.

Dave continued. "Ellie, Aden's daughter, wasn't with him to-day. She stayed home to help take care of the little ones in case Lydia needed to go to the hospital to have the baby."

"She's close to her due date," said Monica. "I sure hope he made it home before she had to go."

"I've been thinking about her lately. If I hadn't been here, I would probably be at their place in Valley View helping Lydia," Leah said.

"All I know is that I'm glad someone got that package back here to me today. I was afraid my plan to help you was going to be a massive failure. I was so disappointed when Albert and Elma didn't sign the papers when we met with them," Dr. Dave said. "Nothing against your mom and dad, but I just hated that, for your sake. I have to say it made me more than a little angry." Sensing he'd said more than he should have, Dave stepped over to the grill and began vigorously scraping it with a stiff bristle brush.

"Well, I'm glad, too, for Leah's sake." Monica looked in Dave's direction. "But I'm sure going to miss having a nanny." She smiled at Leah. Her voice was lilting and pleasant.

Leah sat for a moment trying to absorb the welcome news. Everything she hoped for was finally becoming a reality. After all the questions and doubts it seemed too good to be true. The surgery was going to happen. And soon.

Just then Monica stood up and walked over to the grill where Dave was gathering up his utensils. Monica gave him a big hug and a long mushy kiss. Leah looked away. And then back. They stood there together under the river birch branches, a single body, arms wrapped around each other, a picture of marital bliss.

Leah's heart pounded faster as she gathered up the dishes and cups and made her way back to the kitchen. She was overwhelmed with the news. But she was also thinking about Monica and Dave.

Her parents didn't display their emotions around others like that. But someday, if she had a husband, she'd take every chance to give him a hug and a kiss. Leah rinsed the plates and loaded the dishwasher. Outside the kitchen window, Dave, Monica, and the two little girls danced in the evening shadows, a little community of love. *Someday. Someday I will have a family of my own. Two little girls and a handsome husband. We will eat outdoors on summer evenings. Our children will catch lightning bugs in Mason jars and keep them in their bedroom for a night-light.*

Leah wandered off to her room in the carriage house, feeling at peace with the world. It was true—as *Dawdi* had said— that "abiding bringeth forth much fruit." Her dream was coming true. *Gott* had answered her prayers. Soon she would be straight and strong. Even now she was stronger—not so much in her body, but in her faith. Despite her loneliness this summer in Cleveland, she was gaining confidence in herself. She had managed to belong to this strange world and had done what had been asked of her. She had kept faith when circumstances made her question everything. She was *Gott's* beloved daughter, cared for and cherished, imperfections and all.

CHAPTER 29

Susan Troyer

Sunday, August 8

Dear Leah,

Finally, all the waiting is over! Daett signed the papers so you can have the surgery. I don't know whether to be happy or scared. You are so brave to be living there and having to wait around while everything gets settled.

I can tell you a little bit about what happened. The committee had a special meeting last Friday at Ashery Mills since the church was going to be there on Sunday. According to Dawdi, *it was one of the regular meetings where the Children's Relief Committee approves the medical bills that come in. Thank goodness* Daett *finally told someone our family needs help with this. I was beginning to worry his pride was getting in the way. He's so stubborn sometimes.*

Abe Maust is on that committee. He told Daett *they'd be more than happy to help with those hospital bills and urged him to turn them in. He even took them to the meeting for* Daett.

Abe's Anna went over to the quilt shop that same day for something—she comes over often lately—and bragged that Abe is on the committee. Not as a bishop, of course, just as a community leader. I got to see Fannie in action! Anna came over for her Yoder's Elixir. I heard Fannie go on about you. She laid it on thick, telling Anna how much pain you're in and how you can't work in the garden because of your back and on and on. Not that it isn't true, but you know how Fannie can make a story. She told her about Daett *being stubborn and not wanting to ask for help. I guess Anna once again told her husband what to do. (This time it's a good thing, right?)*

Bishop Maust came over and talked to Daett *that same night. He was out in the pasture that evening fixing the fence, but after he left* Daett *went right into the house and signed everything with* Maemm *and then called Hank Kratzer. The next morning Hank came over and* Daett *just told him to take the big envelope up to Cleveland and give it to the doctor. Hank is old-school just like* Daett. *He didn't want to send it by computer either.*

Susan reread everything she'd written and let out a sigh of relief. It would be wonderful to have Leah back home again where she belonged. She was missing out on so much—and not just the canning. Susan debated what to write next. Should she tell Leah about that trip to Black Steer? Would Leah think she was foolish? Maybe Aaron had already told her.

Why did she keep having these ideas about Fannie and Hank? It was all just in her head.

And then she'd even drawn Ben and Aaron and the rest into it. What had she been thinking? No, she wouldn't write about that. She'd written to the bottom of the page. She'd just sign off there.

Maybe she would tell Leah about it later when this was all over.

It would be so good to have Leah back home again where she belonged. Maybe they would finally have the good times sisters were supposed to have together. They would go to youth groups together, join the young people's volleyball games, and hire a driver to take them shopping. They would be close, share secrets, be best friends.

Susan turned over the page, tapped her pencil for a moment, and ended the letter.

This might be my last letter to you in Cleveland. I'm coming with Maemm *and* Daett *the day before your surgery. We're taking that hospital tour with you. The doctor reserved rooms for us at Ronald McDonald House. Maybe for three nights. Isn't that great? See you soon. I can't wait!*

                                          LOVE, Susan

The rest of the week passed in a blur of activities. *Maemm* fussed over *Dawdi* and filled his pantry with enough food for a week, even though they would be gone for only two or three days. A neighbor offered to check on him. Wednesday evening, the whole family went to Aden and Lydia's in the buggy to drop off the younger Troyer brothers. Jake, Andy, and Adam would stay with their cousins while the rest of the family was in Cleveland.

The next morning, before they headed off to Cleveland, Susan brought *Dawdi* breakfast. He asked Susan to call her parents over to his house. They had already put their overnight bags beside the door and were waiting for Hank while they finished their coffee. They carried their cups with them across the long porch and entered the *Dawdi haus.*

"Susan, girly, would you bring me my Bible? I think we have time for prayers before your driver gets here."

Susan found it on his desk.

"I marked this place for us to read," *Dawdi* said. "This scripture is for us in this time. We're all afraid for Leah. We don't know what is in store, but we abide with *Gott*, who protects us." *Dawdi* tipped his reading glasses low on his nose and lifted his large-print Bible. A sunbeam streamed in the window and cast its glow across *Dawdi* as he read Psalm 91. Susan and her parents sat quietly, listening to *Dawdi's* familiar voice.

"He that dwells in the secret place of the most High shall abide under the shadow of the Almighty. I will say of the LORD, He is my refuge and my fortress: My God; in him will I trust."

Susan's mind wandered as *Dawdi* read. It had been a hard summer, and it wasn't over yet. In just hours, Leah would be in the operating room. *What if it doesn't work? What if something goes wrong? What if she's worse afterwards instead of being better?*

Dawdi was still reading, his words metered by the loud ticking of his clock. "Destruction, pestilence, and punishment" rolled off his tongue in a rhythm that left Susan feeling anxious. Then *Dawdi* paused, as if sensing something important was just ahead. The clock ticked more seconds and *Dawdi* read the assurance they all needed:

"Because he has set his love on me, therefore will I deliver him:
I will set him on high because he has known my name.
He shall call on me, and I will answer him:
I will be with him in trouble; I will deliver him, and honor him.
With long life will I satisfy him, and show him my salvation."
Ps. 91:1-2, 14-16 (KJV)

They sat silently, knowing these words had been their prayer. The clock ticked. Finally, Hank's car tires crunched on the gravel. *Daett* stood. The moment passed and they moved on into the day knowing *Gott's* protection preceded them.

CHAPTER 30

Leah Troyer

Dave and Monica knew how much Leah enjoyed eating out-doors. On the last evening before she checked in to the hospital, they planned a cookout. Dave grilled marinated chicken breasts and expertly roasted a large pan of vegetables. The aroma filled the entire backyard. She would miss these outdoor meals, something her family rarely did at home.

"This is going to be your last meal for a while," Dave said. "No food or drink after midnight tonight." He spoke in a voice usually reserved for his hospital patients but flashed a warm smile in Leah's direction. Leah tried to ignore the nervous feelings she had when she thought about her surgery.

"It's hard to believe this is happening," Leah said. "I'm so thankful for everything. I will never be able to repay you for all you've done for me." Her emotions overflowed and a tear escaped. Thoughts of tomorrow edged into the pleasant family time with the Woodruffs. Leah pushed aside the worrisome thoughts. She resolved to enjoy these last moments of togetherness with the family that had so graciously drawn her in and welcomed her.

"We are so glad you could be with us this summer. We're all going to miss you, terribly," said Monica. "But we'll come and see you in Benville every once in a while."

Leah hoped that would happen, but deep down she knew things would never be the same as they were right now in this

important moment that marked both an ending and a new beginning.

When it was time for dessert, Monica went into the house
and returned with a tall cake covered in creamy white frosting and
decorated with real flowers. "Happy birthday," she said.

Leah didn't realize they knew it was her birthday.

Kylie and Skye trailed their mother, prancing around her in a
delighted dance. "We're going to eat flowers!" Kylie sang.

"Fwowers," echoed Skye.

"For you," Monica said, holding out the cake. "This one isn't
store-bought. I made it myself."

Leah had no idea Monica had been baking. She'd also cleaned
up the kitchen afterward. Monica seemed changed somehow this
evening. She was less moody and, in fact, had a downright sunny
disposition.

"Surely you remembered it's your birthday, today," Dave said.

"How could she forget that?" Monica asked. "The cards and
letters from home were piling up in the mailbox this week."

Leah dropped her head, suddenly shy with all the attention.
"You're right. I got twenty-three cards this week. I didn't forget. But
you didn't need to bother with a cake." Aaron had sent her a letter
every day now for at least two weeks. That was one reason she had
so much mail. She knew he cared for her. She thought of him constantly.

Dave interrupted her thoughts. "It's a milestone birthday.
You're eighteen. An official adult. Congratulations!"

Monica glanced at him affectionately and then turned to Leah.
"Sorry. I forgot to get birthday candles. But we can sing 'Happy
Birthday' anyway."

They gathered around her and the cake and sang while Leah

blushed and watched the two little girls whirling around her in their colorful summer sundresses.

After the song, Monica announced, "This cake is something special. Like you. Have you ever tasted hummingbird cake?"

"I'm not sure," Leah said. "I think my aunt Fannie might have made one."

"I found the recipe online. It's from the *New York Times*. This cake has an interesting history," Monica said. "It's well-known in the south but probably was first made in Jamaica. It was called the Doctor Bird Cake."

"What's a doctor bird?" Dave asked.

"The doctor bird is Jamaica's national bird. It's a type of hummingbird," Monica said. "Enough about the cake. Let's eat it," Monica said. "The birthday girl gets the first piece." She cut into the moist cake and served a slice on a small paper plate. "Bananas, pineapple, and spices. And flowers, too. Enjoy!"

Just then a tiny hummingbird circled the table and flitted briefly over the colorful flowers on the cake. Its wings made a buzzing sound and beat so fast they were a blur.

"It's so tiny," Monica said. "I've never seen a hummingbird that small."

"I think that's a hummingbird moth," Leah said. "I haven't seen one of those for a long time. They're rare."

"Well, I think everyone's wishing you a happy birthday," Dave said. "Even the birds and butterflies."

The girls stared at the tiny moth wide-eyed. They followed its flight with their eyes, listening for the soft whirring of its wings as it flitted around them.

"I think this is a sign. A good one," Monica quickly added. "She's predicting something out of the ordinary."

"It's a sign that changes are coming." Dave winked at the girls who were still staring. They ran to Leah and clung to her skirt, afraid of the strange tiny spectacle.

Leah watched, pondering the ideas Dave and Monica suggested. She had never thought of reading meaning into the appearance of an insect at a picnic.

After dessert, they sat enjoying the cool evening until Monica began clearing the table and Dave corralled the girls to prepare for bedtime. "Hug Leah, girls. It might be a while until you see her again," Dave said.

"Leah, you're excused from helping tonight. You have a big day tomorrow," Monica said. "Off you go. Get a good night's sleep."

Dave chimed in. "Leah, I know you're worried about tomorrow. Everyone gets nervous before surgery, that's only natural. But you're in good hands." The doctor smiled as he held up his hands, palms facing Leah.

Leah swallowed the lump in her throat. "I know I'm in good hands," she said.

"You can ride to the hospital with me tomorrow morning. It's going to be early, so get some rest. We'll leave here at about six," Dave said.

"Okay. I'll be ready," Leah said. And with that she went off to her room. She lay awake for a long time, her mind a stew of memories. Special moments here in Shaker Heights that she would treasure forever. She thought of the little girls, the fun times they'd had playing with toys, splashing in the pool, going to the zoo. She thought of the way Monica and Dave had included her in their conversations, the way they'd praised her work. She would miss this family. Finally, Leah slept fitfully.

When Leah awakened early the next morning, she felt both excited and nervous. She said a little prayer. "*Gott,* please help me today. And thank You. For everything." She dressed quickly. She took a last look at the small table under the window that she'd used for a desk, the cozy reading chair in the corner, the low bookshelf, and the comfortable bed draped with a colorful quilt. She'd miss having a room all to herself. But already this space felt less like home. She'd packed all her belongings into her duffle. Monica would take it to the hospital when she was ready to go home.

Leah said a silent goodbye to this private space, which had offered its solitude and comfort. More than anything, she wanted to have this surgery behind her and to be back home in Benville. At the same time, she'd learned so much about herself—about life—here in Cleveland.

"Goodbye," she whispered to the room. "I will always remember you." With a sigh, she made her way down the stairs. Her pulse quickened in anticipation of all that would happen in the next day or two.

Dave was walking toward her from the house. "Good morning," he said. "Today's your big day." His grin was bright, even in the low light of early morning.

CHAPTER 31

Monica Woodruff

What is the origin of this resentment? The question had seemingly come from nowhere, but for a few days it had followed Monica as she wandered around the house. Now she was home alone while the girls enjoyed a play date.

Tomorrow was the day of Leah's surgery. She was already at the hospital, having left early that morning with Dave.

Monica had planned to watch a chick flick on Netflix, but instead, she sat in the kitchen sobbing for the better part of an hour. She couldn't identify the source of her emotional pain. It wasn't PMS. It wasn't because of Leah. No, it came from a far deeper place beyond the reach of her mind.

Finally, in a daze, Monica got up and moved slowly to the laundry room where she folded towels as if on autopilot. She stopped occasionally to wipe her tears on a soft, warm-from-the-dryer washcloth.

When she'd finished, she dragged herself and the laundry basket upstairs, nearly tripping over a pile of stuffed animals in the middle of the girls' bedroom floor. As if it would somehow ease her despair, she kicked the furry mass out of her way. The stuffies flew this way and that. Paddington landed on his head, crushing his red hat. A giraffe's neck bent into a back flip. The musical unicorn with an almost dead battery gave out a muted ding-dong and flopped against the toy box. As Monica placed clothing in the drawers and put the toys away, she indulged in an irrational internal rant.

I'm a nobody, a giant nothing. Just Dave's housekeeper taking care of everything, somehow managing to fit my plans into your big, important life. Who cares if your dramatic altruism inconveniences me? You even pretended you were doing me a big favor by calling Leah our nanny.

Deep down she knew she was in a pit of self-pity. Leah had never been "underfoot."

She'd been a fabulous nanny and more. Completely unobtrusive as she tidied the kitchen after Monica had spent the afternoon dirtying pots and pans. By now Leah had been admitted and was being prepped for surgery tomorrow morning. Last evening, Leah had swept the kitchen as she did every evening. She'd read stories to the girls, all their favorites, and then said goodnight to everyone. In all these weeks, she had been a calm presence. *So why am I so unhappy, so resentful?*

Dave had left for the hospital earlier than usual, whispering his goodbye while Monica cuddled with the girls, who had a habit of sneaking into their bed most mornings. "Don't forget, I might be late today," he said. "I'm going to stay at the hospital until after 7:00 so I can check on Leah. Her parents will be with her, and I want to see them before I come home."

The resentment had started right then. *Everyone comes before me. Have you ever thought about that, Dave Woodruff? Does it ever bother you that we are left on our own for hours on end? You come home only when the best of you has been given away to strangers. The exhaustion on your face makes me exhausted.*

Her love for Dave sometimes felt like a hollow shell of misery. Dave was a celebrated surgeon at the world-renowned Cleveland General Hospital but still didn't seem to know he'd arrived. And she was living in his shadow, an unfulfilled stay-at-home spouse to his powerful career. That might never change. Why did she hurt so much? The only answer was that she had expected something different from marriage—more togetherness, more romance. Expectations were strange things. They led to daily disappointment and reinforced Monica's lonely reality. She drew in a deep shaky breath, the kind that follows a crying jag.

If anything, having Leah in their home had made her pain more focused and real. Her acceptance of her place in life and her quiet confidence were such a contrast to Monica's dissatisfaction. Resentment continued to build inside her as the days had turned into weeks. At times, she understood the reason Leah was here. Leah needed to have her severe scoliosis corrected before it was too late. But Monica mostly resented the spontaneous decision Dave had made that day at the Children's Relief Auction, seemingly with little regard for her, and her feelings. Feelings she kept hidden from everyone.

Having put the laundry away, Monica made a pot of tea and carried it to the patio that was now shaded in the late morning sun. She had an hour before she needed to pick up Kylie and Skye. On impulse, she grabbed a little book of daily readings that the church women's Bible study had given her.

Monica had never been one for morning devotions, evening devotions, or group Bible studies. God wasn't much of a conscious presence in her life and, in all honesty, for the past few months she'd avoided quiet times of prayer and meditation. Somehow, in the busyness—business—of life it was easy to avoid the solace she knew these quiet reflective moments offered. But today she felt so needy. Maybe there was help on these pages.

Monica curled up in the chaise lounge under the covered patio and breathed in the fresh air of midmorning. She opened the daily reading book to the marked page. She'd experimented with the daily reading for a few days, then dropped the practice in favor of surfing the internet for new recipes. The current date was pages and pages ahead. She tried to relax her body. She sipped tea and prayed for guidance.

God, I'm a total mess. But You know that, don't You? Why am I so resentful and angry about Dave's kindness and generosity? He's a good man—talented, thoughtful, a good father, husband, and provider. I pledged to love him until "death do us part," but I feel dead already. I can't seem to overcome my resentment, these awful feelings I can't control. I don't even know why I'm angry. Please, God, help me. Help me stop being so resentful, so ungrateful for what I have.

Monica found the pages written for today's date. She wondered if there would be some surprising answer, a personal message written there. She hoped for a message from God that would meet her neediness. She wished for an attitude adjustment that would come without her making any effort to create it. Because she didn't have it in her to make the effort lately.

I am the vine, you are the branches, remain in me and you will bring forth fruit.

There were five paragraphs after the italicized Bible verse in which the writer discussed the growth habits of grapevines. Monica read it dutifully and grimaced. She needed far more than this handful of words about agriculture to set her soul right. The tea had cooled to lukewarm. She closed the book. *So much for daily readings. Why did I think I could get my head straight by reading a Bible verse and five paragraphs of platitudes?*

She let the book drop to the ground with a thud and closed her eyes telling her mind to become blank, but it kept pitching random thoughts. She truly wanted help, but the Bible verse didn't work. She dozed until a flock of crows awakened her with their loud cawing from the trees on the other side of the fence. Monica stood, stretched, and followed their sound, feeling amused at their call—their caw—and response. *Maybe a walk will calm me, help me forget all this.*

Monica walked to the edge of their property. The land behind Briarwood was wild, with an age-old neglected wire fence put up decades ago by a farmer. Monica stepped across it easily where the wire had come loose from the rotting fence posts. She entered the woods and wandered. Despite living on Briarwood Street for five years, she had never thought to explore this place. Now she looked around, expecting to see a "No Trespassing" sign, but there wasn't one. She wandered under the tall trees and breathed in the woodsy scent.

As if to catch her attention, a wild grapevine clung resolutely to a tree that appeared beside the narrow path she was following, a path probably made by deer. Little clusters of grapes hung down in front of her, within arm's reach. They were smaller than the grapes she bought for Kylie and Skye and looked weak and unappetizing. And yet they were growing here in the wild. The base of the vine was twisted, the bark peeling away. The branches went every which way, and their tendrils clung to saplings, rotting logs, and even tall weeds.

I am the vine, you are the branches, remain in me and you will bring forth much fruit.

Monica felt something like a shiver run through her. *Could this grapevine be sending her a mystical message? Had God caused her to wander into the woods just now? Was there something here she was supposed to learn, some deeper truth revealed in this wild vine?* She found a spot on a large fallen tree that was beginning to decay and sank onto the mossy surface.

"I am a branch." She repeated the words to herself and let her eyes wander from one branch to another. There were so many branches. They were tangled, untended. But each branch was attached to that large, gnarled root visible a couple of yards away.

Monica sat listening to the sounds of the woods. She breathed in the fragrant green life surrounding her and pulled at the nearest branch. She snapped a tiny cluster of green wild grapes from the vine. She would take it home and put it in a glass vase as a little icon. She would study the vine, be the branch. Try to learn the vine's lesson as life moved forward. Peace would come in little moments like this.

With each deep breath, the resentment and self-pity emptied from her mind and dropped from her shoulders. Change would come. It wouldn't be easy, quick, or smooth, but it was possible with attention to the things that mattered most. She loved Dave and he loved her. They were building a beautiful family together. They were realizing their dreams and growing into the people they were both meant to be.

The hard little grapes were a tactile prayer that rolled sweetly over Monica's fingers. She would return to this letting go each time she looked at the little cluster of wild grapes. She might never fully understand why her resentment was so strong, her compassion so lacking, her self-pity so intense. But she wanted to let it go, to be free from its weight.

Good people she knew seemed to stroll through life with a smile and unwavering positivity. People like Dave—and Aden Weaver. She might never be one of those people. But after this morning, she would repeat the words when the old feelings of resentment called out to her. "I am the vine . . ." That was Jesus saying those words. "You are a branch," He'd said. She looked again at the clinging tendrils, the tender grape leaves, the tiny clusters of fruit, and drank in their meaning.

Yes, I'm connected to God's work in the world, whether I always feel like it or understand how. The simplicity of it all was comforting. And it had come just in time. Tomorrow Leah was having an important surgery performed by Dave's competent hands and his skilled team. Had Leah's presence in their home somehow helped Monica understand her place in the world? While Leah had been with them, she'd been so calm, so capable, so accepting of her lot in life. Perhaps in the end, Leah's simplicity, and the ways of her people, had helped Monica find peace with who she was.

As she slipped through the fence and returned to her backyard, a rightness with the world followed her. It was deeply personal, inexplicable, even holy. She'd heeded the call of a crow, made her way through that small opening, and discovered something true she could hold on to.

CHAPTER 32

Leah Troyer

I t was embarrassing. Bishop Maust stood stiffly above Leah, his beard inches from her chest as she lay naked under a thin hospital gown and heavy layers of a folded flannel sheet. She considered pretending to be asleep, but *Daett* expected her to listen to the bishop's prayer. *Maemm* had written to her in a letter that there would be special prayers before her surgery. She was to give everything over to *Gott,* placing herself in His care.

Leah was closeted in a tiny, curtained enclosure in the pre-op waiting area surrounded by *Maemm, Daett,* Susan, and Fannie. Bishop Maust spoke quietly to them. He had a distinctive scent, a mixture of menthol from his cough drop with a hint of Tide. He assured Leah and her family that *Gott* was with her and would watch over her during surgery. Secretly, Leah would have been happy to have *Gott* watch and let the bishop stay in Benville, but he was doing what *Gott* asked of him. She noticed a bit of scrambled egg stuck in the bishop's beard and tried not to look at Susan. If she did, they might both start laughing.

Bishop Maust grasped Leah's hand and spoke to her in hushed tones. He told her he would pray with them from an old prayer book, a centuries-old prayer for the sick. She silently objected. She wasn't technically sick, after all.

Her parents and Susan huddled close to the gurney. Fannie stood beside *Daett.* Leah was startled when Susan gripped her right hand through the side rails and squeezed tightly. The gesture and Susan's energy comforted her. She felt her mother's hand on her thigh and her father's—a comforting and unfamiliar weight—on her shoulder. The last time she'd heard this prayer was in *Mommi's* room a week before she died. Leah had been thinking about death, in part because earlier she had been informed of a long list of possible complications that could follow her surgery. One of these was death. Dave had reassured her, as had the nurse, that these warnings were a formality and happened rarely. Still, the fear of the unknown flashed through her mind. She pushed it away. The bishop began the prayer.

"Dear merciful Father! You have now visited and laid Leah here, low with sickness and suffering for correction under Your almighty hand. The frailty of imperfect human life may be accusing Leah, and death often stares such a one in the face. We therefore pray to you humbly, with Leah and beside Leah." There was more to the prayer, much more. Leah squeezed her eyes shut tight and listened to the words of the prayer from *Die ernsthafte Christenpflict (Prayer Book for Earnest Christians).*

Please, Gott, don't let me die! I want to live. I want to . . . Leah tuned out the bishop's words and said a prayer of her own that somehow involved Aaron Keim, who crept into her thoughts despite the seriousness of this moment. She felt ashamed that she couldn't keep her mind on spiritual things just now, but a vision of Aaron, his bright blue eyes, and shock of blond hair appeared in her mind. She felt dreamy and a bit foggy—perhaps from the medicine they'd given to relax her. Bishop Maust droned on as Leah drifted in and out of consciousness.

"O heavenly Father! We commend Leah completely into Your hands. O true Savior, return this patient to health. O true Helper in times of trial! Help this weak person. Raise Leah up!"

The bishop cleared his throat. Leah floated into a field of tall grass. Aaron was with her, holding her hand, shading the sun from his eyes. He was saying something, but his words were hard to understand. She would ask him to repeat it later after she awakened from the surgery.

"Because You can do all things abundantly . . . Grant all this out of grace, through Jesus Christ, Your Son, our Lord . . ."

Finally, the prayer came to an end with truly comforting words. Leah heard them and took them into her heart, despite her drifting into sunlight and out again into the fog.

Bishop Maust intoned the final words of the long German prayer. "He lives and reigns with You in the unity of the Holy Spirit, true God unto eternity. Amen." Then he patted her shoulder and the others leaned in to whisper their own words of comfort. A nurse motioned for those gathered around Leah to return to the waiting room. Susan was the last to go, giving her sister's hand an extra squeeze and a mischievous wink before she followed the others. Some of the seriousness lifted.

Then she was wheeled into the cold, brightly lit operating room. "We're putting the anesthesia into your IV now," the technician said through his surgical mask. "Go ahead and count backward from ten for me." Leah took a quick look at her surroundings, bright lights, stainless steel, and masked people wearing scrubs and caps over their hair. She began counting.

"Ten, nine, eig . . ."

CHAPTER 33

Leah Troyer

The cool antiseptic scent of the room was Leah's first sensation as she became conscious. Someone was tucking a very warm blanket tightly around her. Leah opened her eyes to bright light and a nurse wearing blue-framed glasses.

"Good afternoon, Leah Troyer," the nurse said. "You're in the recovery room now. Everything went well. We will let you rest here another hour or so. Doctor Woodruff talked to your parents a while ago. They will be in to see you soon. How are you feeling?"

The nurse's voice was far too loud. Leah tried to answer, but her words came out as a murmur. She wasn't quite awake. Her mind worked slowly as she tried to remember what was happening and why she was there.

The nurse clasped her hands around Leah's feet, making sure the warm blanket was snug against her feet. "Are you warm enough?" The blanket was a solid weight. It felt wonderful. Like being in a cocoon.

"Yes, thank you," Leah mumbled. And then she dozed off.

The next time she awakened, Dr. Dave was standing beside her. His face was a glimpse of normalcy in the otherwise unfamiliar room. He lowered the side rails of her hospital bed and checked her pulse. He looked at the monitors above her bed and then back to her.

"You came through the surgery just fine, Leah. How do you feel?"

Upon awakening this time, Leah suddenly feared that she might not be able to walk. The most concerning risk by far, besides possible death, was that she would be left paralyzed. Her legs felt heavy and motionless under the blankets. *Had the worst happened?* "I'm not sure. Will I be able to walk again?" she mumbled.

"Of course! They will probably have you up and walking later today," Dr. Dave said cheerfully. He stepped to the end of the bed and Leah could feel his hand through the thick blanket. "Wiggle your toes for me."

Leah did as she was told and felt reassured.

"Right now, you're still numb from the surgery and don't feel much. Later on, your back is going to hurt. But we're going to keep up with the pain medication. The nurses will check with you. Let them know if it hurts too much," said Dr. Dave.

"Did you talk to *Maemm* and *Daett* yet?" Leah asked.

"Oh, yes. Right after the surgery. I told them we're going to keep you here in the recovery room a little longer before we let anyone in to see you. We don't want to tire you too soon. You have a horde of family and friends in the waiting room. That's quite the support system out there." Dave's reassurance gave Leah the strength to respond.

"I don't remember anything. Well, nothing after Bishop Maust's prayer."

"I'm sure your family is out there in the waiting room thinking about you and wanting to know you're okay. After this, I'm going to give them another update on you and then your parents can come in here and see you for a bit. The rest of that crowd will need to wait until you're in your room. How does that sound?"

Leah smiled weakly and nodded her gratitude to Dr. Dave. She closed her eyes, but this time she didn't sleep. She was pretending to sleep so she could gather her thoughts about this momentous day that had finally come. This is what she'd been dreading, and now it was over—at least the worst of it.

Lying there in the recovery room, Leah reviewed the strange way she'd come to know Dr. Dave. His face was as familiar to her now as one of her relatives, minus a beard. It seemed so odd to think that the two families had met that day in early June at the Children's Relief Auction. All because of Uncle Aden. Money from that auction would help *Daett* pay the hospital. *Gott* had planned it all; down to making sure she had a bag packed for time away from home. That stay with Aunt Lydia hadn't happened and somehow her parents had agreed to the strange plan. It was so unlike them to make such a quick decision.

And then all those second thoughts, the worries that *Daett* and *Maemm* wouldn't sign the papers. But in the end, they had signed. *Gott* had worked everything out. Leah would have a future free from pain and disability. Her mind drifted to Aaron, as it so often did. Would they have become close if they hadn't written letters to each other this summer? Was that also part of *Gott's* plan?

From the edge of her little reverie, Leah heard Dr. Dave speaking quietly to the nurse. She noticed how his voice had a way of calming her, as it must comfort so many others. Had it been only last evening that they'd celebrated her birthday? That good memory, the hummingbird cake, and the hummingbird moth. Monica had said it predicted something out of the ordinary. But to Leah, what had already happened was extraordinary.

Leah heard the nurse slide a curtain. Then her shoes squeaked as she walked away. *Thank You,* Gott, *for helping me get through this surgery. Thank You for being with me and bringing me here. Thank You . . .* And then Leah drifted, as if on the soft fluffy clouds that glided across the skies at the top of Benville hill. A deep peace came over her as her breath slowed, and sleep overtook her once again.

When she awakened, someone was leaning over her hospital bed. "Are you awake?" a different dark-skinned nurse asked. "Your parents were in here to see you, but you missed them. They didn't have the heart to wake you up. Sorry 'bout that."

She bustled around the bed checking monitors and adjusting things. This nurse was older and had bright, orange-dyed hair. Leah thought it was like the color of *Mommi's* favorite Jello.

But the nurse smiled, notwithstanding her offhand manner and strange appearance.

"What time is it?" Leah asked.

"It's a little after four o'clock, honey. I just came on my shift but I'm not going to see much of you. They told me someone's coming shortly to take you to your room—oh, they're already here. You're going to a room up on the sixth floor."

The door opened and a hospital worker came in. He unlocked the wheels of her bed and soon they were on their way to room 614. Leah watched the ceiling tiles fly past as the man talked about the weather and his children who were going swimming every day this week while they were at day camp. Leah listened, not really understanding all his talk, but enjoying the sound of his voice as they made their way through the hospital halls to the elevator, and finally to the room.

The room was small, the walls were light blue. There were shelves, bright lights, and a tray table near the window. She would be in this room for the next few days. A new nurse got her settled in and announced that Leah's family was waiting in the hall. A different nurse raised the head of the bed, plumped the pillows, and pulled the tray across her lap. "I brought you some Sprite. Does that sound good? Would you like a package of cookies or crackers to hold you over until they bring dinner? You must be hungry."

"I'll take the cookies," Leah said. She sipped her drink and ate the shortbread cookies as she looked out the large window beside her bed. There were tall buildings everywhere and, right in the middle, a huge fancy church with a tall steeple rising above it all. Leah was certain she would never enter the doors of such a church in her lifetime, but even so, it was a reminder of *Gott's* presence here in the hospital. Finally, *Maemm* and *Daett* stepped into the room. "How's our girl?" *Maemm* asked. Her words and the smiles of her parents were the very best gifts of this day so far. But Leah felt certain this was only the beginning of more good things in store.

CHAPTER 34

Susan Troyer

A s she entered the waiting room on the day of Leah's surgery, Susan heard Fannie's loud voice speaking to *Maemm*.

"It's spine surgery!" Fannie exclaimed. "Think of the danger. That poor girl—how can she go through this? She could end up paralyzed—or worse," she stage whispered. "I couldn't sleep a wink last night for worry—poor Leah, how terrible to be here and going under the knife at such a tender age!"

Susan winced at the thought of a knife, then reminded herself that surgeons don't use the knives ordinary people use in the kitchen. Still, the image didn't want to leave her mind. And spinal cord injury. Susan had never thought about that possibility until this very moment. She gave Fannie a horrified look and at once saw her expression reflected in the large mirror on the opposite wall. *Why would they put a mirror in a waiting room?*

Daett held his hat in his hands and shifted in his seat. He was wearing his good everyday pants and a clean, pressed white shirt.

Fannie must have realized she was talking louder than the rest because she finally lowered her voice.

Just then an announcement came over the speaker. "Albert and Elma Troyer, please meet Doctor Woodruff in Room 3-C across from the nurses' station." Susan felt a sick rumble of anxiety in her stomach. Fannie and Susan looked at one another.

Maemm and *Daett* stood. *Daett* placed his hat gently on the

chair where he'd been sitting. Their movements were slow and delib-
erate as if to delay the inevitable. *Dawdi's* scripture aside, it was hard
to "abide." Susan wished she could join her parents, but they hadn't
even looked in her direction. And the announcement didn't include
her. Maybe they were trying to protect her from bad news. Then, a
snatch of *Dawdi's* scripture came back, reassuring her:

> *Those who love me, I will deliver;*
> *I will protect those who know my name. . .*

The day passed in a blur of waiting rooms, the cafeteria, and
short visits with a drowsy Leah. The nurses said she was doing well,
but she didn't look like herself under the harsh hospital lights. It was
a relief when, after supper in the hospital cafeteria, the four of them
could finally take a shuttle to the Ronald McDonald House where
Dr. Woodruff had arranged for them to stay overnight.

———————————

The next day they were back at the hospital. While her parents waited, Susan sat with Fannie. Susan scanned the room looking
for people from Benville. A vanload of relatives and neighbors were
coming to surprise Leah with visits today. Had any of the young people taken off from their jobs? Surely someone her age would be here
to support Leah. Susan stood to stretch her legs. They had only been
here two hours and there was still a long day ahead. She made her
way to the drinking fountain, and in the hallway, Ben Keim met her.

"I didn't know you were here. Where have you been?" Susan
asked. "And where's Aaron?"

"I got lost on the way to the cafeteria," Ben said. "Aaron's coming later. *Daett* needed him in the shop this morning. They sent me for breakfast," he gestured towards the group. "Abe Maust sent me. He has to eat regular because of his diabetes." Ben held up a large paper shopping bag filled with Styrofoam trays. "Let me make this delivery. Then we can talk."

"I brought UNO cards," Susan said.

"Great idea! But will anyone want to play? Everyone seems so quiet in there. I don't see any young people." He motioned to a waiting area off the hallway. It was filled with Leah's relatives and Benville people. "I'll be right back," he said.

Susan leaned against the wall, studying the large room with its substantial wood-paneled pillars, soft lighting, and comfortable chairs. Family groups huddled together in various alcoves holding cell phones, reading magazines, or talking quietly.

Ben returned and stood directly in front of Susan. "You need a break. Let's go outside and get some air," he said.

"I don't know . . . I should be here," Susan said.

"There are so many people here. And everyone has to take turns going in to see her. They were just saying that when I dropped off the food."

"I know you're right. I just feel bad leaving," Susan said.

"It won't matter. You can't do anything anyway. Besides, I have something to tell you." Ben started walking to the elevator and Susan followed. They rode to the ground floor and headed to the main doors. Outside, warm air greeted them. It was a relief after the frigid waiting room. They followed a sidewalk until they came to a small, secluded garden.

Susan plopped down on a bench and Ben straddled the opposite end and faced her.

"So?" Susan asked.

"So what?"

"So what do you have to tell me?"

"Oh, that! It's about Amos Maust," Ben said. "Hard to believe."

Susan thought of Amos, Bishop Maust's wild son. She'd been a little nervous when he drove them to the Black Steer that night. But she also found his rebellion attractive. He was having the time of his life—driving a car, wearing *Englischer* clothes, listening to music, and who knew what else? Besides, he was cute in his camo jacket, blond curls spilling over the corduroy collar.

"What about Amos?" Susan asked. She hadn't seen him since their failed spy mission to Black Steer. Ben saw Amos more often. The guys were always together planning hunting and fishing trips, or at least their hoped-for trips.

"Amos is a loser!" Ben said bluntly.

"No, Amos is sowing his wild oats. You know he's going to come around—they almost always do. He's just tired of living under the bishop's roof, especially one as strict as his *Daett,*" said Susan.

"More than that," said Ben, shaking his head.

"What do you mean?"

"My *Daett* had a meeting with the fire marshal last night—a surprise visit. *Daett* didn't ask for an investigation; he thought the fire was from lightning." Susan nodded in agreement. They both understood Amish ways. There was no insurance company to collect from, so no need to figure out the cause. "But according to Marshal Steiner, they suspect arson," said Ben.

"But everyone thought it was caused by the storm and a lightning strike. Do you mean it wasn't?" Susan gripped the edge of the concrete bench.

"Nope." Ben hesitated, despite the big buildup. Susan waited.

"The fire marshal did a thorough investigation because there were a couple other similar fires in the county. They might all be connected."

"How?" Susan asked.

"Number one: they happen on a stormy night. Number two: it's always an Amish woodshop. And number three: there are always ends of those rattail cigs found on the property."

"So . . . a lot of guys smoke. Lightning strikes during storms. That hardly points to Amos being the guilty party." Susan crossed her arms defensively.

"Not so quick, Susie!" Ben's voice had an uncharacteristically sharp edge.

Susan reached down and yanked a weed from a crack in the sidewalk rather than meet Ben's eyes. Saying Amos intentionally started the fire was ridiculous.

"There has to be more to the story than you're telling me," Susan countered. "I'm not buying it. Sure, Amos is living it up a little too much, but he isn't a firebug! You can't be serious." She turned away from Ben in disgust.

"Wait! There's a number four. There were tracks—boot tracks," Ben said triumphantly.

"Of course. There were boot tracks all over the place after the fire. How would anyone know they belonged to Amos or that they had been made on that very night in June?"

"They were identified as a Patagonia brand, just the kind Amos wore when we went to the Black Steer. Nothing like any guys from around here would wear."

"Ben Keim! I had no idea you noticed men's fashions," Susan teased.

Ben ignored her joke. "I know it was him because I asked him about the boots when I first saw them. He bragged about ordering them on the internet. At the fire, I'd say everyone was wearing the usual Wolverines and Red Wings, their work boots, or athletic shoes. It wasn't a dress-up occasion, Susan." Ben sounded angry. "I'm telling you; Amos' boots aren't the kind you pull on for everyday. They cost way more. I'm sure of it; he was the one that started the fire!"

To Susan, it did appear that Amos was trying to exert his independence from everything Amish, including his choice of clothing and boots. But if this was true, it was heartbreaking. She had to admit that Ben's logic made sense.

"Does the fire chief know it could be Amos? Was he questioned?" Susan asked.

"I don't think so. In case you're wondering, I'm not ratting him out," said Ben.

Susan sighed. She wasn't sure how she felt. *Was it true? And should Ben tell the fire chief?* It might save other families from going through what they'd been through. *But why would Amos do such a thing?*

"You don't need to mention this to anyone," Ben said with an exasperated sigh. "I'm sure it will come out eventually. But Marshal Steiner told *Daett* they saw the same rattails and boot tracks at all these woodshop fires. Amos is going to have to answer for his actions one of these days!"

Susan didn't respond. She liked Amos. The ever-present traffic sounds of Euclid Avenue filled the brief pause in conversation. Then Susan stood, signaling the conversation was over. "You know what? I'm hungry," she said. "Let's find some food." The two made their way back to the hospital and found a fast-food counter. They ordered sandwiches, then tried to figure out which size Starbucks coffee was the small one. Was the "Grande" or the "Venti" the larger one? Neither of them could remember. It smelled so good they decided to go for the "Venti" even though it would have cost a lot less to drink the free coffee in the waiting room.

They carried the coffee back to the waiting area and found seats with their group. Nearby there was a commotion in the hallway and the nurses' station called for a doctor with a foreign-sounding name. Everyone looked up but then realized the announcement was for another family. Susan rummaged in her bag for the UNO cards but thought better of it. She didn't feel like playing a game, knowing her sister was somewhere in a nearby room recovering from having rods inserted into her spine. She pulled a new *Keepers at Home* magazine from her bag and aimlessly paged through it. Ben wandered off, leaving Susan with thoughts that vacillated between her sister and the ugly suspicions about Amos Maust whose father sat a few feet away, chin on his chest, dozing.

To his credit, this was the second day in a row that Bishop Maust had been up at dawn to travel to Cleveland. He'd insisted on praying with Leah and her family before she went into the operating room. Now he was back to visit, Anna Maust at his side. The afternoon wore on and people came and went. Susan waited her turn to see Leah. She sat with the others as they paced, read, dozed, snacked, and visited quietly.

CHAPTER 35

Fannie Troyer

Fannie watched as the Amish friends and relatives waited impatiently for the driver of the sixteen-passenger van. The surgery was over, and all had gone well. Tension drained from the room as Fannie and others returned from quick visits to the patient who was now settled in a room on the sixth floor. Soon Leah would be back home in Benville. Everyone had missed her. It just wasn't the same at home without her.

The driver of the van finally arrived much later than expected, saying he'd been tied up in rush-hour traffic. People gathered their things and followed him to the elevator. Fannie shifted in her seat and looked anxiously in the direction of the farthest corner where Henry had been sitting all afternoon.

She'd planned to ride home with him, but now he'd disappeared. They hadn't spoken about it, and Fannie realized they should have. Because they were together so often lately, she'd assumed he'd be looking out for her. But here at the hospital, Henry kept his distance. He and Aaron had sat off in a far corner, away from the other Amish people. Each time Fannie had looked in his direction he was reading a magazine or a book. He seemed to be avoiding her. Fannie had tried not to let it bother her, but it did. She missed the familiarity between them that happened when the two of them were together. Or was that special bond just in her imagination?

Had he left without her? Was he jealous that she'd come to

Cleveland with the larger group? It had made sense to ride with the
church members and neighbors who had so thoughtfully arranged
the trip. Had she offended Henry somehow? Fannie wasn't usually
shy, but something had kept her in her seat. Why hadn't she asked
Henry when he was going home, and if she could join him?

From the other side of the room, Fannie watched Ben saunter
up to his brother. He punched Aaron's arm and sank into a chair next
to him. He was teasing his older brother about the vase of flowers.
It had sat beside him on the table all afternoon until it seemed part
of the room decorations. Fannie knew otherwise. She wasn't at all
surprised that Aaron was sweet on Leah. What surprised her was his
bold romantic gesture out in the open where all could see, if they
were looking. It was a stark contrast to the way Henry had distanced
himself from her today.

Fannie's ruminations were interrupted when Elma called out
to her. Susan, Elma, and Albert approached Fannie. She stood up and
shook the wrinkles from her skirt. "*Ach*! That's a long time to sit, isn't it?"

"Yes. We've been sitting all day," Elma said. "We're not used to
sitting around, are we?"

"No, we aren't," Fannie agreed.

Albert gripped his hat in both hands as if it gave him much-
needed support. "We're all getting tired. I think we need a break.
We're going to get some supper in the cafeteria. You might as well
come with us."

"You mean right now?" Fannie looked down the hall again,
hoping to see Henry. She wanted to talk to him, but it would be
awkward to refuse to join her family for supper.

"Well, I was planning to go home with Henry. But now I don't
know where he is." Fannie looked around as if he might appear when
she said his name, but he was nowhere in sight.

Elma ignored Fannie's comment. "We should get our supper now before we leave the hospital. I guess you heard we're staying at the Ronald McDonald House overnight."

Fannie nodded. She'd overheard Albert telling the bishop about it.

"Dr. Woodruff arranged it for us," Elma said. "You can stay with us, too. We have three rooms. You can have your own room."

Fannie wasn't used to someone else making plans for her, but apparently, that's what had happened. Her face flushed for no reason—or perhaps it was another one of those hot flashes that came over her sometimes.

"Oh, my!" she exclaimed. "I guess I could stay if you want me to," Fannie said.

"You might as well come along with us and eat," Albert said. "Afterwards, they told us to call a shuttle to take us to the Ronald McDonald House. We told Hank you're staying here tonight."

"Hank's still around here somewhere," Elma said. "He's waiting to take Ben and Aaron home after Aaron visits Leah."

This was all news to Fannie. "I noticed they didn't leave with the others," Fannie said.

"You might just as well stay here in Cleveland with us tonight," Elma urged. "We'll come back and see Leah tomorrow."

Fannie warmed to the idea of seeing Leah again tomorrow. Otherwise, she'd be at home in Benville wondering about her niece. "I guess that would be okay," Fannie said. "You'll come back here tomorrow?"

"Oh, yes. We'll be here bright and early to see how she's doing," Elma said.

The group headed to the cafeteria and Fannie followed Ben, who fell in step beside Susan. Aaron stayed seated and pretended to read the same newspaper that had been on the table all day. He barely looked up as they walked by. Fannie caught a whiff of the fragrant flowers in the vase. *I need to find out what kind of lilies those are. They smell so good. Such a bright pink. I wonder if I could get bulbs and grow them at home.*

In the cafeteria, they went through the serving line looking for something that seemed familiar. It was hard to figure out what to eat in a big cafeteria with so many choices. After Albert paid for their meals they found an empty table in the atrium.

"Leah is doing so well!" Elma said. "The doctor said she will be up and moving around for sure by tomorrow, maybe even later tonight. She wasn't in much pain when we talked to her. I'm so glad this is finally over."

Fannie nodded in agreement. She thought about Aaron with his flowers. Surely everyone knew he'd skipped supper to visit Leah. But no one mentioned it. They sat quietly eating. Fannie had chosen a large slab of meatloaf covered in pasty-looking gravy and a baked potato. "This meatloaf is so bland," she complained. "And the potato is all dried out—must have been sitting there since noon.' Even so, she ate the food on her tray. The pecan pie was slightly better. "It's the wrong time of year for pecan pie," she told the others. "But I guess I'm just in the mood for it."

"If you ask me, the desserts look better than anything else they have here," said Susan.

The rest nodded in agreement.

Fannie looked at her brother, Albert, who nodded and wiped his beard with a thin paper napkin. He wasn't one to talk more than necessary. Elma had once commented that when *Gott* gave out gifts to the Troyer family, he'd bestowed the gift of gab to Fannie. Maybe there wasn't enough left over for Albert. Fannie's younger brother.

At the time, Elma's words had stung, but years had worn away the sharp edges. Fannie was grateful to be included. This was her family. And now they'd invited her to stay overnight with them in

Cleveland. It was their way of telling her just how much she meant to them. When everyone had finished their dessert, Susan gestured toward the large clock that dominated the atrium wall. "We need to get ourselves out of here and onto the shuttle. The last one will be going in a half hour," she said. They cleared the table and walked down the hallway to find the courtesy phone for the shuttle.

The ride through the busy city was like a little tour of Cleveland. The shuttle driver, Raymond, pointed out Playhouse Square with its giant chandelier hanging where two streets crossed. It was held up by large golden beams. Fannie gasped when she saw it.

Raymond assumed his tour guide's voice and gave them the details. "Ladies and gentlemen," he announced. "We are now at the intersection of East 14th Street and Euclid Avenue." He pulled the van into a bus stop and continued. "This GE chandelier was created by the Montreal lighting company, Lumid, and was installed on May 2, 2014. It is twenty feet tall with over 4,200 crystals, each added by hand. Now how would you ladies like to clean that light fixture?"

Fannie smiled at his little joke. The rest sat stone-faced, not sure they should admire such a monstrosity that was "just for show."

"Can you imagine this covered in snow or battered by lake effect winds? But don't you worry," Raymond continued. "Our chandelier is strong enough to weather any Cleveland winter."

Raymond navigated the shuttle back onto the street and continued. "Now you can tell your friends you've seen the world's largest chandelier. It's in the *Guinness Book of World Records* or *Ripley's Believe It or Not*. You'd better believe it."

As they passed under it, Fannie noticed it was already lit although it was barely dusk. The entire street glowed with colorful lights. Everywhere, neon flashed. The streetlights blinked from yellow to red to green along with all the other lights.

It looked like Christmas in Millersburg. At home, the *Englischers* went all out in December, stringing colored lights around their porches and in the trees. The Amish didn't decorate with lights, but they enjoyed them as much as everyone else did. Here in Cleveland, even in summertime, the city sparkled with colored lights. Beside the street, off to the left, a theater façade was bathed in lavender floodlights that distorted everything in the surrounding area.

The shuttle driver expertly took them through this part of his city, pointing out the various theaters and naming them as they passed by. Fannie and the rest didn't have much to say. They didn't know anything about theaters, or Broadway, or the stage. The driver kept talking, out of habit, to pass the time.

Fannie had never been in such a worldly place. Women walked down the street in high heels, wearing flowing blouses and tight pants or miniskirts. Most of the men weren't dressed up. They wore baggy tan shorts and ball caps. Fannie saw a family eating ice cream cones as they leaned against the wall of a theater entrance. A line snaked down the street as theatergoers waited for the doors to open.

The driver grew silent for a time. Albert and Elma stared out the window. Their exhaustion showed on their faces and Fannie felt their discomfort. Susan's eyes shone with excitement as she drank in the colorful streetscape.

"Where are you all from?" Raymond appeared to be determined not to drive across the city in silence.

Fannie caught his eye in the mirror above the windshield. She thought he was directing his question to her.

"We're from Benville, two hours south of here," she said.

Raymond drummed his fingers on the steering wheel. "Never heard of it," he said.

"What's it close to I might o' heard of?"

"Well," said Fannie, "did you ever hear of Sugarcreek, Ohio?"

"Yeah, believe I have. I know someone who went there to the Swiss Festival not long ago."

"We're not Swiss, so we don't go. Anyways, we're too busy in the summer to take off for something like that," Fannie said.

Raymond nodded with understanding. "I'm sure you are," he said.

Now that the conversation had started, Fannie kept going. "It's a lot of fuss for the *Englischers*, though. We're from Benville, about twenty miles from Sugarcreek. Everyone knows about Sugarcreek. It's famous."

"Really? Now what's Sugarcreek famous for, other than the Swiss Festival?" Raymond asked.

"You mean you don't know?" Fannie asked. "Why, Sugarcreek is the home of the world's largest cuckoo clock." The others looked at her with surprise. They likely thought she was bragging, or being too friendly with strangers, but she didn't care. Raymond was nice and he was trying to make this an enjoyable ride for them.

"Ah, yes!" the driver exclaimed. He pounded the steering wheel with his fist, accidentally blowing the horn. "We're O-H-I-O, the best and the biggest—at least for chandeliers and cuckoo clocks!"

Everyone laughed. After that, the atmosphere in the shuttle changed. As they continued through the city to their destination, everyone appeared to relax and take in this strange, colorful world they'd entered only yesterday.

Thinking about it later, Fannie wondered if Elma and Albert had invited her precisely because they knew she could manage awkward conversations with strangers. Fannie was pleased with herself and her little joke. Didn't it just prove that there was always something you could find to talk about, no matter how different you were from others?

CHAPTER 36

Aaron Keim

A fter weeks of waiting to see Leah, on the day after her surgery, Aaron was stuck at home minding the K&T Woodshop and waiting to load a truck. And the driver, Jim Somebody, was late—much later than he'd promised. This was part of Aaron and his *Daett's* monthly routine now. On the day Aaron's *Daett* went to collect sharpened saw blades and repaired routers from a place on the other side of Holmes County, Aaron was in charge for the morning. Unfortunately, that was today, of all days.

The neighborhood was quiet since so many had gone to Cleveland to visit Leah and sit with her family at the hospital. They'd left at 5 a.m. in a white sixteen-passenger van, more than a dozen people, including some Troyer relatives. Their bishop, Abe Maust, was in Cleveland for the second day in a row.

Leah was never far from Aaron's thoughts, even though he was stuck at home. He'd prayed silently for Leah yesterday at 9 a.m., the time her surgery was supposed to take place. And today, while he was disappointed he couldn't be there, he also enjoyed being responsible for the woodshop all on his own.

Aaron shuffled the delivery papers and double-checked to make sure every piece was labeled and properly wrapped for shipment. After making sure everything was in order, he sat at the large oak desk, handmade by his *Daett* almost four decades ago. Aaron ran his fingers over the small, charred area on the side. He was glad he'd saved the old desk from the fire. Aaron imagined himself in charge of the woodshop. He imagined a busy home where Leah made a good noontime dinner . . . and he imagined more of his future, all of it centered on Leah, who would become his wife, and this shop, which would be their families' livelihood.

Aaron's mind wandered as he drummed his fingers on the slightly greasy desktop. Ever since Leah had gone to Cleveland, their relationship had been unfolding in letters that passed between them. Ben, who always got to the mailbox first, teased him about it. Aaron just ignored him and shoved the letters into his pocket to read later when he had time to himself. He wanted to be alone to savor Leah's beautiful handwriting and sweet words.

Looking back now, Aaron thought it must have started that day when the four of them—the two Troyer sisters and the two Keim brothers—rode to Mt. Hope on their bikes. Until that day, Aaron had always thought Leah had her eye on Ben. But Ben was too impulsive and talkative for a quiet girl like Leah. *Daett* always said that opposites attract. If that were true, Aaron would like *Susan* best, not Leah. But over the summer Ben had made a point of seeking out Susan, probably to keep her mind off her worries about Leah.

Aaron was annoyed with Ben's constant visits to Fannie's shop when Susan worked. Ben needed to keep his mind on his work. Lately, furniture orders arrived regularly for the K&T Woodshop. Deadlines loomed. The *Englischers* wanted their new furniture delivered on time, well before their Thanksgiving dinners and Christmas celebrations.

There were now almost more orders than the shop could complete in a timely manner. *Daett* had put Aaron in charge of tracking the details of custom orders. He knew which base went with which top, what kind of bevel was ordered for each table edge, and the customer's desired color from stain samples that ranged from light nutmeg to deep onyx. One small mistake could mean a beautiful piece made at K&T ended up being donated to a charity auction or sent to an outlet where it sold for far less than the original order.

Aaron looked around the shop with satisfaction. Although he'd never say it aloud, it was probably a good thing the old shop had burned that night in mid-June. The community had quickly come together to rebuild, and the new workshop was far more spacious and better arranged for their current level of production. Aaron had been only five years old when *Daett* decided to quit working for a neighboring woodshop and begin his own. Aaron had grown up in the shop. He loved the smell of fresh wood shavings and the smooth feel of a sanded tabletop beneath his fingers. He thrived on the challenge of creating a new design when a vendor requested something unusual.

Even more, Aaron liked talking to the dealers who stopped in to place an order or pick up custom pieces. From them he learned about new construction methods, designs, and colors dealers predicted would be popular for the next season. Since the fire, *Daett* had turned more of this work over to Aaron. He was the eldest son who would one day manage K&T when *Daett* slowed down and was ready to pass the business on to the younger generation. *Daett* spoke of it more and more—ideas about traveling out West to visit relatives. He'd been saying he'd like to simply cut firewood from the woods, go hunting and fishing, and step away from all the responsibility.

Aaron and Ben were still young and horsed around, but sometimes Aaron wished his brother would keep his mouth shut and keep his mind on his work. For instance, Ben gossiped about the fire marshal's suspicions. Went so far as to say that it was probably Amos who started the fire. In Aaron's opinion, there was nothing gained from tattling gossip. Aaron had been taken aback when Marshal Steiner suggested the possibility of arson, but the more he thought of it, the more it made sense.

Amos was trouble. *What would cause him to do such a thing?* Aaron puzzled over it for days. When he'd written Leah about it, in confidence of course, she'd suggested Amos might have a mental health problem or even be using drugs. That wouldn't have occurred to Aaron, but he trusted Leah's compassionate understanding of human nature. Maybe her suffering had made her wise in that way. Maybe Amos needed more help than people knew.

Aaron's thoughts were interrupted when, at nearly noon, a large truck made its way up the driveway and backed up to the loading dock. Jim got out and tried to visit good-naturedly as usual, but today Aaron wasn't in the mood. He wanted to get the delivery out of the way so he could go to the hospital to see Leah. *Daett* had agreed to the trip if Aaron could find someone to take him. It didn't take long for Jim to figure out that Aaron was all business today. He silently checked over the delivery list and helped Aaron load the truck.

"Okay, I'll see you next month," Jim said as he pulled down the box truck's overhead door. Aaron suspected what Jim had on his mind—a large Amish-style meal and raisin pie. That might be why he waited until almost noon to come. The shop workers had joined him once or twice, but that wasn't about to happen today.

"I have to go make a call now," Aaron said. He was hoping Jim would take the hint and leave.

"Sure. Calling your girl?" He was always joking around like that, but today it got on Aaron's nerves.

"Nah, I just need to call the driver. The family is up in Cleveland because our neighbor had surgery yesterday." Enough said. Jim got in the truck and pulled away from the loading dock, waving out the window as he left for his date with mashed potatoes and raisin pie—the best in the county.

Aaron went to the office, found the cell phone in the desk, and made his call. "Hello, Hank? Aaron Keim, here. Remember me?"

"Sure! Fannie's neighbor, right?"

"Right. I wondered if you'd have time to take me somewhere."

"You're in luck, Aaron. I've been sitting at home all morning."

"Fannie and Susan and other neighbors went up to Cleveland because Leah Troyer had a big surgery yesterday. You probably know about that, right?" Aaron had no doubt Hank knew. Surely, Fannie had filled his ear about it for weeks.

"Oh, yes, of course. Been thinking about that family today, for sure," Hank said. "You heard anything yet?"

"No, nothing so far," Aaron said.

"Okay. I'll head right over there," Hank said, sparing Aaron anymore explanation. "You ready right now?"

"*Yah.* I'll grab a bite and see you as soon as you can make it."

Aaron went to the house, washed up, and slapped together a thick ham sandwich with Swiss cheese and plenty of mustard.

The rest of the day was his. *Gott* willing, he would see Leah this evening. One quick visit was all he hoped for. There would be others around, wanting to visit her. Everyone cared for her so much. Aaron had prayed for her so often, ever since this day was first planned. He believed it was *Gott's* will for Leah to have this surgery. He admired her faith and knew Leah had strength enough to endure this hard thing—with *Gott's* help.

Aaron imagined the look that would pass between them in the hospital. He was a little nervous to see her; worried she was in pain. *Would she be as glad to see him as he was to finally visit her?* Oh, how he hoped everything would fall into place. He would look into her eyes, maybe hold her hand, and all his thoughts for the future would somehow connect with her future. That is, *Gott* willing.

In Cleveland, Hank dropped Aaron off at the entrance to Cleveland General Hospital before driving to the parking deck. It was a relief to finally arrive at the hospital. He had not imagined how huge this place was, despite Leah's description in her letters. He was completely out of his element. He took it all in as he stood in the cool shadows of the tall buildings and watched people navigate the revolving door. Finally, he took on the challenge. He felt like he had swallowed a stone, and it was sitting in his gut making him nauseous. Once inside the cavernous lobby, he stood looking this way and that, not knowing what to do.

There was a gift shop to his left and he walked toward it, giving himself time to get his bearings. He wandered in and picked up a Hershey bar and a pack of gum. As he was paying, he noticed glass shelves lined with vases of flowers behind glass doors.

"I think I'd like to get flowers, if they're for sale," Aaron said. His words sounded strange, a little hollow. He was blushing with embarrassment. But the clerk didn't seem to notice.

"Of course," she said with a smile. "Should I help you find something in there?" She gestured towards the display.

"Yes, please. I don't know what to get." He felt every bit like the country hayseed he feared he was. Still, the smiling clerk didn't seem to let on that she thought there was anything odd in his behavior. They stepped toward the glass case, and he noticed the prices of the large bouquets. They were out of the question—given the few bills in his pocket. Maybe the clerk sensed this.

"The stargazer lily bud vase is a popular one. They are so fragrant!" the clerk exclaimed as she opened the door and reached in. The air was instantly filled with a delightful aroma. Aaron took the smooth glass vase in his hand. He made his purchase, heady with the scent of the flowers and the energy of his new-found self-confidence. As he carried the flowers into the lobby, he saw Hank strolling down the hallway. Hank did not comment on the flowers and simply asked, "Do you know where the family is waiting?"

"I'm not sure," said Aaron.

Hank took charge. "I'll go ask where they are." He moved toward the main desk and Aaron followed close behind. Soon they were on an elevator going to the sixth floor. The stargazer filled the elevator with something Aaron associated with hope, with love, and with a passage to maturity. Now all he had to do was stay calm and composed when the group in the waiting room saw him carrying a vase of gift shop flowers.

Let them tease me. Let them make a fuss. What do I care? My girl had surgery yesterday. With all she's going through, it shouldn't bother me if someone notices I care for her. As Aaron and Hank approached the waiting room, they passed Albert and Elma who were heading in the opposite direction. They barely glanced at the two men as they passed. Hank found a chair away from the large group of Amish and sighed as he eased into it. He unfolded a newspaper he was carrying and asked Aaron if he wanted to read the sports section. Aaron placed the stargazer on the nearby table and sank into a chair near Hank, gratefully accepting the paper.

He glanced again at the Troyers who were now leaning on the counter at the nurses' station. *What was going on? Was everything okay?* He opened his Hershey bar and offered a piece to Hank. He tried to concentrate on the paper. But he was only pretending. *Gott, please be with Leah. Please let her be okay.*

The Troyers left the nurses' station and walked towards Aaron and Hank who quickly asked, "What's the report on our girl?"

"She's doing just fine. We're heading to the cafeteria now and then out to the Ronald McDonald House for the night. She might be sleeping now, but I'm sure they'll let you in to see her if you want to." Leah's *Daett* addressed his words to both of them.

Aaron hoped Hank would stay put, content to read the newspaper. After such a long summer, Aaron wanted Leah all to himself this afternoon.

CHAPTER 37

Fannie Troyer

After a cold breakfast, Elma and Albert were ready to return to the hospital. The trip there was uneventful, and they quickly made their way to the sixth floor. The nurse greeted them with the news that Leah was making great progress. She'd even walked a few steps the previous evening. The little group sat around Leah's bed, looking at the hospital equipment and talking about the flowers. "Where did these come from?" Elma asked.

"Aaron brought them for me." Leah blushed and smiled at Susan. Albert and Elma didn't let on that they were pleased that a young man had brought Leah flowers—or that he'd come to visit her for that matter. Fannie knew they were secretly glad for Aaron's interest in Leah. Albert would never say it, but Fannie knew he didn't want Leah to end up unmarried and alone like his sister Fannie. But Fannie had few regrets about how her life had turned out.

Just then Dr. Woodruff appeared in the doorway. "Good morning, everyone! How's our patient feeling this morning?" He walked over to the bed and peered at Leah who gave him a big smile. "I'd like to examine Leah and then go over some post-op instructions with Leah and her parents, if you don't mind." He looked in the direction of Susan and Fannie, who quickly gathered their things and left for the waiting area where they helped themselves to a free coffee. It wasn't very hot and was too strong, but they drank some of it anyway to pass the time.

Finally, Albert and Elma came out of Leah's room. Elma greeted them. "It's going to be a while until Leah is completely healed and
able to do much work. She's going to need help with simple things
like tying her shoes for a time." Her face was full of concern. "The
doctor wants her to stay in the hospital a few more days to be sure
she gets a good start on her physical therapy."

"I thought she'd be home in a couple of days," said Fannie.

"No, it's going to be at least ten days, according to Dr. Woodruff," Elma said. "She can't lift anything heavier than a coffee cup
and shouldn't be bending over. She has to get in and out of bed in
a certain way." Elma shook her head. Worry bubbled up and spread
across her face. "The therapy people will make sure she doesn't hurt
herself. There's a lot to remember."

Albert nodded. "The doctor suggested we stay here with her a
couple more days at least."   Fannie clutched her little black handbag
tightly. Her willowy frame stiffened. "I'm not staying here much longer. I've got a shop to run. And I'm going to need Susan this week, at
least later on." She added the last part to soften words that came out
more harshly than intended. Sitting around in the hospital wasn't
her cup of tea.

"We understand, Fannie," Albert said. "You don't need to stay
on our account. I'm tired of Cleveland, too."

Elma nodded in agreement. "The two of you should head back
home later today," she said. "We don't all need to be here. There are
things to be tended to at home."

Fannie felt relieved.

"Susan can help you some this week, but she will also need
to be at home looking after *Dawdi* and the boys," Elma reminded
her. "We shouldn't take advantage of the neighbors more than necessary."

Near lunchtime, the group made their way to the cafeteria again, dreading the endless choices and confusion of the place. In the entryway corridor, Fannie stopped at what seemed to be the only pay phone in the entire hospital. She called Henry, thankful she didn't need to borrow Albert's K&T Woodshop cell phone he'd brought with him to Cleveland. He frowned on using it for personal calls, except in an emergency.

"Hello, Henry. It's me. Can you come and take Susan and me back to Benville today?"

"I sure can!" His answer came swiftly, with not a hint of reserve. He sounded happy to hear her voice. Perhaps her worries about him snubbing her were all for naught.

She rejoined Susan and her parents who were talking to Monica and her daughters.

They'd come to visit Leah. The girls were clutching a basket of candy that had shiny metallic balloons attached to it with ribbons. They danced around their mother banging the balloons into her face. "Stop it now!" she demanded. The girls slowed but they still ran in circles around the group standing there in the hallway.

"There are some smaller restaurants and fast food if you go down that way," Monica said. "It's ridiculous, but this immense hospital even has junk food." She led them down the hall and turned a corner. There in front of them was what looked like the commercial section of a small town, with fast food places, a gift shop, and a pharmacy. Monica and the girls left, and the group found a Burger King. They ordered their favorites, then sat eating and people-watching. Bystanders stared at them because of their strange clothes. And they stared at others who looked just as strange to them.

Finally, the Troyer parents went back to Leah's room. Susan and Fannie sat on a padded bench near the main doors waiting for Henry's van. They didn't wait long.

"How's our girl getting along?" Henry asked as soon as Fannie had settled herself in the front seat. She breathed a sigh in response, happy for the return of the Henry she knew and relieved to be heading for home.

"I didn't know it was going to be so long until Leah could come home. We thought it would just be a couple of days, but I guess she will be in the hospital for a few more days. It's a serious surgery," said Fannie.

"Yes, I imagine so. She's a strong girl with a lot of courage."

Fannie liked the way Henry always said something pleasant in reply to her news. He had a way of making people feel comfortable. It was as if he was one of them.

"Now you girls, don't chatter too much until I get out of this mess and find the expressway," Henry cautioned. He turned up the radio slightly. "WQMX Medina—This is *your* country radio station." They drove down Euclid Avenue to the soothing strains of John Denver, easing them out of town. *Country roads, take me home, to the place, I belong . . .* They wouldn't be going quite as far as West Virginia but thank goodness they were on their way home.

In Benville, Henry dropped Susan off at her house first. Susan climbed out of the van with her backpack and Toby sniffed her shoes. Everyone waved goodbye. Then Henry and Fannie made the short trip to her place. He pulled up under the big pine tree and opened the windows. "Well," he said, "you're back from the big city. How does it feel to be home?"

"I was never so glad to be home as I am today," said Fannie.

"I could never live in a city. All that noise and commotion. It's too much."

"When I was a professor," Henry said, "I used to like visiting cities now and again for conferences. But today it feels better to be here under your pine tree with the windows down." The pine's fragrance was pungent and tangy. They listened to the soughing of the wind in the old boughs.

"Would you like to come in for a little?" Fannie asked.

"You know, I don't mind if I do," Henry said. "I could use a cold beer." He was joking of course.

"Oh, Henry!" she said, fanning her face with her apron. "You know I don't have such things in my house. But come in and I will see what I can find."

Fannie bustled around in the cool kitchen, opening windows and shooing out flies. She set a cookie jar on the table and told Henry he should help himself. She heated a kettle and added a scoop of spicy powder to two mugs. "This is Friendship Tea," she said. "I *know* it's better than Budweiser."

"How do you know?" Henry asked.

"I'll never tell," she teased.

He ate the cookies and drank the warm tea. Fannie found a small wheel of Swiss cheese and a loaf of homemade bread. She opened a pint of bread and butter pickles. She brought them each a slice of watermelon on a plate. The two sat at the table comfortably slathering butter on the bread and savoring the sweet goodness of their togetherness. They ate their simple supper as if they were a long-married couple blessed with a quiet evening at home.

"I'd better be going now," Henry said after they'd eaten. "I'd stay longer, but I wouldn't want those young Troyer boys to think I'm courting their aunt. Thank you for this wonderful meal. And for the good company."

Fannie ignored the "courting" comment. She was long past that time of her life. And courting was such an old-fashioned word, anyway.

"You're welcome, any time," she said.

CHAPTER 38

Leah Troyer

The day of surgery had passed in a blur with intermittent visits from *Maemm* and *Daett*, along with those of Susan and Fannie. They were her support team. They had stood looking down at her, a bit more quiet than usual. Leah tried to ease their discomfort. "I made it through the surgery. Don't mind all these machines and beeps," she said. "The nurses say I'm doing great."

"I'm so glad it's finally over with," said *Maemm*. She looked tired. They all did. "I have a few cards here that the neighbors gave me to bring along."

She busied herself opening them, handing them to Leah, who read each one and handed it back to *Maemm*. Susan lined them up on a shelf where Leah could see them. *Daett* stood holding his hat in both hands. He looked with concern at his daughter but didn't say much. He was clearly out of his element.

"What a relief," Fannie said. She plopped herself down on the end of the bed. Leah winced at the sudden change in position.

"I don't think you should sit on her bed," *Maemm* said.

Fannie stood up quickly. "I'm so sorry. I wasn't thinking. Of course not."

"There's a chair," Susan said, gesturing. But no one wanted to sit in the big hospital chair. They stood over Leah and vied for the chance to tell her news from Benville.

The nurse returned. "On a scale of one to ten, how would you rate your pain right now?" she asked.

Leah hesitated. "Maybe an eight? A seven?"

"Okay. I'm going to add something to your IV. It's a bit soon to start you on pain pills," said the nurse.

Taking that as a sign, the family left soon afterward.

Around five o'clock, Susan popped in to deliver a chocolate sundae. "We checked and the nurse said it is okay for you to have this," Susan said. "Dessert first. They're going to bring you a supper tray soon."

Leah thanked her and adjusted her bed. Leah held the ice cream cup in her hand and took small bites while she listened to Susan's tale about rearranging the quilts in Fannie's shop. Ben's role in the ordeal made them all laugh, but when Leah laughed, she cringed from the stabbing pain in her back.

"I think our ten minutes is up," Susan said. "You need to get some rest."

When they were gone, Leah set the ice cream cup aside and closed her eyes. The room was finally quiet. The pain was less now, and Leah was thankful for a break from her caring family.

She welcomed the relaxed feeling and dozed.

That first day was a blur, marked by nurses coming and going, asking her questions, and checking her in between short visits from *Maemm, Daett,* Susan and Fannie. The following day was different. Susan reported that the waiting room was packed with visitors from Benville. She'd already seen many of them as they'd crowded into her tiny room to wish her well. They came in groups of two or three, and sometimes more. Aunts and uncles, and church friends. They stayed only long enough to reassure themselves that Leah was okay. When they left, they wished her well and said they were praying for her.

Leah listened and nodded. She said little but felt a flood of gratitude for all the people who cared about her. As for the news from home some shared, she'd already learned most of it from Aaron's daily letters the past couple of weeks.

There was a dull ache in Leah's back and a bulky compression contraption on both legs. The nurse had explained these prevented dangerous blood clots. She pulled the sheet and blanket up to her chin. The hospital room with pale blue walls was cold. She dozed, a result of the pain medicine and her busy day of hosting visitors.

"Look at you! What are all these contraptions?"

Leah heard Aaron's voice and opened her eyes. At first, she thought it was a dream. But it wasn't. Aaron was standing close to her bedside with both hands behind his back. "Looks like you had chocolate cake. You should have saved a taste for me." His bluest eyes sparkled, even in the dim light of the hospital room. "Everyone tells me you're doing *goot* and came through it just fine. Does it hurt much?"

Leah ignored the question she'd answered so often today. It was so good to see him. "Oh, hi . . . I didn't know you were coming. I thought by now everyone had left except for *Maemm* and *Daett* and Susan and Fannie. They're staying at the Ronald McDonald House overnight."

Aaron's face broke into the mischievous grin Leah remembered from back when they were still children on the school playground. He looked as if he was going to say something funny.

"I smell something. Are you wearing perfume?" After she said it, she felt silly. Of course, men don't wear perfume. She was at a loss for words in his presence. The summer sun had bronzed Aaron's skin. His hair had bleached to golden, and his muscles bulged under his thin summer shirt. She admired him as he towered over her, forgetting for a moment that she lay helpless, swathed in a hospital gown, her hair covered with a plain green scarf, knotted behind her head at the nape of her neck.

"So, you smell perfume? I don't think so. My aftershave wore off long ago."

"I don't know, something smells like a candle, or maybe flowers."

"Flowers? What kind of flowers?"

Leah felt silly now. But she still thought she smelled flowers.

Aaron slowly brought a tall glass vase from behind his back and placed it on the tray table. Leah's eyes filled with tears as she took in the beautiful stalk of lilies. "Oh! That's what I smelled!" *Why am I crying? The flowers make me happy.* Aaron picked the vase up again and held the flowers close to her face. She drank in their spicy fragrance. He pulled a faded blue bandana from his pocket and handed it to her. This made Leah cry even more. Once she started crying, the tensions of the last two days overtook her, and she couldn't stop. Aaron stood by, looking helpless.

Leah dabbed her eyes with Aaron's handkerchief. She breathed in the lingering scent of his aftershave. It was hard to stop crying. Suddenly, she felt completely exhausted. She was ready for this whole summer to be behind her. She dabbed at her eyes, trying to stop her tears. Her breath came out in little bursts. She sniffled and looked at Aaron who was shifting from one foot to the other. He seemed unsure how to act.

A wave of pity and affection swept over Leah. She composed herself enough to speak. "I'm so sorry! I don't know why I'm crying. The flowers are beautiful. What a nice surprise!" Leah managed to take a deep breath. "I guess everything just caught up with me. I feel so happy it's over and relieved it went okay. I know everyone was praying and I think I had faith; I wanted to have faith that our prayers would be answered, but it was so scary."

"Leah, everyone says you are so brave," Aaron said. "Not just anyone would have taken this risk or accepted the doctor's offer, but you didn't let fear stop you. I know it was scary." Leah handed the bandana back. Aaron took it and somehow kept hold of her hand as he stood over her, his eyes locked onto hers. She lost herself in those blue pools of tenderness.

His hand felt rough and warm wrapped around her smooth, cool one. "Leah, I waited all day to see you. I wanted to see you alone, without all the Benville folks looking over my shoulder and listening to my every word. If they get to thinking we're a couple, they'd have way too much fun with that." He looked around nervously, as if he was worried someone would overhear him, then let go of her hand and picked up his hat.

Leah smiled. He was certainly right. She thought of the Benville crowd, the church people, and relatives. They liked to gossip about the young people.

"Thank you for all your letters. After reading them, I probably already knew everything my visitors told me today, but I didn't let on. The way you write made me smile every time." Leah paused a moment, remembering the warm feelings that rushed through her each afternoon when she'd opened another envelope and saw his pages of neat handwriting on lined notebook paper. "It made me a little less homesick after I started getting your letters almost every day. Thank goodness for Mr. Miller's letter writing lessons and Miss Good's penmanship classes."

Aaron nodded in agreement. "I can't stay long, Leah. I don't want to keep Hank waiting. He mentioned rush-hour traffic. He was so nice to bring me up here this afternoon. *Daett* had to be out of the shop today, so I couldn't leave for the hospital until the truck came to pick up an order."

Leah nodded. "I'm just so glad you came. I missed you." Leah hoped her words weren't too bold. But she sensed, just from their letters that she and Aaron had something special.

"I wanted to say something else, Leah. Before I leave. I've been thinking about it for a while now. *Daett* helped me get a buggy horse this summer and I'm getting him used to going on the road. I was hoping when you're better—and back home—we can spend time together. We could go on the Holmes County trail and have a picnic. How does that sound?"

Aaron's face had gotten red as he'd said all of this. His words came out in a rush as if he feared he wouldn't get everything said.

Leah had suspected this would happen eventually, but his declaration here in the hospital took her off guard. She blushed and brushed a wisp of hair away from her forehead. "Aaron, of course, that would be wonderful. I would like to spend time with you. It will be *goot* to talk to each other instead of writing letters."

"It sure will be," Aaron said. His relief was obvious in his voice. He grabbed her hand again and held it tightly. "You know, Leah, your crooked back wouldn't have mattered to me, but I'm happy for you. For us. Because we're closer now. From the letters."

Leah nodded and her eyes filled with tears again. She knew it was true. She held onto his words as he let go of her hand.

"Okay, I need to shove off. Let me know how everything goes. Write soon."

"I will. It won't be long until I'm back home," Leah said.

Then he was gone. Leah replayed the sound of Aaron's voice in her mind, determined to remember his words, each thing he'd said.

As she closed her eyes, the scent of Aaron's stargazer lilies ushered in the sweet beginning of her new life. He was no longer simply a neighbor or a friend from school. He had given her flowers, wiped her tears, and asked her to be his girl. She'd survived the surgery and would stand straight and tall beside him.

Her body relaxed into the softness beneath her until she drifted peacefully to sleep, finally feeling warm, loved, and happier than she'd been in months.

CHAPTER 39

Hank Kratzer

I t was a quiet morning in Honey Run. Hank Kratzer brewed a pot of coffee and carried his cup, along with a gigantic, frosted cinnamon roll, to the small patio outside his door. The air was filled with the scents of summer—butterfly bush, bee balm, garden phlox, and honeysuckle.

Hank enjoyed the little garden planted around his entryway by the former resident, Mrs. Barnes.

On the advice of her daughter who had overseen the sale of the condo, he'd placed a hummingbird feeder on the iron hook. Now his tiny outdoor café was whirring with the wingbeats of the lively, delicate creatures. They darted back and forth sipping nectar from the flowers and then from the feeder. While he savored the sweetness of the cinnamon roll between sips of the smooth coffee, he soaked up the sun and the fragrance of his small corner of paradise. When the phone rang, it was from a woodworker who had business to do in Walnut Creek.

"I'm afraid it's going to take a while today," he said. "But would you be able to wait around for me? I need to get back home as soon as the meeting is over. My brother and his family from Maryland are expected at about 4:00 in the afternoon."

"Of course. I can do that. I'll be there in a half hour." Hank didn't hurry to finish his coffee. That was something he was learning—to live more slowly.

When he was ready, he put the rest of the sweet roll away and grabbed his straw hat, his cell phone, and his keys. The trip was uneventful, and his passenger wasn't conversant, leaving Hank to his own thoughts. He mulled over his questions. Why did the Amish religion have so many rules? He thought about Fannie and her family, about Leah. How was she getting along in the hospital rehab in Cleveland? Fannie would keep him updated. No question about that.

As he drove, he gathered in the sights along Route 241, which was bounded on both sides by Amish homes resplendent with large flowering gardens, fields of grain stacked in shocks, and horses grazing in white-fenced pastures. The horses must be happy not to have to travel to Walnut Creek dragging a buggy on a hot, humid day like this one.

Hank dropped off his passenger at a huge storefront that had an even larger warehouse behind it.

"I will call when I'm done," his passenger said. "You don't have to wait here if you have something to do for a couple of hours."

Hank knew exactly what to do. As soon as the man was inside the door, he turned around and drove back to Route 241. At the Amish Culture Museum, he parked his car and went inside. A blast of cool air welcomed him as he opened the door. A polished handmade walnut desk in front of him was staffed by an older Mennonite woman.

"Welcome! Can I help you find something today?" she asked. "Do you want to purchase a tour?"

"No, not right now. Do you mind if I browse in your bookshop?"

"Of course not! Make yourself at home," she said. "Feel free to find a comfortable chair and read if you find something that interests you."

He scouted the shelves, noticing the artistically bound books, some with German titles. He noted a collection of hymn books and colorful coffee table books. He picked up a couple of them, including a book of beautiful photographs and a more scholarly one by an author with a PhD. The history and culture of Ohio's Amish communities interested him, and he settled into a comfortable sofa conveniently arranged in front of the bookshelves.

A revolutionary religious and social movement, Anabaptism originated in the 1520s in Europe. Members of the movement were persecuted by everyone—both Catholic and Reformation churches. These ancestors of today's Mennonite and Amish groups fled Europe to become landowners in Pennsylvania and then drifted westward, settling in the Appalachian foothills.

He looked up from the book and rested his eyes on the landscape visible through the window. The Amish must have felt at home when they found this geography. It was so typical of Alsace, one of the places those ancestors had left. But what was so radical about their beliefs?

He continued reading, paging ahead from time to time, feeding his curiosity with details, history, and bits of theology. An elderly Amish gentleman approached him. "*Vass gleichsht du s'best dya?* Maybe reading?" The Amish man, it seemed, was asking him what he liked to do best.

Hank realized he could understand this simple question.

"*Yah, laysa bichah!*" Hank responded in Pennsylvania Dutch.

The man looked at him in surprise.

"You're right. I do like to read. This is fascinating." Hank held up the book. "You have some interesting books here."

The man sank down on an overstuffed chair across from Hank and stretched out his legs.

Hank noticed his crisply pressed shirt, a steely gray color.

"We like people to be informed," the man said. "That's why I volunteer as a docent here. And you couldn't find some of these books about anywhere else. We try to have materials here to help tourists who want to learn about the Amish." He paused. "But I don't think you're a tourist, are you? You just spoke a little *Deutsch*."

Hank leaned forward and sighed. "I wish I could speak it," Hank said. "There are times it would help me. I retired here. I live in the Honey Run condos and drive the Amish. Sometimes I'm curious to know what they're talking about."

"It's not that hard for some people to catch on. Did you ever study German in school? Or Latin, maybe?"

The man seemed thoughtful and well-read, a good conversationalist. Hank felt as if he was conversing with one of his colleagues from OU. "I took some German when I was getting ready to write my dissertation. I don't remember much now. And, of course, back when I was in high school everyone had to take Latin. It's the root of many languages and helps one understand the meaning of many common English words." He felt comfortable here, almost as if he was back in the university library, or a faculty lounge.

The conversation continued to unspool into the afternoon. "Maybe you can tell me this," Hank said. "Why does everyone dress so much the same? And not just the clothes, but it seems like everyone lives in a similar way."

The man rubbed his hands together and looked down as if he was thinking how to answer. "*Demut ist die schonste Tugend.* Do you know what that means?"

"I'm afraid I don't." Hank took a guess. "Something about beauty, maybe?"

The Amish gentleman stood and went to a shelf. He pulled down a book and opened it to a page written in German. "This is a hymn in the Amish songbook *Liedersammlung*. It says humility is the most beautiful virtue. Jesus said the meek will inherit the earth. We're known as the Plain people because we value humility." His eyes twinkled. "We're so humble that our hymn about humility goes on for eight verses."

Hank laughed along with his new friend.

"The worst sin is *hohchmoot*. Pride."

The man turned serious again. "We embrace a life of simplicity, but things still are complicated. We have our problems just like everyone else."

"I am learning that," Hank said. "I drive for this one woman, an older unmarried lady. Her niece has a disability. Everyone is so concerned for her because she's away from home right now. She had surgery to correct a spinal curvature. It seemed like such a big decision for them."

"*Ach!* Yes. What to do? We don't want to see our *kinnah* suffer when there's a way out. So many families have problems. Health problems. Even mental health problems, drugs, and alcohol." He shook his head and Hank thought of the Amish people he knew.

The two gray-haired men sat quietly, as if in prayer. Hank felt the sadness of life and knew it was shared by this Amish stranger.

"If you want to understand the Amish, the first thing to know is the importance of our spiritual life in the community. It's referred to sometimes as *gelassanheit*."

A flash of recognition crossed Hank's face. "*Gelassen*, that's the past participle of *lassen*. Doesn't that mean something like leaving behind?"

The man nodded his head. "Well, you do remember your German," he said approvingly. "So far, so good. *Gelassen* can also be used as an adjective. As such it means unhurried, calm, easygoing."

"So it means laid back?" Hank asked. He smiled at his clever translation.

"Something like that," the man said. "It's self-abandonment. Adding the suffix *heit* to *gelassen* turns our adjective into a noun."

"I get it. It's like in English when the word helpful becomes helpfulness." Hank was beginning to make the connection.

The Amish man stroked his beard as he searched for an explanation. "If you look it up in a dictionary, you'll find a definition such as serenity. But as the Amish use it, it has a much bigger meaning. *Gelassenheit* is sometimes used to describe the life of the Anabaptists. It can mean self-surrender, resignation, yieldedness, being open to God's will, being willing to suffer for your faith, and even, after all of that, it can mean peace, calmness."

Hank thought of Fannie and her family, the peace he felt when he sat in her kitchen in the tiny cluster of homes named Benville. It was a community where people knew one another and supported and helped each other when trouble came.

The man leaned forward, placing his elbows on his knees. "We try to live as Jesus taught and the community helps us do that. We try to be peaceful people. Maybe you read about peace and nonresistance in that book. I think there's a chapter about it, including some history about our ancestors' refusal to fight in wars, for instance."

"I didn't get that far yet. I think I need to buy this book before I leave," Hank said.

"That's a good one. You will get a good idea of our faith if you read that one. It's more scholarly, with lots of footnotes and a glossary. But I can see you won't have any trouble."

"I'm learning so much. And this helps. Thank you." Hank swept his hand to include the man and the bookshelves behind him.

The man continued. "The thing most strangers see first when they meet the Amish is the way we practice separation from the world. Our clothes, our way of life, our limits on the use of technology. We do these things to stay separate. To keep our identity, our faith." His voice was hushed, and his words seemed to circle above and around them for a moment or two.

"Thank you for helping me understand," Hank said. "I like the way you explained this to me."

"That's why I'm here. I want people to learn about us and our ways. So many just see the clothes and the horses and such, but don't bother learning what it means. I'm glad you came in today."

"Me, too," Hank said. "This has been so helpful."

The grandfather clock in the entryway chimed 3:30. Hank looked at his watch. Just then his cell phone buzzed, and he closed the book he was reading. He decided to buy that one book. He'd read it from cover to cover, footnotes and all.

His new friend handed him another small book, an *Amish Dictionary*. "Here, you can just have one of these. You will make better use of it than most of our customers do, I'm sure."

"Thanks!" said Hank. "I need to be getting on now. Thank you so much . . ." Now he realized there had never been a proper introduction. He felt as if they were becoming great friends, and yet he didn't even know the man's name. It was part of this simple life, perhaps, ignoring social conventions, introductions, and the expected gestures. "I'm sorry; I don't think I ever got your name. Mine's Hank Kratzer."

"The name's Good, Daniel Good. Here's my card." He handed Hank a white calling card printed in formal black lettering. "Thanks for coming in today. You're welcome anytime. I'm usually here on Thursday if you'd like to talk some more."

"Pleased to meet you, Mr. Good. You helped me understand things I wondered about." Hank tucked the card inside the book. "I'll read this. I'm sure I'll have more questions when I come back next time."

"Any time. It's been a pleasure meeting you." His handshake was firm, and he looked his new friend in the eye, smiling as he spoke.

"Now I know where to come when I have a long wait in Walnut Creek." Hank headed to the reception desk and paid for his book.

Five minutes later, he pulled up to his destination and parked his van among the long line of other cars and vans waiting in the parking lot. Soon the woodworker came out of the building carrying a box of wood finish products and a stack of brochures and catalogs. He deposited them on the back seat and climbed into the van without saying a word.

Whether his passenger was troubled or was simply an introvert wasn't clear. But it gave Hank time to compose his thoughts and begin writing another journal entry in his head as he drove.

I am finally getting my questions answered. This Amish life I see and am part of every day is much more rooted in history than I'd first suspected. I met a new friend today. Daniel Good. He spoke to me in Deutsch, and I understood! I never imagined I would be able to catch on. Hank drove towards Benville, winding his way up the quiet road, watching the heat shimmer off the fields.

Gelassenheit. *It's yieldedness. Being laid back. Who would think that is part of one's spiritual life, their belief system? I am learning that very thing here, though.*

In the rearview mirror, a Harley appeared and gunned around Hank's van. He gripped the steering wheel. The passenger barely seemed to notice.

When I was young, I was easygoing and carefree. But life's sadness, losing Elaine, has changed everything. I feel cynical and burdened by the weight of the world, the evils of our time. It can be so oppressive. Honestly, I must have been drawn to Amish Country in the hope of escaping some of that. The Amish don't consume so much news. Daniel Good talked about being separate from the world, talked about calmness, and peace. And I think I felt some of that today as I sat in the Amish Culture Museum with Daniel. Gelassenheit.

Hank thought about the many things he'd learned today about Amish life. He practiced a couple more Pennsylvania Dutch phrases in his mind.

As they turned onto the final road, a white van with Maryland plates was directly in front of them. "Looks like the relatives made it," his passenger said gesturing to the vehicle.

"Perfect timing. I hope you folks have a good visit." Hank turned into the driveway and parked his minivan.

"Yep!" The man pressed two twenty-dollar bills into Hank's hand. "Thanks for waiting for me," he said.

"I was glad to do it, and thank you," Hank answered.

CHAPTER 40

Leah Troyer

I t had been less than a week since she'd entered the rehab unit and Leah was impatient for her release. The past two nights she'd dreamed of riding in the open buggy with Aaron. It was the perfect way to travel during late summer and early autumn days. She dreamed of sitting close beside him as they made their way through the beautiful hills of Holmes County where all the gardens were in full bloom.

In her dream, she saw brilliant colors swirling together in a whorl of sunlight—her mother's gladiolus, the roses, and petunias, a flood of red, pink, and purple. She awakened, thinking she smelled the scent of sweet corn as it was pulled from its green husks before dinner. Her spirit was light as she remembered the freedom, the abandon she felt in that dream. But when she was fully awake, she was still in Cleveland dreaming of home.

On the first day of rehabilitation, the therapist had instructed Leah about simple movements such as getting in and out of bed and how to sit in a chair. They warned against lifting and carrying things while she was still healing. It seemed strange to have nothing to do except to learn how to stand and sit and walk without hurting herself. Between therapy sessions, she rested, read, and wrote thank-you notes. She dutifully took walks up and down the hallways when prompted by the nurse.

The soon-familiar routine consisted of practicing movements to protect her back and at the same time strengthening her muscles.

She was eager to move, but at times her muscles tensed, and she wanted to cry from the pain. She stopped the tears and reminded herself that, as the nurses and therapists told her, healing takes time and patience.

Time crept slowly in rehab with hours spent waiting for Jenny, the head therapist, to make recommendations to the staff for "next steps." Then she spent time in the therapy area before going back to her room for lunch and a nap. Leah did as she was told, sometimes wincing as she moved about.

"It's normal to feel some twinges of pain in your back muscles, particularly in the shoulder area," Jenny told her. "The nurse is checking with you about your pain medicine regularly, right?"

Leah nodded. "I have some pain, but it's not too bad most of the time," she said.

"That is what we're looking for. We want to get you moving, so be sure to keep the pain under control."

Leah didn't express her worries, but sometimes she felt unsure she would ever be as strong and straight as everyone said she would be. She felt weak and tired, even though everyone complimented her on her excellent post-surgery progress.

"Most of Dr. Woodruff's patients don't come here for rehab," Jenny told Leah. "But he said the severity of your curvature, the complexity of your surgery, and the distance between the hospital and home was a concern. He wanted us to keep an eye on you for a few more days." Jenny must have known how badly Leah wanted to leave. "I understand you're a special patient of his, so we'd better take good care of you."

Leah smiled weakly. She wasn't sure how to respond.

On the third day of her stay, Jenny came into the room with another therapist. "This is Maggie," Jenny said by way of introduction. "She's a specialist in muscle therapy. Dr. Woodruff suggested we bring her in to work with you a bit."

Leah glanced at Maggie who flashed a bright smile. She looked strong despite her short stature and petite frame.

"Jenny tells me you're experiencing a great deal of tension and tightness in your back and shoulder muscles," Maggie said. "That's not surprising since you have been out of alignment for so long." She crouched down to eye level beside Leah's chair as she said this.

Leah liked Maggie. "I wasn't strong enough to do some things at home. *Maemm* always gave me the easy chores. She didn't want me to work in the garden."

"I understand. She was trying to protect you. But now you are going to be able to do physical things you could not do before. I predict that by next summer you will be out in the garden pulling weeds like everyone else." Leah laughed. So did Maggie and Jenny.

Maggie explained what she would do. "Sometimes when people have pain it is caused by tight muscles. It might be due to earlier injuries or from your previous skeletal limitation created by your body over many years. I'd like to loosen up some of your neck and back muscles using something we call muscle therapy."

"I've never heard of it," Leah said. "But if you and Dr. Woodruff think it can help, I'm willing to try it."

"Good," Maggie said. "When we get to the therapy room, I'm going to use gentle pressure on your back to determine areas where your muscles are tight, or possibly frozen. My compressions, along with your focused attention to breathing, will release those areas that are immobile. It should provide pain relief and allow better movement for you."

Jenny left and Maggie walked with Leah to the therapy room with its mirrored walls. Exercise equipment and machines filled the center of the room. It was quiet here now. Most patients were in their rooms at this time of the day. Maggie led Leah to a low table. As Maggie adjusted it, Leah saw herself in the large mirrors. Until now, she'd always avoided looking at herself. She'd kept busy following therapy instructions, not wanting to see her body in those huge mirrors.

Now she felt curious. She looked closely at her tall stature, her slim, balanced waistline. She noticed with surprise her womanly figure, her erect posture. Finally, her eyes fell to the drooping hemline of her dress. *Maemm* had done what she could to camouflage her crooked back when they made her dresses. That was such a loving gesture. But all *Maemm's* pinning and fussing to make her dresses fit would now become a memory. This dress sagged differently, now that she was straight. And taller. Again, adjustments were needed. But she would do it gladly. *Maemm* and Susan would be happy to help. A feeling of gratitude washed over Leah.

"Okay, I think I'm ready now," said Maggie. Leah sat on the table while Maggie pressed on her muscles, questioning and probing as she evaluated. Leah watched herself and Maggie in the mirror as Maggie instructed her to do simple movements incorporated with a breathing technique. With each breath, Leah grew stronger in body and spirit.

When she got back to her room, she'd intended to take a nap, but instead, an aide delivered another stack of cards and letters. Leah had learned that someone, possibly Fannie, had put an announcement in *The Budget*, the Amish newspaper. Letters and cards were coming from Amish communities all over the country. Leah opened the envelopes and admired the beautiful cards, many handmade. She read the notes, each unique and interesting. The writers explained how they were related to her, wrote about their activities, or just described the weather, gardens, and crops. Most everyone said they were praying. Others wrote a Bible verse at the bottom of the letter.

Susan called just before dinnertime. Leah suspected her family had created a schedule because someone called nearly every afternoon. She knew Aaron wasn't on that list because he called every evening, sometimes late at night. Leah felt closer to Aaron each time they talked. Although they had been together throughout their school years, they now knew one another so much better than they ever did when they'd sat beside one another in Hill Top School. Leah and Aaron had grown up. They were no longer the innocent children they had been back then; they were more than "just friends" now. Leah was sure of it.

At the end of her first full week in the rehab unit, the entire Woodruff family came to visit. It was Friday evening, and they brought a large pizza, a container of sweet tea, and fancy cupcakes Monica had baked and decorated. The girls sat on the end of Leah's bed facing each other, playing with toys they'd brought along. Monica, Dr. Dave, and Leah sat in a semicircle in front of the large window. They ate the pizza and watched the sun drop down over the city as the lights came on. The tall buildings sparkled with light. Between them, the sunset glowed orange and gold, streaked with shades of blue and periwinkle.

As she took in the view, Leah thought of all that had changed for her in this one short summer. She had been thrown headlong into an unfamiliar world and had managed to enjoy it, despite the challenges. She had survived uncertainties and learned to be more comfortable with herself—the person *Gott* had created her to be.

She felt secure in her faith. As *Dawdi* had once reminded her, she was *Gott's* beloved daughter. And she felt a deep love, the love of both *Gott* and her community. She would never again feel as lonely as she once had.

Watching the sun drop behind the tall buildings was a contrast to watching a sunset at home. There, you could sometimes see the fiery red ball sinking slowly over the pasture field until it was only a thin orange crescent on the horizon. In the country, the evening air was fresh and cool with a damp earthiness that wafted from the mown grass. Tomato vines were heavy with fruit, and bean plants were still blooming and sprouting new beans that had to be picked every couple of days.

The pea vines were decaying on the compost pile to enrich the soil they would become part of in the next season. The air was heavy with the scent of mingled growth and decay. The flowers were still lush and at their most brilliant. Fannie's hanging baskets of red and white petunias would be trailing onto the porch railing by now. If she thought about them, Leah could imagine their fragrance, the creaking of the porch swing, and the soft light of evening. She longed to be outdoors. For ten days she hadn't left this huge hospital that covered an entire city block.

"I'm tired of being cooped up inside," she told her visitors. "I know I need to be here, and I am so thankful for everything that's happened. Sometimes, I still can't believe it all worked out the way it did."

"We're glad you accepted our offer," said Dr. Dave. "You were very brave to leave your home and family to spend this summer in the city. I know it hasn't been easy, and yet here you are. But not for long," Dr. Dave added. "Sounds like you're ready to go home."

"Oh, yes. I am. When do you think I can go?"

"How about tomorrow?" Dr. Dave said with a grin. "The reports are all good. I see no reason to keep you longer than necessary. You've been working hard in rehab, and they say you're ready. So tomorrow it is."

Leah felt a rush of joy. "Tomorrow? That's wonderful."

"We brought that bag of belongings you packed before you came in for surgery. Didn't you see it?" He pointed to Leah's duffle beside the door where they'd dropped it as they entered. Leah hadn't noticed it until now.

"I arranged for a medical transport to take you home to Benville tomorrow. I let your parents know they should expect you around noon."

Even though she'd anticipated going home soon, she hadn't thought much about the details of when—or how—she would get there.

"The hospital has a transportation program, so I took the liberty of scheduling them for tomorrow at 10:00. They will make sure you're comfortable for the ride home and we won't risk an untimely injury. I'm sure whoever is driving will enjoy a chance to leave the city and see your Amish Country. I know it's beautiful this time of year."

Leah nodded. "Oh, yes! It is!"

Dr. Dave gave Leah final instructions and an appointment card for a follow-up visit to his office in mid-October. It would be a year until her body was fully recovered and there would be two appointments between now and then. "Don't let them make you do a lot of work for the next while. Take it easy. Enjoy it while you can!"

Leah smiled, knowing everyone would make sure she didn't overdo it.

Soon the Woodruff family said their goodbyes. Everyone was a little tearful. The girls hugged Leah's legs and showered her with kisses. Monica took her hand. Tears welled up in her eyes and in Leah's, too, and then they hugged. They wouldn't see one another again for a long time—maybe for months. The doctor took her hand in his, looked her in the eye, and said his goodbyes. Leah walked with them to the elevator door where they stood and talked awhile longer. She thanked them all once again. Her words were simple, but they came from her heart. And then they were gone.

It was dark outside and nearly bedtime when Leah returned to her room. She efficiently gathered all the cards and letters she'd received and put them in a bag. She laid out her clothes for tomorrow, including the pink canvas slip-on shoes from Monica. Once she got home, she probably wouldn't wear them much. They'd be saved for special times. She folded the lounge pants and their matching pieces and put them together in the bottom of the reusable shopping bag Monica had left in the room for her. On top of her clothes, she placed the vase that Aaron had given her. She would treasure that vase always—a special reminder of his thoughtfulness.

The next morning, Leah awakened early. She showered and dressed, then picked at her breakfast tray and watched the clock. The digital numbers changed so slowly. She picked up *The Budget*, but she'd read all of it already. Soon a nurse came to check her temperature and blood pressure and have her sign the release forms. Leah scanned the pages quickly and carefully wrote her name at the bottom. She was eighteen and could sign the papers herself now.

An aide came in with a wheelchair and they made their way to the elevator and down to the lobby area where they met the van that would take her home. Soon they were out of the city, onto an expressway, and into the fresh countryside where the sun gleamed bright over mowed hayfields and rows of tall corn. Everything was green and lush to Leah's eyes, more beautiful than it had ever been.

By noon, Leah was back in Benville, carefully climbing the steps to the porch. *Maemm* and Leah's younger brothers came out of the kitchen to greet her. Adam looked her up and down and broke into a huge grin. "You're tall now!" he exclaimed. "They made you taller!"

"You're taller, too," Leah teased him back. "Look at your pants. I can see your ankles." Everyone laughed. It was so good to be together again.

The flowers were as beautiful as in Leah's dream, maybe more beautiful. Blossoms cascaded over the edges of flowerpots. The fence had been freshly painted. Toby wagged his tail in greeting, sniffed Leah's skirt, and then looked subdued as if he knew better than to jump or try to play with his long-lost friend. He followed her around the rest of the day, her protector and guard.

Susan and *Dawdi* made their way across the long porch that served as a bridge between the *Dawdi haus* and the Troyers' larger home. He was using his cane and was slower than before, but *Dawdi's* smile was as warm and bright as ever. Before they all sat down, Leah glanced momentarily at the grapevines in the side yard. They were well-tended and hanging full of concord grapes.

The early summer pruning had made *Dawdi's* vines fruitful for another year. Their lessons were still lodged in Leah's heart where they would remain. She couldn't wait to sit with him—just the two of them—and tell him about Cleveland. Even more, she looked forward to his lessons, the truth he spoke so easily and with such kindness. But for now, the whole family gathered there to visit on the porch.

Later, when she was settled in, *Maemm* told Leah that even though church would be at the K&T shop, Leah should stay home and rest tomorrow morning. The morning service would be followed by a young people's Hymn Sing later in the day. Leah needed to rest in the morning. Later she could gather with the young people for the singing. According to Susan, they'd planned an ice cream supper in Leah's honor. After so many days of inactivity and the excitement of being home again, Leah was thankful for *Maemm's* suggestion. She was already tired, and bedtime was still a long way off.

That evening, the family gathered around the table for a Saturday night supper. *Maemm* and Susan had cooked sausages and fried potatoes. There was a large bowl of fresh cabbage slaw, and thick slices of homemade bread with some of the peanut butter spread they'd made for tomorrow's church dinner. There were cookies and cut-up fresh fruit in a glass bowl. Once they'd all gathered around the table, *Daett* bowed his head. Usually, they just prayed silently, but on this evening *Daett* prayed a prayer of thanksgiving for the food and for Leah's safe return.

———————————

On Sunday morning, as planned, Leah stayed at home while the rest went to K&T where the men had set up the benches for church. Even *Dawdi* went since it was so close. At home, Leah sat in the front room reading *Family Life*, an Amish magazine. Through the open windows, she heard her congregation singing. She looked around the familiar room. Hand-loomed rugs were scattered on the hardwood floor. There was no television or radio, no draperies or mini blinds. A clock ticked as she rocked back and forth in *Maemm's* favorite rocking chair draped with a shawl. The woodstove was cold in summer and topped with a bright new dishtowel and a bouquet of zinnias and wildflowers. Leah breathed in the deep peace that is best found in the calm familiarity of home.

That evening, Amish young people from around the county came to Benville for the singing. Ben and Susan, with Aaron's help, had moved a recliner to the shop. Leah sat there comfortably all evening, off to the side, but very much a part of everything. Most of the others sat on benches sharing the English hymnbooks—girls on one side and boys on the other. They sang one song after another—the old Gospel songs "My Faith Looks Up to Thee," "Sweet Hour of Prayer," and "Bringing in the Sheaves." They sang slowly and heartily, letting their voices soar into the summer breezes.

Leah's heart pounded when Aaron took his turn leading the singing. She didn't remember him doing this before. His face was more expressive than the others, his voice stronger. From time to time he glanced at Leah, catching her eye, and holding on for a moment as if to signal their bond, a connection they had proven across miles of separation during this long summer.

It seemed that all of Holmes County was singing in gratitude for Leah's healing and safe return. Leah was sure that Benville, Ohio, was one of the most beautiful places on earth. And its inhabitants, she among them, most blessed. Their music drifted across the pastures and gardens. It floated on the breeze to Clear Creek Road, wafting across the horses grazing in the pasture. They swatted flies with their tails in the rhythms of the evening. Barn swallows swooped down into third-cutting hay, drying in the field, awaiting tomorrow's harvest. Finally, the singing ended and they closed, as they always did, with "Blest Be the Tie That Binds."

After the young people had finished singing, there was homemade ice cream, fruit, and chocolate for toppings. Earlier that evening, the neighbor women had mixed the ice cream using fresh eggs, cream, and sugar. The men had churned it outside in the yard while the young people sang. Girls brought out plastic containers of salty chopped nuts, sprinkles, pretzels, and chips. There was an entire table filled with cookies and cakes.

No big announcement was made, that wasn't the Amish way. Yet Leah knew this party had been planned to welcome her home. Aaron and Ben pulled benches and folding chairs into a semi-circle around Leah. The others gathered to form a line and fill their bowls with the homemade ice cream. There was chatter, joking, and laughter as the young people dipped into toppings and loaded their plates with snacks.

Leah rested, not ready to stand in line. She saw the frivolity and was part of it even though she sat on the sidelines. "May I take your order, Miss Leah?" Aaron asked. He bent over to speak with her. He was so close she could smell his aftershave, a hint of rosemary and eucalyptus. Already she recognized this scent as belonging solely to him.

"Oh, yes! Thank you!" said Leah. It was an inconspicuous moment between the two of them. Conversations hovered around them in the newly built, clean-swept woodshop. For a moment, time stood still. Aaron's hand reached out to cover Leah's. His fingers curled around her hand where it rested on the arm of the chair, and he gave a gentle squeeze. In the warmth of his touch and the fire in his cobalt-colored eyes, Leah caught a glimpse of a future she had once not believed possible. Her gaze met his and held him, revealing the depths of her finally opened heart.

THE END

ABOUT THE AUTHOR

Joanne Lehman's Amish-themed fiction is grounded in her rural Mennonite roots. Rich in descriptive detail, her lyrical fiction explores hope, healing, and forgiveness—always with a dash of romance. She grew up on a chicken farm in Columbiana, Ohio, next door to Appalachia, where she wandered the fields and woods barefoot and swam in the farm pond. Life revolved around church, cousins, and grandparents.

Joanne earned an MFA in creative writing and has worked as an adjunct English instructor, journalist, and community relations specialist. She is an award-winning author of three poetry chapbooks, a novel, *Kairos*, and a collection of creative nonfiction. Joanne has published poetry, essays, and articles in literary journals, religious periodicals, and local newspapers.

An incurable procrastinator, Joanne relies on a wide assortment of passions and hobbies to avoid writing. These include cycling on rail trails, doing Pilates and water aerobics, thrift shopping, traveling abroad, and baking desserts with zucchini or rhubarb as an ingredient. She is equally skilled at charcuterie and cheesy potatoes and can cut a pie into seven pieces. Joanne and her husband, Ralph Lehman, live comfortably in their *Dawdi haus* in Wooster, Ohio. They have two children, four grandchildren, and nine great-grandchildren.

BENVILLE COMMUNITY SERIES

Word of mouth is crucial for any author to succeed. If you enjoyed *Leah's Faith* please leave a review online, wherever you are able, even if it's just a sentence or two. It would make all the difference and would be much appreciated.

Thanks!

Joanne Lehman